A FATHER-SON LOVE TRIANGLE AND THE POWER AND PULL OF FIRST LOVE

FOR LOVE OF BILLIE

PATRICIA VIDO

Grunge Muffin Press

First Edition
Copyright © 2026 by Patricia Vido
Cover and internal design by Meredith S. K. Boas

Paperback ISBN: 978-1-971167-00-8
Ebook ISBN: 978-1-971167-01-5

For Love of Billie is a work of fiction. Names, characters, places, and incidents are
products of the author's imagination or are used fictitiously. Any resemblance to actual
events, locales, or persons, living or dead, are entirely coincidental.

Excerpt from "Death Is Nothing at All" by Henry Scott Holland

Published by Grunge Muffin Press
215 W Main St., Elkton, Maryland 21921
(443-252-5800)
grungemuffinpress.com

Library of Congress Control Number: 2025923665

*For Rudy
who always believed I would do it
and in memory of
Naomi 'Ni' Carlson
who resolved to wear out, not rust out.*

CHAPTER ONE

I scooped a spoonful of cereal and studied the what's-wrong-with-this-picture drawing on the back of the box. A broom stored in the refrigerator. Books shelved under the sink. The wall clock without its hour hand.

Tick. Tick. Tick.

Mom shattered the silence. "I don't know why you think you have to go, Aidan," she said to Dad. "You don't get overtime."

Bang! Dad gaveled his mug on the counter and turned to face her. If he was counting, he didn't make it to ten. "Now what, Monica? What do you nee—"

Mom waved her hand to cut him off. She didn't need anything. She wanted him to not want to go, but couldn't or wouldn't ask him to stay, so every Saturday, Dad visited three or four of the advertising accounts he serviced for *The Danton Monitor*, our hometown daily newspaper, and every Saturday Mom picked at him for it like I'd pick at a scab.

The first time he took me with him on what he called his rounds, Dad said, "People want to be heard, Finn. I try to listen."

Then, grinning and poking me in the ribs, he added, "Besides, when I stop in to shoot the breeze on the weekend, I sell more ads during the week."

A second-grade teacher in my elementary school, Mom talked and expected others to heed.

"Ready to go, Finn?" Dad asked, as though we were setting off on an adventure rather than a ride around town.

I slurped the last of the milk from my bowl, wiped my mouth with the back of my hand, and nearly knocked over my chair as I pushed it back and jumped up from the seat. "Ready, Dad!"

Mom motioned me to her side, swept the mop of sun-bleached hair from my forehead, and mused, "Where has the time gone, Finn? When did you get so big?" I didn't understand her thinking. I'd worn out the previous year's shirts, pants, and jacket before she could hand them down to Rand and Rudd, the scruffy younger Jones twins at school, and I was sure I'd still be the shortest kid in my class when I started sixth grade in a week.

Every day I stood tall and sat up straight, and I'd asked Dad if there was a rack or some other equipment to stretch me at Gus's Gym where he lifted weights. He'd stifled a laugh and told me not to worry. "You'll have another growth spurt," he said. "You could end up taller than me." But I was afraid I was done growing, afraid I'd be "Shrimp" or "Short Stuff" or worse, ignored.

Mom sighed, gave my bangs another brushback, and issued Dad an order: "Get his hair cut while you're out or he won't be able to see the board in school."

When Dad snapped to attention, saluted Mom, and said, "Aye, aye, Cap'n," I froze. His teasing could ease the tension or set her off again. As she leapt from her chair and swatted his back with the rolled-up morning paper, I sucked in a breath, then exhaled, relieved, when she laughed with him and shooed us from the house.

The air outside steamed like a shower, and my faded black *Star Wars* T-shirt stuck to my back. We slid into Dad's seven-year-old Fairlane and rolled down the windows because the air conditioning was shot. Mom's car was the newer Ford station wagon in the one-stall garage behind our nearly hundred-year-old house.

"I'd be embarrassed to drive this car the way you keep it," Dad said the day he discovered "Wash me" scrawled in the dust on the wagon's rear window.

Mom snapped. "I don't care what it looks like as long as it gets me where I want to go."

Dad fired back. "Well, it won't get you anywhere if you forget to fill the tank."

"One time. That only happened once," Mom said, sputtering like the car when it had run out of gas on our way to school. If he hadn't driven by, Dad never would have known. Mom would have called anyone else for help, and she'd have told me, "Let's not bother your dad about this."

Dad started the car, backed down the driveway, and drove to the other end of our block. In front of my grandpa Dom's house, Dad turned and sped downhill into the new day. He grinned as I waved my arm out the window like he did and echoed his shouts: "Hello, Maple Lawn. Wake up, Washington Avenue." On Main Street he parked between the sprawling newspaper plant and Sam's sliver of a barbershop. "Let's stop in at the paper," he said. "Then we'll go get your hair cut."

After he unlocked the office door, I ran ahead to the ad department, but stopped short when I spied a woman I didn't know sitting at the clunky industrial-style desk abutting Dad's.

A dust-flecked shaft of sunlight lit her copper-colored hair like a halo and I swear she had the face of the statue of the Little Flower in church.

She must be holy.

"Billie," Dad said as he came up behind me and rested his hands on my shoulders. "This is my son, Finn."

I caught a whiff of the sweet, spicy jasmine that climbed Grandpa's back porch post and gazed into her green eyes like we were in a staring contest. Billie blinked first with long lashes that were thick and dark, and when she said my name in a breathy voice, I thrummed like a white-hot lightsaber.

CHAPTER TWO

No, Billie wasn't a saint.

She was one of "them," employees of the Louden Company, the *Monitor*'s new owner. They'd come to conform the *Monitor* to Louden corporate standards, but Dad said the company was more interested in our paper's state-of-the-art four-color press and location north of Pittsburgh's interstate highways. Danton was one of the sites chosen to print and distribute a new kind of newspaper covering the whole country for readers nationwide. The *Monitor* was a sideline.

In the newsroom, the out-of-town editors introduced the glory obit, a feature story incorporating the details of death of important people like a borough councilman and the retired superintendent of schools. In phone calls and letters to the editor, longtime *Monitor* subscribers like Grandpa complained. Dad said people in Danton didn't like the idea of anyone receiving special treatment at the end of life no matter how significant their accomplishments or interesting the stories. They thought Death should be the Great Equalizer.

While some of the ad salesmen were worried about their jobs, Dad wasn't concerned about his. Billie had discovered why. "Everyone says you're the best salesman here, Aidan," she said to Dad. "What's your secret?"

"No secret," Dad said, shrugging off her compliment. "I just do my job."

"Well, can I shadow you someday? To see for myself?" Billie asked.

I wasn't surprised that Dad put off my haircut and invited her to join us. No time like the present—that was his motto. It must have been Billie's too because she jumped up from her chair ready to go.

"It'll be hot in our car, though," Dad warned her. "The air's on the fritz."

"Oh, we can take mine," Billie said. She grabbed her purse, led us outside to a brand-new candy-apple red Camaro, and giggled when Dad stopped and stared and wolf whistled like a bug-eyed cartoon character. "Do you like it?" she asked him. "I just got it. Before I left Florida."

"You left Florida for western Pennsylvania?" Dad asked, like he couldn't believe it.

Billie shrugged. "It was time for a change." She said she'd worked for four years at her hometown newspaper after high school and transferred to the Louden flagship paper in Tampa for the past three. That made her twenty-five, ten years younger than Dad and Mom, and would make her thirteen years older than me—once I turned twelve in two months.

"Well, I hope you'll like it here," Dad said. "We do, huh, Finn?"

I nodded like a bobblehead.

When Dad opened the passenger door, I dove into the sleek black leather interior. Instantly, the new-car smell overpowered Billie's perfume. Perched on the edge of the rear seat, I gripped the bucket seat backs and scrutinized the dash, determined to memorize every detail.

As Dad and Billie got into the car, I slid back—straight into a real-life what's wrong with this picture. Oh, there were three of us and I was sitting in back as usual, but Dad wasn't driving and Mom wasn't there. My neck prickled as though Sam, the barber, were buzzing it with his clippers, but Dad settled into his seat as easily as he relaxed in his recliner at home. If an indicator had flashed, he'd missed it. "Don't ignore the check engine light or you'll have bigger problems down the road," he'd often told Mom. I would have warned him that something was wrong, but like the boy on the cereal box at breakfast, I was mute, immobile. Only my eyes moved, darting from Billie to Dad and back to Billie again.

"It's so hilly here," Billie said, looking around as she started the car.

Dad chuckled. "Yes. That's western Pennsylvania."

"And the streets are so wide and curvy."

"You noticed," he said, cocking his head like he did whenever someone surprised—and pleased—him with an observation. Billie beamed.

Then, turning to look as she backed up her car, she winked at me. Like a shot, it knocked me back in my seat and scrambled my senses. When Dad or Grandpa winked at me, it was to let me in on the joke when they told a tall tale, but Billie hadn't said anything and she didn't look like she was kidding. Dazed, I kept an eye on her as she drove. She glanced frequently at Dad, who talked like a tour guide.

"You've heard of Olmstead? The famous landscape architect who designed Central Park? He laid out Danton too. That's why we have these wide, winding streets and the tall maples to shade them. And at the turn of the century, Danton had the world's largest sheet steel mill." Leaning back in his seat, Dad spoke to me over his shoulder. "Tell Billie where the workers came from, Finn."

"Germany, Italy, Ireland, and Poland," I recited.

"Are you the local historian?" Billie asked Dad. From her teasing tone and his self-conscious smoothing of his cowlick, she might have winked at him too.

"Sorry," he said, shaking his head. "I talk too much."

"No," Billie countered. "You know so much."

"Well," Dad said, "I'm interested in history. And science—"

"And everything else," I said, piping up.

"Ooh," Billie cooed. "A Renaissance man."

Again, Dad smoothed that tuft of hair Mom told him people only noticed because he was always touching it.

He pointed out the Victorian and Queen Anne–style houses commissioned by the mill owner for his workers and churches like St. Anthony's and Our Lady of Czestochowa built by the immigrants themselves. "People are assimilated today," he told Billie. "If they go to church at all, they go to the nearest one, not necessarily the one built by their ancestors."

At our own church, the wrinkled old ladies giggled like girls when Dad teased them, and in town, whenever he encountered the gaunt, grizzled man everyone called The Pointer, Dad never crossed the street to avoid him. He walked right up to the old man, looked where he gestured, and nodded at the gibberish he spoke. People noticed that, and while they admired my mother, they embraced my dad.

Dad liked to recall the morning he drove into Danton for the first time and saw Mom's hometown materialize through the river's thin mist.

"Brigadoon? Ha. That's a laugh," Mom said dismissively. "There's nothing remarkable about this place."

Mom was right about a lot of things, but she was wrong about that. Besides the usual swings and seesaws, our community park had amazing attractions that could transport kids far beyond Danton's borders. My friends and I patrolled foreign battlefields in the decommissioned Sherman tank and rode the rails like brakemen in the Conrail caboose bolted to a bed of track. We crawled through the belly of the Sabre jet to the cockpit, then bailed out like paratroopers, zipping down the slide that protruded from the jet's nose like an insect's proboscis. At a pond on the outskirts of town, we scooped minnows, and on the train tracks, we laid pennies for the passing freights to flatten. Everyone knew everyone else, and we kids could roam all over town.

I willed Billie to feel the magic.

As we approached Simpson's Ford dealership, Dad's largest account and the one he made sure to visit every Saturday, Dad pointed and I shouted, "Billie, stop!" After she parked, I darted from her car to the gleaming pewter-and-black Mustang hatchback inside the showroom. With its red and orange racing stripes and stenciled images of galloping horses, it was a replica of that year's Indy pace car. We'd been waiting weeks for it to arrive.

"Hop in, Finn," said one of the salesmen as he opened the driver's-side door. I scrambled onto a seat upholstered in a dizzying black-and-white houndstooth, grabbed the wheel, and turned it from side to side leaning into imaginary curves. "So, Aidan," the salesman said to Dad, grinning and rubbing his hands together, "what'll it take to get you into the driver's seat?"

"Sorry," Dad said, striking a hands-up pose. "I'm a family man. It's strictly sedans for me."

As though Billie were a new hire rather than a temporary Louden transfer, the salesman said, "Nice to meet you. Billie, is it? Stick with Aidan, here. He'll show you the ropes."

Mr. Simpson made the same assumption about Billie when Dad introduced them. "You'll learn a lot from Aidan here," he told her. "I've tried to get him to come work for me, but he says he'd rather be out and about."

At the door to the garage, I inhaled the intoxicating mix of gas and oil and exhaust and ran to a service bay where Mom's older brother, my uncle Pete, was prone over an engine. When Dad introduced them and Billie stuck out her hand to shake his, Pete smiled what Mom called his lady-killer smile. "Another time maybe?" he asked, holding up his grease-blackened hands. Billie giggled, Pete laughed with her, and Dad said we'd better get going, we'd see Pete later. "Might not have a picnic supper tonight," Pete said, jerking his thumb toward the radio on a nearby workbench. "They say a storm's coming."

"Hard to believe the way it looks now," Dad said. Outside the garage, the sun beat down from a cloudless sky.

As we started to leave, Mr. Simpson called to Dad from the showroom door, and Dad gave him a thumbs-up when Mr. Simpson said, "Save us a spot in that Labor Day ad supplement, Aidan. We'll have the copy for you next week."

Awed, Billie said, "You didn't even have to ask."

Dad just grinned, suggested lunch though it wasn't yet noon, and directed Billie back into town to Jake's, a bar down the street from the newspaper.

It took a minute for my eyes to adjust to the bar's dark interior, and I gagged at the stale beer smell. I trailed Dad and Billie past the long row of bar stools, a few occupied by off-the-night-shift millworkers hunched over their bottles of Iron City beer and empty shot glasses.

In the small dining area at the back, Dad chose a laminate table that teetered. Instead of moving to another, he and Billie sat there rocking the table back and forth like it was the funniest thing in the world. Even after Jake brought their beers, my Coke, and our capicola and provolone sandwiches, they played with the table like a couple of kids. If it had been one of my friends and me, Dad would have bawled us out and told us to stop carrying on, but with Billie he just laughed.

When Dad cracked a joke and Billie giggled, leaning closer to him, it was like a movie camera zoomed in on them for a close-up and cut me out of the shot. I got that two's-company-three's-a-crowd feeling and nudged Dad to insert myself back into the scene. "We should go," I said. "We only made one stop."

"In a minute," Dad said, but he didn't look at me. His eyes were on Billie. I eyed her too, then got up to fire darts at the board on the wall. After a few of the darts missed the target and stuck in the wall above, below, or beside the board, Jake came to the table, glowered at me, and asked, "Getcha anything else, Aidan?" Finally, Dad got up to leave.

Back in Billie's car, we rode through the west side of town, the area eastside residents considered "the wrong side of the tracks." Developed later and without a grand plan, the west side had smaller lots and plainer houses than those in our neighborhood. Storefronts were drab and some were empty. Good thing Dad didn't say any of that to Billie because she pointed up Seventh Street where she said she was renting a cute little apartment in a house at the top of the hill.

"You're not staying at the motel with the rest of them?" Dad asked her.

"Oh, no. I wanted my own place," Billie said. Again, she asked Dad about his record ad sales.

"I don't think of myself as a salesman," he said.

"What?" Billie sounded confused.

"I'm a problem solver," Dad said. "I listen to what owners and managers say they need and show them how advertising can help them get it."

"But—"

"Trust me," he said, "the commissions follow." Then he posed the question that troubled his coworkers. "About those layoff rumors, should the ad department be worried?"

"Well, you shouldn't," Billie said confidently. "Corporate will probably offer you a transfer to one of the metro papers."

"Oh, I'll never leave Danton," Dad said. He didn't add what he'd often told Mom and me, that he thought it was better to be the big fish in a small pond.

"How about you, Finn?" Billie asked, her eyes seeking mine in the mirror again. "Do you want to work at the newspaper like your dad?"

He and I answered simultaneously.

"Not in the ad department," Dad said.

"I want to be a reporter," I said.

My pulse quickened as I pictured the newsroom where the teletype machine rattled and the police scanner squawked. Yes, Dad had a point when he said the ads he sold helped pay staff salaries, but to me, writers were the most important people at the paper. They investigated everything so the *Monitor* could confirm or deny, praise or criticize, expose events or keep them off the record. The paper had power, and its reporters got the glory. "They're the first ones to find things out and they get to tell everyone else," I said, eager for Billie's reaction.

"Well, I think they're nosy," she said. "I would never speak to a reporter."

Oof! Her blunt reply was a gut punch and I blurted my surprise. "That's what my mom says."

"Well, she's right," Billie said.

No, she's wrong. You're wrong, Billie. I stared at the back of her head as though I could bore through and change her mind but gave up and looked out the window. I couldn't believe it. I didn't think Billie was like Mom. I didn't want her to be like Mom.

CHAPTER THREE

WHEN BILLIE ROUNDED A CURVE AND SPOTTED BREWERS, she squealed, "Ice cream. Let's stop."

I expected Dad to say, "No, it's custard," and tell Billie how egg yolk made Brewers' treats richer, denser, and creamier than ice cream, but he didn't correct her the way he'd corrected me as a kid. She made the sharp left turn and her car bounced in the ruts of the dirt and gravel parking lot.

At small screened windows on either side of the squat whitewashed cement block stand, we ordered, and then picked up our cones, three tall twists of chocolate and vanilla custard. While we ate, sitting in a row on a picnic table top, the sun went into hiding and the air held its breath. Then, as the wind picked up, leaves quivered and curled inward exposing their pale undersides—a sure sign of impending rain.

When Billie finished her cone and jogged into the adjacent field calling me to follow, I hesitated, but just for a second. Her summons seemed innocent enough. She was acting like a kid herself raising her arms and dropping them like she was conducting a band or an orchestra, and as though on her cue, thunder rumbled. I imitated her movements until threatening indigo clouds clumped together and sagged from the sky. Was Billie conjuring a storm? Until then, I'd assumed Dad was teasing when he warned me about imps or pixies disguised as beautiful women: "They unleash terrible trouble in the lives of men, Finn, and because of their power, resistance is futile." A lightning bolt flashed and more thunder rolled. Trees rocked, fanning the sky with their branches.

"Let's get in the car," Dad called, worry in his raised voice. I ran to him, but when I looked back, Billie was still twirling in the field. Shouting her name, Dad ran to her. He grabbed her hand, pulled her back to the car, and told her to drive to the far end of the parking lot. "We've got to get away from these trees," he said. Scooting across the backseat from one window to the other, I thrilled at the intensifying fury outside. As Billie parked and turned off the engine, big scattered drops of rain thudded the roof and hood of her car. More thunder boomed on the heels of another lightning flash, and she and I both jumped. "Don't worry. It'll be okay," Dad said, but it wasn't.

Like the spray and rotating brushes in a carwash, rain lashed the front and sides of Billie's car, obscuring our view. The wind roared, raising the hairs on the back of my neck. Then, like the time Mom's car hit a patch of black ice and did a donut, a powerful wind gust slammed Billie's car and shoved it, juddered it. We all yelled, and I grabbed Dad around his neck. He braced himself with his right hand on the dash and Billie grabbed his left. She looked scared, so maybe she hadn't whipped up the storm after all or maybe she was sorry she had. We all held on until the car stopped shaking.

"Whew. Boy, that was something, huh?" Dad said. "It's all over now, though. Nothing to worry about. Everybody all right?" With a "heh, heh, heh," he tried to make light of the situation, but his wordiness gave him away. Dad talked even more than usual when events made him twitchy.

When the rain stopped and the sky lightened, we got out of the car. Muddy water churned in the swollen creek alongside the custard stand. Severed tree limbs littered the ground. Ripped from the top of the building, the big neon cone sign was stuck upside down a few yards away, its curlicued peak buried in mud. At the sight of a huge uprooted oak lying on its side, I shuddered and Billie gasped. We exchanged our last look of the day—that sober combination of horror and relief survivors share. No, it was more than that. I owed her my life. If she hadn't moved her car, that tree would have flattened us. Never mind that it was Dad who told her to move it.

"We'd better get going," Dad said. I could tell he was shaken too because he didn't take time to school Billie about the smell the squall had left behind, the clean-air, wet-earth scent of rain mixed with ozone, geosmin, and plant oils—petrichor.

As she drove, Billie swerved to avoid big branches on the road. Around a bend, a fallen tree about two feet in diameter blocked our path, and Dad talked Billie through a detour back onto our route. Amid downed wires, scattered shingles, and siding stripped from houses, clusters of people stared into the distance as though they weren't ready to take in the damage right in front of them. Dad voiced their shock and his own when he said, "I've never seen anything like this."

"Was it a tornado?" Billie asked.

"Too late in the season," Dad said. "Wind shear, more likely. Christ!"

I leaned around Dad and gaped through the windshield at the wide ribbon of destruction that made him curse. Stripped of their leaves, bare trees on the hillside bent at their waists as though trying to hide their shame. The scene stunned us into silence.

When Billie dropped us off at the paper, Dad said goodbye through the passenger window, and when she reached out, he did too. I expected them to shake, pumping once or twice before letting go, but they held on, their clasped hands like two puzzle pieces fitted together and pressed into place. I was standing right beside him, but I may as well have been invisible. Even if I'd been taller, I doubt Billie would have seen me. Her eyes were locked on Dad's until he withdrew his hand and said, "Be careful going home."

As she drove away, I wasn't worried anymore that there might be something wrong with it—I just wanted to stay in the picture. And Dad didn't have to say, "Don't tell." I wouldn't bother Mom about Billie.

CHAPTER FOUR

Strewn with debris, swaths of Danton were as desolate as the televised aftermath of any forest fire, hurricane, or earthquake from across the country or around the world, but when Dad turned his car onto our street, flashing red lights and the backup beeping of an ambulance in Grandpa's driveway distracted me from the devastation. The ambulance lurched to a stop, and when the rear door opened, an EMT inside held Mom's hand as she stepped down and out of the vehicle. Grim-faced, she strode to Dad's side of the car. He rolled down his window and asked, "What happened?"

Gripping the door panel, but looking like she wanted to throttle Dad, Mom ignored his question to ask one of her own. "Where were you? Oh, never mind. Follow the ambulance. They're taking Dad to the hospital." Grandpa? What happened to Grandpa? After Mom wrenched open the rear door and settled on the back seat, she asked again, "Where have you been all this time?" Then, with a glance toward me, she demanded, "And why isn't Finn's hair cut? What have you been doing all day?" Why was she so concerned about us if Grandpa was hurt?

Compared to Mom, Dad was calm. In the way he'd keep me from flying forward after a sudden stop, he extended his right arm and a pointed finger across my chest. It was like he was saying, "I've got this, Finn," so I kept quiet. When Dad asked, "What happened to Dom?" and directed Mom's attention back to Grandpa, she stopped her interrogation.

"That big tree in back fell and pinned him under the branches," she said. "I don't know what possessed him to go out in that storm."

As I pictured Grandpa on the ground, my chest heaved like Mom's. If I'd been with him, I could have helped him, and I should have been with him—not riding around town with Dad and Billie. I used to spend every Saturday morning with Grandpa, skipping alongside as he ambled the six blocks to Antonelli's Bakery. I puffed out my chest when he crooned like Frank or Dean or Perry for people on the street. But at the beginning of summer, when a quartet of teenagers mimicked Grandpa's singing and snickered, I'd asked to go to work with Dad. Sure, I wanted to be noticed, but not if it was because people were laughing at me.

Dad tailed the ambulance, its lights flashing and siren shrieking, down the hill and across the bridge to the hospital. Many more trees had fallen, two of them on cars. A chainsaw jangled in the distance. Our car was quiet. No one said a word. At the hospital, Dad dropped Mom and me off at the emergency entrance behind the ambulance, and when the driver and attendant eased Grandpa out on a wheeled stretcher, I stepped back. Strapped down, he lay motionless with his eyes closed and an oxygen mask over his pale, pinched face.

When Dad joined us in the waiting area, he tried to reassure Mom. "Don't worry. Dom's a tough old bird," he said, but she headed back outside where she paced on the sidewalk. Mom hated hospitals. She always said nothing good ever happened in one, except for my being born, although even that was terrifying at first. When a nurse said we could go see Grandpa, Dad tapped the window to motion Mom back inside, and we followed the nurse to a curtained bay in the ER. As she listened to the doctor, Mom kneaded my shoulders, and I winced but didn't wriggle away. I figured it was my penance for leaving Grandpa all alone, and I braced myself to bear it.

"He was lucky," a doctor said, addressing Mom. "No broken bones, just a couple of bruised ribs. But he hit his head when he fell, so we should keep him overnight."

"No, I want to go home," Grandpa said, as he grasped the rail and rolled onto his side. "Yeow," he bellowed. Mom released me, rushed over to him, and eased him onto his back.

"Listen to the doctor, Dad," she told Grandpa. "We'll get you in the morning." Freed from her grasp, I hunched then flexed my shoulders to try to relax them.

"Will Grandpa be all right?" I asked her as we left the hospital.

"The doctor thinks so, but say a prayer for him," Mom said lightly, as though it was a suggestion not a directive. The doctor must have lifted her worries, but mine still weighed me down. That night I prayed like a broken record: Please let Grandpa be all right. I promise I'll hang out with him more. Then, picturing Billie in the ad office, I added: Just not on Saturday mornings.

CHAPTER FIVE

Riding home in the passenger seat of Mom's car the next day, Grandpa surveyed the damage around town without speaking. At his house, the tree had spared his garage but crushed the vine-draped pergola over the backyard patio. I handed him the newspaper as he settled into his chair. He stared at the photos on the front page and lamented the loss of life detailed under the "Two Dead in Violent Storm" banner headline. Huddled in a first-floor utility room, a young couple and their dog had been crushed to death when the roof of their house caved in.

Dad flipped through the coverage on all three of the Pittsburgh TV stations. Some people interviewed swore they'd seen a funnel cloud, but according to the weather service, it was straight-line winds like Dad had told Billie. Graphics on TV and in the newspaper illustrated how a cluster of storms formed a squall line with Danton at dead center. Some of the gusts were clocked at a hundred miles an hour. In an aerial shot of a nearby mobile home park, trailers, trucks, and cars were scattered like Legos and Hot Wheels in a sandbox.

In his homily that morning, Father Damian had compared the wind to the Holy Spirit, but it didn't go over with the congregation. "No, it was a devil wind, Father," Mrs. Petrosky said after Mass, crying and shaking her finger in the pastor's face. Her daughter and son-in-law were the two people who'd been killed.

Dad challenged Father Damian too. "If it was a cleansing wind, Father, what did we do to deserve all this destruction? Are we too proud of the place where we live? Is that a sin?" When Mom elbowed him to be quiet, Dad said, "What, Monica? He's got me thinking."

For the first few days, residents worked hard on cleanup, but then they slacked off. Shoulders slumped and faces wore the defeated looks that always followed a big Friday night high school football loss. It was as though people sensed that along with the surface damage, our foundation had been undermined too. When a seven-year-old boy disappeared from his home one idyllic autumn afternoon, and searchers found his abandoned bike, parents curtailed our formerly free roaming. Before leaving home, we had to tell them where we were going, take a friend, and call when we arrived.

The TV stations descended as they had after the storm, but their few minutes of coverage couldn't match the *Monitor*'s. Reporters interviewed the boy's parents and neighbors, school administrators, local and state police, even the FBI. Their stories filled whole pages of the paper for weeks. They wanted to talk to the boy's teacher, but Mom refused. She said the coverage was turning into a circus and she didn't want any part of it, but I overheard her tell Dad she didn't know what to say. A new year had just started, the boy was new to the school, and she hadn't had the chance to learn anything significant about him.

"You would have," Dad said, in a reassuring voice.

Mom kept the few worksheets the boy had completed and

looked at them every night before she graded the day's papers. In church, she lit a candle for him like she was grieving another son, a brother I'd never known. The boy's name was Hudson—"a name he'd never have the chance to grow into," Grandpa said, his voice thick with emotion.

Evil's intrusion made our once-inviting town turn its back. Residents withdrew from their sidewalks and porches. The welcome signs at our borders faded, and no one bothered to touch them up. Instead of stopping, prospective visitors kept on going. Danton deteriorated, losing population and its position of influence among the other municipalities in the county. When I said my prayers at night, I apologized to Captain Danton, who'd established the town, and Olmstead, who'd embellished it. It felt like we'd let them down.

Our new sixth grade teacher Mr. Weiss told us it was superstitious to think the wind blew anything away from or into our town, but his assessment dealt Danton a different blow. He said the mill laid off a third of its workforce because of nationwide trouble in the steel industry, and with the exciting opening of a strip mall and cineplex in a neighboring township, our movie theater and downtown businesses would close. "The storm was just a coincidence," Mr. Weiss said. "It's the times that are changing."

CHAPTER SIX

Despite his still-sore ribs, Grandpa insisted on walking to Antonelli's to buy the ciabatta for a fall picnic, our last of the year. He steadied himself with a hand on my shoulder as he stepped over upheaved slabs of sidewalk. Along with the bread, he bought me a roll to eat while we sat for a rest on the window ledge outside the bakery. Then he gave me the change—a quarter, a nickel, and three pennies—one of them as shiny as Billie's coppery hair.

"Think that's a brand-new one?" he asked, pointing to that penny.

I peered at the date. "Yes. It says 1979." He didn't have to tell me it might be lucky or that I ought to save it. I put the other four coins in the left pocket of my cargo shorts and fingered the bright penny before tucking it into the pocket on my right. Billie. She was right there with me again.

Except for an occasional exhaled "ah," Grandpa shuffled home in silence, and I was free to flip uninterrupted through my stored images: Billie wearing a halo of sunlight in the ad department, Billie whirling under blue-black clouds before the storm, Billie winking at me. Suddenly, I remembered Dad winking at Mom once and Mom kissing him. Whoa! Is that what Billie wants? Kissing Billie wouldn't be like kissing a girl, but I didn't think it would be like kissing Mom either. I glanced at Grandpa, but he hadn't noticed my agitation. I matched my breathing to his to try to calm myself and cool down, but it was a struggle because Billie walked beside me all the way home.

In my room, I put the penny in my box of treasures with Uncle Pete's dog tags and two silver dollars from Grandpa. I was still staring at it when Mom called to me that it was time to go eat.

The whole family had gathered in Grandpa's backyard, including my aunts Rina and Rachele, Mom's younger sisters, who worked for the county and shared an apartment in the county seat. Uncle Pete surprised me when he motioned me over to sit next to him at the picnic table. Usually, he sat off by himself on the retaining wall of stacked railroad ties. Mom said that was because he got sad and felt bad remembering friends who'd died in the war he'd survived.

For a change, though, Pete was sociable. "Tell me again," he said to Dad as we started to eat. "Who's the new girl?" What? How did he even remember her from our brief stop in the garage at Simpson's?

"Her name's Billie," Dad said, giving Pete a long look, then a wink. "Why? You interested?"

Pete didn't answer. Instead, he grabbed me around my neck, pushed my face into his lap, and drummed the back of my head with his knuckles. That wasn't funny the first time he'd done it, and it had gotten old fast.

"Ow. Quit it, Pete," I yelled. "Mom!" I thought she'd come to my rescue and tell him to stop, but she just laughed along with everyone else. When Pete let me up, I scowled and slid away from him. It wasn't the manhandling that bothered me. It was his curiosity about Billie. I didn't want to think about him putting the moves on her.

After we finished eating, Grandpa sipped his grappa and reminisced about the grandma I'd never known, the dark-haired beauty at the tailor shop who'd measured his in-seam on their first meeting. "She was very professional, but I had to step back," he said. "I was afraid she would feel the effect her touch was having on me."

"Dad!" gasped my aunts, as though they were shocked, as though they'd never heard that story before. Everyone else laughed, but then grew quiet. My grandmother had died of cancer before I was born. Mom said it was because Grandma offered herself up so God would protect Pete in Vietnam. When Pete came home and Grandma went to the doctor, it was too late for any treatment to save her.

"I fell apart, but you took charge of everything, Monica," Grandpa said to Mom. "You saved us."

"She saved me too," Dad said, because it was Mom who'd told him about the ad sales job at the newspaper in their college town when he'd run out of money and had to drop out of school.

"But you saved Finn," Mom said, gazing at Dad with an awe that never diminished no matter how many times she told the story of my premature birth. "When the doctors said it would be touch and go for the first three days, Aidan went to the hospital chapel. He said, 'God, I never knew my father and you took my mother too soon. You owe me my son.' That's how he prayed. Brazenly," Mom breathed.

Dad said it was a tribute to God, not an affront, to pray that way. It was a conviction that God could do whatever you asked and would do it if you were sincere. "But if it turns out there's a price for my prayer, I'll gladly pay it. You. Are. Worth it," he said, pointing at me three times for emphasis. I tapped my chest twice and pointed at Dad the way he'd taught me when I was little. Everyone laughed except Dad and me. It was how he showed he loved me and how I showed I loved him back.

I'd seen the photos taken of me—reddish-brown and wrinkly with a concave chest—and heard the details so many times that I could have recounted them myself as though I remembered and was reliving my earliest days in the NICU, but I never got the chance. It wasn't just my story. It was my family's story too.

"Finn was so tiny," Rina and Rachele said in tandem the way they did everything. They were our Greek chorus.

Rina: "While he was in the hospital—"

Rachele: "Two babies died."

Rina: "But Finn wasn't sick like they were—"

Rachele: "His lungs just had to develop. He had to grow."

"I was terrified when Finn stopped breathing or his heart rate dropped and he turned that dusky color," Mom said. "Nurses rushed to rub his chest or give him a burst of oxygen through that bag valve mask."

Grandpa skipped to the happy ending. "It was a scary start that October 12," he said, looking at me like he still couldn't believe I'd survived, "but 1967 turned out to be the best year ever."

Misty-eyed and sniffing, my aunts wrapped up the experience. "We had the best Thanksgiving because Finn was the reason to be thankful. The best Christmas because Finn was the present, and the best New Year's Eve because Finn was finally home."

My lungs had matured and I'd gained enough weight to be discharged without a monitor. Mom draped a banner printed with 1968 over my bare chest, and Dad took a photo of me with Grandpa dressed as Father Time.

I preferred those recollections about my past to speculation about—and expectations for—my future.

Dad was solemn. "Finn, you were spared for a purpose."

"But remember how he struggled," Grandpa said. "Maybe surviving was his big achievement."

Aunt Rina picked up on that. "Maybe we should give him—"

"A break," said Aunt Rachele.

Pete snorted. "You mean coddle him."

Mom reaffirmed Dad's pronouncement. "Aidan's right," she said. "I chose Finn's name for its meaning, not just to go with Maguire. Finn will be the hero of his life."

As a kid, I played at being a hero, stabbing the air to slay imaginary monsters with a toy plastic sword and swinging like Spider-Man from the ladder-like monkey bars in the park. I swooped to the rescue and escaped unscathed, never doubting whether I was strong or courageous enough to save the day.

But earlier that summer of 1979 when the third floor of a burning apartment building collapsed and trapped three Danton firefighters in a four-alarm blaze, I learned heroes could be ordinary people who took risks and made sacrifices. Sometimes, while trying to save others, they died. During the televised memorial service, a chaplain lauded each victim for laying down his life for a friend, but all the building's residents had escaped the fire. There hadn't been anyone for the firemen to save.

Confused, I said, "They died for nothing."

"But that doesn't diminish their bravery," Mom said.

I wanted to be brave, but I didn't want to die. "Does that mean I can't be a hero?" I asked.

"No," Dad said. "It means you're human."

Finn. Fair hero. For the first time I considered that in christening me, Mom had saddled me with a burden too heavy to bear.

CHAPTER SEVEN

In the office next Saturday morning, Dad showed Billie how to create an ad on the page layout terminal, his sculpted forearm on display as he reached from behind her to tap the keyboard and point at the screen. Cripe. He was practically lying on top of her.

Listing in his wobbly swivel chair, I shot a crumpled piece of paper into his wastebasket, pushed my foot against his desk, and spun the chair around. "Two points," I shouted, raising my arms overhead and glancing at Billie to confirm I'd captured her attention. When I dropped my arms, my right elbow brushed against the pen and pencil holder I made for Dad when I was a kid, and the cup flew onto the floor where it clattered and scattered its contents. Dad slammed his hand on Billie's desk and yelled at me to quit screwing around and pick up his stuff. Hot with embarrassment, I slid from his chair, but as I crouched on the floor, he apologized to Billie for losing his temper, and when I reached my hand up like a puppeteer to set the cup back on his desk, they laughed.

"C'mon," Dad said, helping me up from the floor. "We'd better get going and let Billie get her work done."

We'd walked halfway to the door when I remembered and ran back to tell Billie my class was coming to the paper on a field trip. She said she'd watch for me on the tour, and she was as good as her word.

As my group filed into the ad department a few weeks later, Billie craned her neck toward us, then waved when I stepped out from behind the other kids. I didn't see Dad, and I paid no attention to what Walt, Dad's boss, told us about advertising. His voice was background noise. Too soon we were sent up the stairs to the newsroom, and I discovered I wasn't the only one who'd been eying Billie. "Who was that downstairs?" a kid from the other sixth-grade class hissed. Like a snake.

I tried to sound casual. "Billie. She works with my dad."

"Yeah? She's a babe," he said.

"Shut up. You don't know her," I said, louder than I should have. He backed off, the other kids backed away, and I straightened up, afraid Mr. Weiss had heard, but he was absorbed in the editor's talk. I wouldn't be punished or made to apologize. And why should I? That kid had a lot of nerve thinking he could say anything about Billie.

At the tour's end in the cavernous press room, the mammoth press rattled and whirred as it devoured the giant roll of newsprint and spewed out the day's news, but I'd lost interest, disappointed that I'd have to leave the paper without seeing Billie again. Then, when I glanced up to where the folded newspapers began their descent, Billie waved to me from the glass-enclosed catwalk above the press. My heart soared but then plummeted when Dad walked through the door behind her, pointed at me, and mouthed, "Hey, Finn." Whatever he said to Billie made her laugh, put her hand on his arm, and divert her attention from me. I frowned as my hands formed fists. He ruined the picture I was taking of her in my mind.

At supper that evening, Dad asked how I'd liked the tour.

"It was okay," I said.

"Just okay? You love the paper. What happened?"

I asked to leave the table.

"What's with him?" Dad asked Mom as I went upstairs to my room.

"He's growing up. Asserting his independence," she said.

But it wasn't that, or if it was, it was Dad too. He got to be with Billie all day every day and still he had to horn in on my few minutes to catch her eye. In my room, I dove onto my bed and planted my face in the spread. I didn't want to hate him. He'd never hurt or embarrassed me like dads who were mean or fat or loud. I wouldn't have met Billie without him, and without him, I wouldn't get to see her again. I couldn't confront him, couldn't keep him from Billie, but I didn't have to go downstairs to watch TV with him, and I didn't have to say good night. Hours later, when he knocked on the door of my room and opened it, I pretended to be asleep.

CHAPTER EIGHT

One fall Friday after school, I almost ran into Billie as I rounded a corner in the grocery store. Looking past me, she asked if I was there with Dad.

"No, my mom," I said, just as Mom steered her loaded cart into the aisle.

"Hi. I'm Billie from the paper," Billie said, switching her plastic carryall to her left hand so she could shake Mom's hand with her right.

"Well, hello, Billie from the paper," Mom repeated. Billie smiled as though she didn't notice, or didn't mind, that Mom had mimicked her. Her carryall held a frozen pizza and a thick paperback with a cover drawing of a rugged-faced man grasping a bare-shouldered woman. It wasn't the sort of book my mother read.

In her wrinkle-free suit, heels, and still-fresh makeup, Billie could have been starting the workday rather than ending it. After seven hours with her second graders, Mom's mousy hair was disheveled, her lipstick faded. She wore her comfortable flat shoes and a rumpled corduroy jumper with *A-B-C* and *1-2-3* embroidered on the bib. "My friends say you look like a walking bulletin board," I'd told her once. She laughed and said she liked to dress for her pupils because they got excited when they recognized letters and numbers.

On our way out of the store Mom muttered, "Where have I smelled that perfume before?"

"At Grandpa's," I said. She stopped and looked at me like she didn't get it. "His flowers. On the back porch."

That focused her attention. "And what else do you know about Billie?" she asked.

I squirmed under her scrutiny, then shrugged. "She's nice."

At supper that evening Mom told Dad, "I met Billie today."

"Oh, yeah?" he said, his eyes on his food.

"Finn says he sees her at the paper on Saturdays," Mom said.

"I guess she's there sometimes," Dad said, but Billie was in the office every Saturday. "Say, this chicken is good, Monica," Dad said as he stood up, grabbed his plate, and hurried into the kitchen to get a second helping.

A few weeks later as a teammate's dad drove some of us home from a soccer scrimmage at another school, we passed a house on the west side of town.

"Isn't that your dad's car?" one of the kids asked me. "What's it doing there?"

I didn't say anything. It was Dad's car parked in the driveway all right, behind a car that looked like Billie's, but I didn't know the answer to the second question. If that was where Billie lived, I bristled at the thought of Dad going to see her without me and at the sticky situation it put him in. He had to know it was something people would notice, pretend not to, but then gossip about later. A better, braver son might have confronted his father and alerted his mother, but that could have changed things, and I wanted things to stay the same.

When Dad came home with a bunch of flowers for her, Mom asked, "What's the occasion?"

"Can't you just accept them?" Dad asked, sounding miffed.

"Yes, I can," she said. Then, after kissing him and sniffing his neck, she said, "You smell like jasmine. Did you stop at my dad's?"

"Dom's?" Dad did a double take, then recovered. "No," he said. "The flower shop."

Over Thanksgiving vacation, Billie's father came to town, and Dad and I met him in the office. As I ran up to greet Billie, her dad stepped back and gave me a quizzical look, but nodded when she introduced us and shook Dad's hand. He didn't stay long after we arrived. Dad was at his desk at the other end of the office, and I was at a computer near the front door furiously tapping the keys with two fingers like reporters I'd seen in the newsroom. As Billie's dad put on his overcoat and headed for the door, he sounded stern. "What's going on here, Billie? Is this going to turn out like Tampa?"

"Shh," she said.

"No," he said. "It's time to move on. There's no future for you here."

His words pricked and I panicked. I didn't want Billie to leave Danton. I peeked around the terminal to check her reaction. When she looked away and didn't answer him, her dad grumped. "Well, you make your bed, you lie in it," he said and left. That struck me as funny and I typed the line until Dad said it was time for us to go too.

You make your bed you lie in it.

You make your bed you lie in it.

You make your bed you lie

In my own bed that night, the words came to me again:

What's going on here, Billie? She'd worked at the newspaper in Tampa. Had she known an ad salesman there too? Did he have a son? For the first time, I tried to imagine Billie's life before she'd come to Danton. She'd talked to other people, maybe given them rides in her car, and maybe even liked them as much as she liked Dad and me. I'd thought we were special, but maybe we weren't. Maybe we were like anybody else.

CHAPTER NINE

On the Saturday before Christmas, I was special again, or at least special enough for Billie to give me a present. She laughed when I ripped off the big red bow and silver paper, dove to my knees, and stared at the boxed model of the Millennium Falcon.

"Do you like it, Finn?" Billie asked as she hovered. "You love *Star Wars*, right?"

I was so preoccupied Dad had to prompt me. "What do you say, Finn?"

"Thanks, Billie," I said, gazing at her in wonder for knowing just what I'd wanted and with gratitude for her giving it to me.

Weeks before when I'd asked Mom for the starship, she'd said, "I don't know. It's expensive. Don't get your hopes up." Since that's what she said every year before she surprised me with what I most wanted on Christmas morning, I was pretty sure I was going to get it, but thanks to Billie, I wouldn't have to wonder and, even better, I wouldn't have to wait. Eager to assemble the model by adding the landing gear and radar dish, I examined the picture on the box.

Billie had a gift for Dad too, a book of Irish poems, sayings, and blessings with his name printed in gold on a corner of the forest green cover. He cradled the book as he turned the gilt-edged pages and read aloud some of the passages about troubles and roaming, being strong and at peace.

"Do you like it, Aidan?" Billie asked him in that airy voice.

"I do," Dad said, but instead of taking it with him, he slipped the book into his desk drawer before we left the office.

At home, I thrust the box containing the Falcon into Mom's face.

"Where did that come from?" she said flatly, and after I told her, "Well, it looks like you got what you wanted."

Instead of helping her decorate the tree, I assembled my model. If it had been her gift to me, Mom would have shown more interest. She would have asked Dad to supervise and told me to be careful to follow directions, but as it was, she let me put it together all by myself. When I was done, some of the decals were crooked, but I didn't care, and she didn't criticize. She was the proud parent again telling me I'd done a nice job.

Before I fell asleep that night, I overheard my parents talking in their room.

"How much time do you spend with Billie?" Mom asked Dad. I caught my breath and rolled from side to side cocooning myself in the covers.

"You know I'm out of the office most of the day," Dad said. Hmm. He didn't answer her question.

"And why did she buy Finn that present?" Mom asked.

"I don't know," Dad said, sounding like he might be getting worked up. "He talks about that *Star Wars* stuff all the time. I don't think she meant anything by it."

"So, what are we going to give him now? Nothing can compete with that."

That calmed Dad down. "You'll think of something, Mon. C'mon, give me a kiss. Let's go to sleep."

I cringed at Mom's reply. "I'll have to return the one I bought him. Or maybe I'll wrap it up for Rand and Rudd."

"Who?" Dad asked.

"The Jones twins at school. They don't have much. I give them Finn's hand-me-downs every year at the start of school," Mom said. "Well, except for this year because he wore everything out."

"Do you think two of them can share one toy?" Dad asked again. "Won't they fight over it?"

"I'll get a second one, then," Mom said. "I hope they're not sold out."

How it must have hurt her to be deprived of giving me the one present I wanted that year. Still, she didn't say or do anything to make me feel guilty. More so than Luke and Han, Princess Leia, Chewy, and the droids under the tree on Christmas morning, that was her gift to me.

I'd planned to show Billie my assembled Millennium Falcon after the holidays, but it snowed all Friday night and by Saturday morning, we'd gotten the predicted foot of snow. Dad prowled the kitchen. He pushed the curtains aside and peered out the window as the snow picked up again.

"Don't get any ideas," Mom said. "You can't go out today."

"No, I guess not," Dad said, plunging his hands into his pockets.

When the wall phone rang, Mom picked up the receiver, clamped it to her ear with her shoulder, and said hello as she walked to the sink. She repeated the greeting, then retraced her steps to replace the receiver on the phone.

"Wrong number?" Dad asked.

"They didn't say," Mom answered.

"Huh." His bewildered expression matched hers.

In the afternoon, Mom made popcorn for us. "Coming," Dad said, when I called him to watch TV with me, but he didn't come, not right away. When I went to the kitchen to microwave another bag, he was on the phone leaning against the wall with his back toward me. I hadn't heard the phone ring. He must have made the call. "Me too," he said, before hanging up.

"Who were you talking to, Da—" A crack of thunder cut me off and Dad and I both jumped. He glanced at the phone as though it had been the source of the boom, then shook his head and gave a nervous laugh.

The last of the Louden employees were due to leave Danton by the end of January. The advertising staff was gone except for Billie, and I didn't want her to leave. I'd stopped thinking of her as one of "them." Instead, she'd become one of us. She belonged in Danton or at least at the paper, but when neither she nor Dad seemed concerned, I decided it was up to me to keep her from going.

Yes, I know. I should have saved my demand for an even greater need someday, but by then, Billie was like the gospel: on my mind, on my lips, and in my heart. I imitated Dad, the way he'd interceded for me when I was born: God, you owe me. Make Billie stay.

And it worked.

A week later Dad and I were back in the office when Billie told him, "Walt says I can have a job here if I want it."

"But you wanted to move up in the company," Dad said, sounding surprised.

"That's what I thought I wanted," she said, emphasizing "thought."

"So, will you stay?" Dad asked.

"I will," Billie said smiling. Happiness blew me up like a

balloon.

But in church the next morning, I deflated. It was the triangle-shaped stained-glass window above the altar that did it, the all-seeing Eye of God, looking sad like Mom whenever I did something wrong and she said she was disappointed in me. It was just an image, not really God, but I addressed it anyway: Don't look at me like that. I didn't do anything. It was a coincidence, like Mr. Weiss said about the storm. I didn't take back my petition, though. I was desperate for Billie to stay. Things had worked out for Dad when he'd prayed for me in the NICU, so maybe things would work out for me too.

But I'd forgotten what Dad had said. There might be a price to pay for my prayer.

CHAPTER TEN

On Valentine's Day, yes, Valentine's Day, I woke to a different kind of thunderclap and an aftermath more devastating than any storm. "You sonofabitch! You bastard!" Mom shouted. She'd never said anything so vicious. Even Dad didn't use those words.

"Monica, don't," he said, sounding like he was dodging hits heavier than those from a rolled-up newspaper. "Calm down. Let's talk about this."

"Calm down? Calm down?" Her furor increased with every word. "There's nothing to talk about. Get out! Get the hell out and stay out!" The slamming of their bedroom door down the hall made mine vibrate too.

On my back in bed, I curled my pillow over my ears and stared at the pale blue ceiling where Mom had painted clouds before I was born. Happy little clouds, she called them. Over time I'd discerned images in the wispy white paint and I rolled to my side, turned on my bedside table lamp, and searched the ceiling. There they were, the familiar shapes of a sailboat, a galloping horse, a spaceship.

When my door emitted a horror-movie creak, I released the pillow and drew the covers to my chin. "Time to get up, Finn," Dad said, looking in. "I've got to go to work. I'll see you." When? That's what I wanted to know given what I'd heard, but he was gone before I could ask.

It hit me then, as sharp and certain as Mom's cry. Billie. The commotion had something to do with Billie.

I ate breakfast alone, dressed, and waited in my room, steering clear of Mom until it was time to leave for school. I didn't want her erupting at me too. As she drove, she clutched the steering wheel and clenched her jaw, and when she stopped the car to let me out in the gray slush at the school's upper-grade entrance, she didn't say goodbye or tell me to have a good day or anything.

When she'd told Dad to get out, did she mean for good? Where would he go? Would he come back to see me like he said? My head hurt, then my stomach hurt, but I wasn't sick. I was worried. Well, worried sick. But by our class's Valentine's party at the end of the day, I was mad like Mom. I'd figured it out. Dad would go to Billie's. Without me.

CHAPTER ELEVEN

"Bee mine" read the extra-large valentine I opened from Francine. "Oooo, she likes you," the guys said, laughing and jostling me. I shrugged them off and shoved the card into a paper bag with the smaller cards from the rest of my classmates.

At home, I rubbed my finger over the fuzzy yellow-and-black coating on the bumblebee's body. Francine's name inside the card and the X and O above it gave me a bit of the glow the day was meant to inspire. I put the card in my box of treasures with the pennies that reminded me of Billie. By then I'd collected five.

Dad didn't come home that evening. After supper, Mom served me a piece of the heart-shaped cake with pink icing she'd baked the night before. She didn't have any cake herself, and she didn't remind me to do my homework or even ask if I had any to do. Sitting at the dining room table grading papers, she didn't notice that I'd watched three sitcoms instead of my usual one, but as the theme song for a fourth sounded, she jumped up, shut off the TV, and sent me to bed. "What were you thinking?"

she scolded, as though I'd done something wrong by trying to disappear for a while into other people's lives.

The next day brought the same silent ride to school, but at the end of the day, Mom said, "Your dad called. He said he'll come see you when we get home."

When Dad pulled into the driveway behind us, Mom went straight into the house without acknowledging him and Dad stayed in the car. He'd been gone less than a day and a half, but it seemed longer. When I got into the passenger seat, Dad reached out to me, but then pulled back his hand as though it had met a force field, and when he asked where I wanted to eat, it was with where-would-you-like-to formality rather than hey-how-about-we-go familiarity. At the KFC, he didn't banter with the teenagers behind the counter, and he didn't speak to any of the other customers or even look at them as we weaved our way to an empty table. Sheepish rather than self-assured, he wasn't a stranger, but he wasn't quite Dad either.

When he dropped me off at home, surrendering me to Mom again, he said, "I'll be back to see you soon. Okay?"

I wanted to know if I was right about him and Billie, so I asked, "Where did you go, Dad? Where are you staying?"

He winced, but brushed me off with, "Oh, don't worry about me."

That evening, when Mom tried to explain their separation, she emboldened me to ask about it. "It's like a time-out," she said.

"Are you getting a divor—"

"No," she said sharply. Then she softened. "I don't want you to worry. And I want you to remember, none of this is your fault."

But if Billie had come between Mom and Dad, and if it was my prayer that had made Billie stay, maybe I was to blame. And I did worry, mostly about Mom.

At school, I'd tell Mr. Weiss I needed to go to the bathroom but I'd sneak down to the school's primary grade wing and peek in on Mom's classroom. It was a swirl of activity when her second graders were present, but when they left for art or music instruction elsewhere in the building, she sat at her desk looking lost.

"Are you all right?" Mom asked me one evening. "Maybe you need a checkup. Mr. Weiss says you ask to use the restroom several times a day."

Busted. I'd have to stop spying on her. She'd have to be all right on her own.

We were all on our own. Oh, I still had a mom and a dad, but not a family. My parents didn't have to divorce for their bond to dissolve. It happened as soon as Dad went out the door. From that point, they were defined by their relationship to me, not each other. I'd thought they knew everything and could talk about anything, but neither offered any more explanation for Mom's outburst and Dad's leaving. I had to give them credit, though. Dad didn't badmouth Mom. Mom stopped criticizing Dad. If people gossiped about my parents privately, they didn't let on in public. Mom remained respected. Dad was still well liked.

It took Mom three weeks and an intervention from Grandpa to let me spend every other weekend with Dad. "Your father loves you. I can't keep you from him. It wouldn't be right," she said, paraphrasing Grandpa, but based on the rest of what I'd overheard, Mom had another motivation. "Maybe you're right," she told Grandpa. "Maybe having Finn around will remind Aidan he's still a father, still a husband."

As Dad drove me to his new home that Friday evening, he said, "It's better this way." He must have meant it was better that he and Mom weren't arguing, but to me it was better because of Billie. At the house where I'd seen their two cars parked in the fall, she stood on the landing of the weathered gray stairway. The fur-trimmed hood of her white parka framed her face and the exterior light lit it. She clapped her gloved hands and called to me as I started to climb. I couldn't get to her fast enough. "Relax, you two," Dad said, laughing when we reached her.

She led us inside the apartment, which was tucked under a sloped roof, and showed me around. It didn't take long. "This is the kitchen, of course. And the living room is in there," she said, pointing through a doorway to a smaller, dimly lit room. Down a short hallway at the other end of the kitchen were a bathroom and bedroom. The kitchen had an oval maple table and four matching chairs, one of them pinned against the wall by the table. That made sense. We'd only need three. Hanging at windows in the door and over the sink were snow white curtains printed with a border of bright red hearts. In fact, there were hearts everywhere. The TV sat on a wooden stand with heart-shaped cutouts. Hearts decorated the towels in the bathroom, a throw on the couch, the quilt in the bedroom, and the pot holding a spider plant in the kitchen window.

I was surprised the décor didn't bother Dad. When my aunts had asked Mom why she always chose stripes and plaids for our house, Mom said, "Aidan says, 'No hearts and flowers, Monica. Not if you expect me to stay here—and sleep here.'"

For supper, we ate Chinese food Billie ordered from a nearby takeout restaurant. She opened the tightly packed white cardboard containers releasing steam and spicy aromas, and spooned white rice, vegetables, and beef in a brown sauce into three bowls. Challenging Dad and me to eat with chopsticks, she showed us how to use them by scooping a pepper and a bit of rice up along the inside of her bowl and into her mouth. It was awkward but when I did it, Billie gave me a high five. Dad switched to a fork, but at least he ate the food. "You know I don't like Chinese," he'd always told Mom, but as far as I knew he'd never even tried it.

When Billie broke open her cookie and examined the bit of paper inside, she covered her face as though she were embarrassed by the fortune. Dad took it from her and read, "People are naturally attracted to you." He grinned, and said, "Well, that's certainly true."

When he looked at his own fortune, he hesitated the way Billie had. "Read it, Dad," I said.

"If you have something good in your life, don't let it go," he read, then stared at the paper for a while as though trying to figure out what that something might be.

Dad and Billie agreed my fortune was the best because it held a promise: "You will have a dream and it will come true." They left their papers on the table to be tossed out with the empty food cartons, but I put mine in my pocket to transfer to my box of treasures at home.

After supper, we sat in a row on the couch and watched TV. I didn't get to sit in the middle like I did at home. Dad did. He stretched his arms across the back of the couch and rested a hand on Billie's shoulder. I was sorry for having fun while Mom was at home alone, but then the Dr. David Banner character got mad, bulked up into the Incredible Hulk, threw a man off a roof, and made me forget about everything except the TV show. At ten, Billie produced a pillow, sheet, and blanket and made up a bed for me on the couch. When she said, "Good night, sleep tight," just like Mom, I wished she hadn't. It reminded me that Mom would pass my empty room on the way to her own.

When I got home on Sunday, there was a major change, although I didn't notice it right away. After church and lunch, I had to unpack, take the clothes I'd worn on the weekend to the washer in the basement, and start my homework. It was dinner time before I realized that like Dad, his photo on the buffet was gone too. After we ate, I checked the stairway wall. The old collage frames had been replaced by new ones with photos of

Mom, me, Grandpa, Pete, and my aunts—everyone but Dad. Mom must have worked on them all weekend. She was wrong to try to make Dad disappear, but I didn't say anything. I didn't want her to get mad at me, too. I didn't realize she might also be hurt.

CHAPTER TWELVE

On my second Saturday at the apartment, Dad took me to check out a nearby street of shops. The condensation on the plate-glass windows of one obscured my view, but the "Bip-bip-pow, waca-waca-waca" emanating from the building was unmistakable. I yanked open the door, gawked at the shrieking video games, and claimed the last available machine. With quarters from Dad, I fired the laser cannon at rows of aliens descending on the screen.

When Dad asked behind me, "Do you want to play too?" I turned, and the invaders slipped away from me in a game-over fizzle. Oh, no, Dad. Not him. It was Jeff from school, the one kid we all tried to avoid. A head taller than me, he stole food from trays in the cafeteria and shoved guys around when teachers weren't looking. When he said he'd play, Dad went to the cashier to exchange a few more bills for quarters.

While we waited, Jeff advanced a little too close for comfort and gave me a hard look. "You live around here now?" he asked. What? Was he going to tell me to stay off his turf?

I stepped back and tried to stay calm. "No. My dad does."

"What about your mom?" he asked.

"She's at home," I said, as Dad returned with a handful of coins and said he'd see me back at the apartment when I was done playing. What? No. Wait, Dad. Don't leave me. Jeff pocketed all but one of his quarters. That one he flipped and snagged midair, eyeing me the whole time. Yeah, kid, I may have half the coins, but I hold all the cards. He was a cold-hearted killer. If I coughed up my quarters, would he let me live? When he advanced on me again, I gulped and shut my eyes, but he brushed by me.

"You play pinball?" he asked.

Grateful to still be standing, I opened my eyes. "Some," I said, but not too well, Jeff discovered.

When he played, he was in control. His eyes roamed the table of the colorful Bally's Evel Knievel game anticipating the ball's movements. He calmly tapped the cabinet buttons, and the flippers responded, catching the ball in just the right spot to fling it back up among the bumpers where it ricocheted with a ding, ding, ding, driving up the score. When he stepped aside to give me a turn, he stayed just as engaged, telling me, "Aim for the spinner that's lit," and when I tilted, he shrugged off my loss. "Don't worry. You'll get the hang of it," he said with a confidence that made me a believer.

When we ran out of quarters, Jeff pulled a dollar from his pocket and bought us each a slice of pepperoni pizza. "Your mom's the best teacher," he said out of the blue as we ate.

That puzzled me. "But you never had her."

"I see her in the halls. She never yells. My mom yells all the time." He didn't say anything about a dad. "So, what's the deal?" he asked. "Did your parents break up?"

If anyone else had asked, I might have snapped, "None of your business," but something about Jeff made me think he could size up the situation for me. Neither Mom nor Dad had offered a satisfactory explanation. I might as well find out what Jeff would say.

"They had a fight and she told him to leave," I said, searching his face for his reaction.

"Why? What'd he do?" he asked.

Too late to stop now. "I don't know for sure," I said, "but I think it had something to do with Billie."

"Who's Billie?"

How to describe her? "A lady Dad works with."

"Did he move in with her?" Taking my silence for confirmation, he said, "Yeah, then they'll probably split up."

The initial pang Jeff's bluntness produced made me sorry I'd let him weigh in, but he sounded so matter-of-fact, like a separation, and maybe even a divorce, were no big deal, so maybe they weren't. Maybe Jeff wasn't just taller and stronger than me, but wiser too.

When we'd finished eating and he got up to leave, I followed him outside. He didn't have a hat or gloves, so I left mine in my jacket pockets, and when he shoved his hands in the pockets of his jeans, I did that too. At an apartment building halfway around the block, Jeff ducked into a below-ground entryway. He leaned against the brick wall, pulled a crushed pack of cigarettes out of his jacket pocket, and offered me one of the last two.

When I'd tried to smoke once with some other kids, I'd almost choked, but I didn't want to refuse. After Jeff lit a match and my cigarette, I took a drag, coughed, but only once, and then puffed like Jeff three or four times before an old man yelled down from a second-story window for us to beat it.

I crushed my cigarette with a twist of the ball of my foot like Jeff did and walked away beside him, matching his stride, imitating his swagger. He headed to a playground with a set of eight swings, though only five of them had seats. He flipped over the snow-covered seat of one, sat on the dry side, and turned around several times twisting the chains. I did the same with another swing and when the chains were twisted tight, we lifted our feet and spiraled as the swings unwound, leaving me dizzy—and feeling free.

"Will you be here next weekend?" Jeff asked.

"No. Every other," I said.

"That's where I live," he said, pointing to one in a long line of blackened redbrick row homes across the street. "Maybe when you come, we can do stuff."

"Okay," I said, drawing out the word as I considered his invitation, and then, "Yeah," when I realized I wasn't afraid of him anymore. And for once, I wasn't worried about being short. If I was with Jeff, no one would miss or dare to dismiss me.

"But don't make your mom feel bad when you leave your house," Jeff said.

"Huh?" His sudden seriousness surprised me.

"Don't run out of the house all excited to see your dad," he said. "Pretend like you forgot he was coming or like you're only going with him because you have to."

I tried to remember how I'd left home the day before. "But won't that make my dad feel bad?" I asked Jeff.

"Nah. Dads can take it," he said.

When I returned to the apartment, it was dim and so quiet that, at first, I thought Dad and Billie had gone out, but as I walked farther into the kitchen, I heard muted voices coming from the bedroom. "Knock first," I'd been told at home after walking in on Mom and Dad once. I was torn between wanting to pound on the door and yell for Dad and Billie to come out and wanting to slink away. After the boost I'd gotten from being with Jeff, I felt cut down to size again, cut out of the picture. I'd thought I had a place in the apartment, but now I wasn't sure. When Dad opened the door, I flinched.

"What are you doing there, Finn?" he asked, making it sound like I was spying or listening in, but I wasn't. Not on purpose anyway.

It was Billie who made me feel welcome again. She made the macaroni and cheese from the blue box I liked even better than the kind Mom made from scratch. Then, while we ate, she asked me about the arcade, and I told her about Jeff. When we watched TV, she leaned across Dad to ask if I liked the show or wanted to change the channel, and she refilled the snack bowl as soon as I emptied it.

At ten, Billie made up my bed for me again. While I'd told Mom to stop saying that babyish snug-as-a-bug-in-a-rug thing, I wouldn't have minded hearing it from Billie, and as for what Jeff said about how to leave Mom, it would be hard to pretend I was anything but happy coming to spend every other weekend with Billie and Dad. I mean Dad and Billie.

I'd been sitting with Jeff at lunch for a few weeks when Mom said she was surprised to hear it. "His teacher says he's not a good influence."

"I don't care," I said, annoyed that I'd been ratted out. "He's my friend."

"Since when?" she asked.

I considered how to answer. "Since we played video games at the arcade."

"Oh. When you were with your dad," she said. "Well, we should have him come here."

When I invited him to our house, Jeff hesitated. "She won't make me do homework, will she?"

I laughed, and rushed to reassure him. "No. No homework on Friday or Saturday. Only on Sunday."

We were shooting hoops in the driveway Saturday afternoon when Mom came out on the back porch to drive Jeff home. After watching us for a few minutes, she said, "You're really good, Jeff." He straightened up, standing even taller, drove toward the basket, shot the ball over my head, and—swish—through the net.

After we dropped Jeff off at his house, I told Mom what I'd heard from kids in Jeff's room that week. "Jeff got kicked out of class again."

"What do you mean 'again'?" she asked. "What happened?"

"Well, when the teacher calls on him, Jeff makes a joke instead of answering, and when the whole class laughs, she says, 'Okay, mister, down to the principal's office with you.' So, he gets up to leave, but makes a face behind her back, and everyone laughs again."

"I see," Mom said.

No student had ever been transferred from one class to another in the middle of the school year, but a few days after I'd told Mom about Jeff, he was moved into Mr. Weiss's room with me. Mr. Weiss never questioned him in front of the class. Instead, he stood by Jeff's desk to talk to him. After a few days, Jeff said Mom was now one of the two best teachers at school, and Mr. Weiss was the best teacher he ever had.

When Jeff came to our house a second time, he spent almost as much time with Mom as with me. She asked him to read aloud from one of the Narnia books so she could hear how it sounded and decide whether her second graders would like the story. When he stumbled over "prosperity" and "indigence," she showed him how to sound out the words and guess at their meaning from the context, and she gave him a paperback dictionary to take home along with the book.

"When you look up a new word, Jeff, it's yours forever," she said.

When she put it that way, using a dictionary sounded less like a chore and more like an adventure. Jeff bought her explanation too, but I was confused and embarrassed by the look of adoration that lit his face. He was my friend. She was my mother. What was going on?

CHAPTER THIRTEEN

ONE FRIDAY NIGHT BILLIE POPPED A TAPE INTO HER boombox and pulled Dad to his feet. "Dance with me, Aidan," she said. Their bodies pressed together, they moved like one person, not two—one person who'd forgotten about me.

But when that song ended and another began, Billie asked me if I wanted to dance. Dad faded away as she took my hands in hers. Looking down at our feet, I followed her steps making the outline of a rectangle on the floor. The box step, she called it. When she put my left hand on her back at her waist, it drew me closer to her, not as close as Dad had been, but close enough for me to feel woozy and wonder why.

"Hold me firmly so you can guide me. Oops. Too tight, Finn," she said with a giggle, then, "There, that's better," when I relaxed my grip. She put her left hand on my shoulder and took my left hand in her right. "Ready?" she asked. I nodded but looked down again to keep from staring at her chest. When she said, "Look up," I raised my eyes to hers. "Remember those steps, but relax. You want to glide," she said, pairing the word with the smooth slide of her foot.

Whether from the beat of the music, the lyrics about love, or being close to Billie, I went straight from woozy to sweaty and shaky. That's when Dad came up behind me, tapped me on my shoulder, and took Billie out of my arms. "This is what you do, Finn, when some guy has been dancing too long with your girl. It's called cutting in," he said, chortling like a cartoon villain as he danced Billie away from me. He twirled her around, and then held her as she bent backward over his arm like they were a professional dance team or something. I plunked down at the table and glared at him, whether because he'd laughed at me or taken Billie away or both.

When I punched the stop button, I thought he'd get the message, but Dad kept dancing without the music, exaggerating his moves, frustrating me even more. Billie laughed and danced along with him for a bit, but then stopped. She came back to me, opened a nearby cabinet door, and suggested we play one of the games stored inside.

We danced with Billie almost every weekend I spent at the apartment. When it was my turn, Dad would let us go for a while before cutting in and taking Billie away from me, always at the wrong time, although from his perspective, it might have been in the nick of time.

Another weekend, a surprise bounded down the steps as Dad parked in the apartment driveway. "A dog," I cried as I leapt from the car and it leapt into my arms, slathering my face with its tongue.

"She likes you, Finn," Billie said, smiling. "Do you want to name her?"

The offer was a big deal, almost like the dog would be as much mine as Billie's, like we would be sharing her. I had to pick the perfect name. When Billie nuzzled her pet and her hair blended with the dog's fur, I had it.

"Ginger," I said. Billie sat back on her heels and quirked her head like the dog. "She's the same color as your hair."

"You're right," Billie said laughing. "Ginger it is."

The shape of Ginger's head and her long-haired coat showed traces of spaniel, but she was not a pedigreed dog. Billie got her from the animal shelter.

"They're the best dogs," Dad always said. "Grateful for the love you show them."

"You love mutts because you are one. A lovable mutt," Mom used to say, teasing him.

When I'd asked for a dog, Mom said we couldn't get one because no one was home during the day to take care of a pet, but no one was home at the apartment either. During the week, Ginger stayed in a big wire crate with bowls for food and water. Billie walked her in the morning before she went to work, late in the day when she came home, and after driving to the apartment on her lunch hour.

That weekend, Dad had a surprise for me too—a new bat, glove, and a pack of six baseballs. "Now you won't have to drag your stuff from home if you want to play ball with your friend," he said. I preferred another explanation. Having something of mine at the apartment made me part of it, not just a visitor, and when I had to go home, Billie and Dad had a reminder of me—even if the equipment was stored in a built-in wooden box under the steps outside.

One Saturday afternoon when Billie said I could take Ginger for a walk, I walked her over to Jeff's house, and together we walked her around the block. In front of the arcade, as I was handing the leash to Jeff, a car passed us, and Ginger took off after it. She yanked the leash from my hand and dashed dangerously close to the car. "Ginger, come back," I yelled as Jeff and I raced after her. I thought the driver would hear us—or Ginger's barking—and stop, but he kept going. As Ginger fell behind, the car swerved, and the rear wheel caught her. There was a yelp, a thud, and Ginger lay panting and whimpering in the street. "No!" I yelled and ran even faster. When I reached her, I dove to my knees, moaning, "No. Oh, no." Her big brown eyes asked a question I couldn't answer, and I put my arms around her but looked away.

Other cars screeched to a stop, a door slammed, and a driver ran to us. "We'll have to move her, but carefully," he said, as he worked his arms under Ginger's body, lifted and carried her to the grassy area between the curb and sidewalk. He smoothed his hand over Ginger's head, soothed her with, "There, there, girl," and moved his hands all over her body. When he touched her left front leg, she gave a pitiful cry. "Feels like it's broken," he said. "You should get her to a vet."

"Billie," I breathed, even as I dreaded delivering the news that Ginger was hurt.

"Go get her," Jeff said. "I'll stay here."

Dismissing the Good Samaritan's offer of a ride, I ran as fast as I could to the apartment, stopped for a second to catch my breath at the base of the stairs, and then raced to the top.

"What's wrong?" Dad asked when I burst through the door.

"Ginger," I gasped.

"Oh, no," Billie said. "Where is she?"

I sucked in, then expelled another breath. "The arcade."

"I'll get the car," Dad said, but Billie ran out of the house down the steps and I took off after her.

When we reached them, Jeff was smoothing Ginger's coat, and when the dog saw Billie, she whimpered and pedaled her front legs trying to get up. Billie cuddled her pet and cooed to her where she lay in the grass. When Dad arrived, the driver who'd stopped helped him get Ginger into the back seat. Billie got in beside her, and I sat in front with Dad.

As I waved goodbye to Jeff, Dad reproached me and left me

shaken. "How'd you let that happen, Finn?"

"It's okay, it's okay," Billie said, but she was talking to Ginger, not Dad or me.

Ginger did have a broken leg, but no other injuries. The vet we took her to applied a splint, said she'd learn to limp on three legs until it healed, and she'd be fine.

Back at the apartment, Billie carried Ginger up the steps and into the bedroom. Dad said he'd better take me home because Bille was upset. I braced for a lecture, but he didn't say anything else until he pulled up in front of our house and the scaffolding erected in front of it. "What's going on?" he asked.

"Mom's getting the house painted," I said, and then, because he'd made me feel bad about Ginger, "She said she had to do it because you aren't around anymore."

Dad white-knuckled the steering wheel as he stared at the house, and I jumped out of the car.

"Finn, wait," he said, just before I slammed the door. "What color?"

"Blue," I said. "Her favorite."

At school, I told Jeff I didn't know when I'd be back in his neighborhood.

"It wasn't your fault," he said. "Just a bad break."

Mom took my side too. "Accidents happen," she said. I don't know what she told Dad, but in another couple of weeks I got to go back to the apartment. It was the only time Billie wasn't waiting for me on the landing, the only time I dragged my feet going up the stairs.

Inside, I asked her, "Are you still mad at me?"

"Oh, I wasn't mad, Finn," she said. "I was worried about Ginger, but she's all right. That's all that matters." As though weighing whether she should continue, she paused. "It was your dad who thought you had to learn a lesson."

And Dad who'd kept me from Billie.

CHAPTER FOURTEEN

AT THE APARTMENT ONE SATURDAY NIGHT AFTER SCHOOL had started, I got sick, sicker than I'd ever been. As the pain intensified, I pressed my hands into my abdomen and pushed Ginger away when she tried to jump up on me.

That brought Billie to my side. "What's wrong, Finn?" she asked, as I doubled over on a kitchen chair.

When I groaned, "My stomach," she called Dad, and when a wave of nausea engulfed me, I groaned again. "I'm going to puke."

"Let's get you to the bathroom," Dad said, trying to help me up.

"I can't," I whimpered, deadweight in Dad's arms. Billie ran out of the kitchen and back in seconds with a bath towel. She folded it in half, laid it in my lap, and knelt on the floor in front of me.

"I'll hold it for you if you have to throw up," she said. I didn't want to, not in front of her. I moaned and shook my head. "It's all right," she said. "Go ahead. It will make you feel better."

As though her words were a finger stuck down my throat, I gagged, my stomach convulsed, and I puked in the towel. Hanging there, grossed out by the puddle of chunks, I shuddered and hurled again, twice. Billie wiped my mouth with a clean corner of the towel and waited. My stomach contracted and again I gagged, but nothing came up. I wasn't better, though. The pain persisted along with the heaves and my mewling. Billie balled up the towel, set it on the floor under the table, and put her hand on my forehead. "He's hot, like he has a fever," she said to Dad, and to me, "Where does it hurt, Finn?" When I pressed my hands on my lower right side, she grabbed Dad's arm, and her soothing voice turned urgent. "It might be his appendix, Aidan. You'd better get him to the hospital."

When Dad scooped me in his arms and ran out of the house down the steps, I was in too much pain to protest being carried like a baby. Billie ran behind us, then darted around Dad to open the passenger door for me. I curled up on the seat, and when Dad got in behind the wheel, he slammed his door, propped my head on his thigh, and started the car. When Billie knocked on his window, he shouted, "Gotta go," backed up out of the driveway, and pulled into the street.

Was he upset with Billie now?

As he drove, Dad steered with his left hand and kept his right on me, rubbing my arm. Nervous or worried or both, he talked nonstop. "Sorry you're hurting, bud. There's not much traffic now. We'll be there in no time. I'll call your mom as soon as we get there."

At the hospital, Dad pulled up outside the emergency entrance and ran inside carrying me again. "Help. Need some help here," he called, and a nurse ran toward us. "His appendix," he said, when she asked what was wrong. He laid me on the cot in one of the curtained-off spaces, and, moaning, I rolled onto my side. When the nurse took my blood pressure, the cuff's tight squeeze distracted me for a moment, but then a doctor came in and pressed on my belly.

"Yeow!" I howled like Grandpa did in the hospital after the storm.

"Call the surgeon," the doctor ordered the nurse.

Later, when Mom peeked around the curtain then yanked it aside to enter, I launched myself into her arms, held tight, and cried. I didn't care who saw or heard. "It's okay, Finn," she said, her voice soothing like Billie's. "Your Dad and I are here. You'll be all right."

It took me a while to wake up after the surgery. At the voices and beeping noises, I tried to open my eyes, but I couldn't lift my lids. It felt like they'd been glued shut.

"It's all over," someone said.

"Mom?"

"I'm here," she said, exhaling deeply.

"Dad?"

"Right here, bud."

Billie? Did I say her name or just think it?

When I was discharged two days later, Dad drove Mom and me home and stayed with us all day. My belly was swollen and still tender, but I didn't want to go to bed. I lay on the couch with my head on Dad's thigh like when he'd driven me to the hospital. Mom sat at the other end of the sofa, my feet in her lap. It was like they couldn't get close enough and couldn't keep their hands off me. Dad patted, stroked, and jostled my arm. When Mom checked my forehead for fever, she used her lips instead of her hand. It was an excuse to kiss me, and even Dad kissed me when it was time for him to leave.

They both wanted to be home with me for the rest of the week, but it was the start of a new school year for Mom, and Dad had to sell extra ads for a special supplement in the paper, so Grandpa came to stay with me. When he told me my appendix had nearly burst, all the touching and hugging and kissing made sense. "We might have lost you," he said, putting an arm around me and kissing me himself on the top of my head. After a pause, as though weighing his words, he added, "I probably shouldn't say anything, and don't get your hopes up just yet, but I wouldn't be surprised if this gets your mom and dad back together again."

My stomach churned as though I was getting sick all over again. A reconciliation was what I should want, but then how would I get to see—

"It's lucky your dad got you to the hospital in time," Grandpa said.

But it was Billie, Billie who'd told Dad to take me.

I spent a second day on the couch and again after she came home, Mom hovered. Dad was back too after work, but like a guest not a member of the family. He rang the bell even though the front door was open and we could see each other through the storm door. "Look who's here," Mom said to me when she went to the door and stood aside to let Dad enter. Before going back to the kitchen, she told him, "You can stay and eat with Finn if you want. It's just that macaroni and cheese from the box, but he likes it."

That gave me the segue to ask Dad about Billie, but when I did, he said, "Don't worry about Billie. Just concentrate on getting better." But I did worry that in dismissing my question Dad was dismissing Billie too.

The next day events snowballed. Mom made Dad's favorite food, shepherd's pie, and sat to eat with us at the dining room table. They conversed like a couple in a TV commercial. Dad complimented Mom's cooking and Mom offered him a second helping. If Dad noticed his photo missing from the buffet, he didn't let on.

After dinner, Jeff brought my homework assignments and said, "Hey, maybe your mom and dad will get back together." Again, it was what I should want, but . . .

On Saturday morning, I felt well enough to get out of the house, and Dad and I walked to Grandpa's. "How's it going?" Grandpa asked, setting his newspaper aside.

"I'm working on it," Dad said. I assumed he meant the sales campaign at the paper.

After another week, Mom said I was recovered enough to resume a regular schedule. When Dad came to pick me up, she was working in the yard. Packing in my room, I heard them through my open windows.

"The house looks nice, Monica," Dad said.

Her response was matter-of-fact. "It needed new paint."

"And that blue's a good color," he said, offering another compliment.

"Now you like it," Mom said. "You fought me on it for months."

"I know," Dad said. "I guess I just couldn't picture it." She must have turned away from him because he said, "Wait, I want to ask you something." And then, "I want to come home." My chest pounding, I tiptoed to my window, pushed the curtain aside, and looked down on them.

"That's not a question," Mom replied.

Dad moved toward her and made his pitch quickly. "I'll leave the paper. Sell cars at Simpson's. Can I come home, Monica?"

"Why?" she asked.

"You," he said without hesitation, "and Finn. You're my family." It was the right answer. Surely, she'd say yes. Instead, she asked, "Have you left her?" and when Dad didn't reply, Mom said, "Well, do that, and then ask me." She sounded confident, like she'd known all along Dad would want to come home again. But it had been months since we'd been a family, and for the last few, Mom had seemed just fine on her own. Did she really want Dad back? Or did she just want him to not be with Billie?

The storm door opened and slammed shut. "Finn," Mom called from the bottom of the stairs. "Your dad's here." I expelled the breath I didn't realize I'd been holding and collapsed on the edge of my bed as my legs gave way.

Later, when Dad pulled up to the apartment and Billie ran down the steps to my side of the car, I told her, "I'm all right," but I wasn't. I was afraid to warn her that Dad wanted to leave, so I concentrated on reminding him how great things were with her.

"Billie's a good cook, isn't she, Dad?" I said when she served us ground beef mixed with some ingredients from a box.

She laughed. "Oh, Finn, I am not. I can't make anything from scratch."

"Dance," I told them on Saturday night, and while Dad danced with Billie when she reached for him, it was at arm's length, and he didn't cut in when she danced with me. When we watched TV, he let me sit between them on the sofa, but I couldn't enjoy it. It was another troubling sign. He was pulling away from Billie. I tried to beam a warning to her, but it didn't work. She didn't get it.

"Is something wrong?" she asked me. "You're so quiet."

I pressed Ginger against the ache in my chest and begged to take her to church on Sunday for the blessing of animals. We couldn't go in the afternoon like everyone else because then I would be with Mom, but I was sure Father Damian would bless Ginger before Mass. Dad didn't commit. "We'll see," he said.

During the night, I woke with the urge to pee and made my way like a blind man through the kitchen and down the hall. I stopped when I saw the sliver of light under the closed bathroom door. I almost knocked, but then Billie opened it. She pulled the door wide, glanced back at the mirror, and then turned toward me.

"Finn!" She gasped. She was naked.

She ducked back behind the door and closed it, but too late. I'd seen everything. The triangle-shaped patch of reddish-brown hair glistening between her legs. The dark rings around her pointy nipples. Breasts like the supple balloons filled near to bursting for summertime water battles with Jeff. I stared open-mouthed at the closed door, the way I'd stared after getting a glimpse at one of the men's magazines in the barbershop. Billie was a centerfold come to life. When she opened the door again, she was dressed in her robe. "It's all yours," she said lightly, stepping out of the bathroom as though nothing had happened.

My face and body burned. In the seconds it took to reach the toilet, I freed myself from my pajama bottoms, then lifted the seat, and released a stream. Relieved, I tried to relax, willing my shaking to stop, my breathing to return to normal. Seeing Billie like that was an accident, so why did I feel like I'd done something wrong?

When I opened the door, Billie was there. "Can't sleep?" she asked, bending down, trying to get me to look at her. "How about some milk?" In the kitchen, she sat with me at the table while we sipped from the mugs she'd warmed in the microwave. When she asked if I was okay, I nodded, but kept my eyes on my cup.

"What's going on?" Spooked by Dad's sudden appearance behind me, I almost spilled my milk.

"We just woke up," Billie told him. "We're trying the warm milk trick to get back to sleep. Right, Finn?" Right. I nodded again.

"Go back to bed, Billie. I'll stay with him," Dad said. As he sat down, Billie got up, and I raised my eyes to hers. Her expression confirmed it. We had a secret to keep.

"Bad dream, bud?" Dad asked.

"No. I'm all right." I didn't want to deal with him.

"Good. It's way too early." As he walked me back to the couch, his face practically disappeared behind a boisterous yawn. He waited until I got under the covers, turned off the light in the kitchen, and went back to bed. With Billie.

I lay still, my eyes wide in the darkness, as I imagined Billie in the bathroom, in the kitchen, dancing, watching TV—naked in every scene. Growing hard, I worked my hand through the fly of my pajama pants. It was okay to touch myself there if I was alone, Mom had told me when I was little. "It's a private thing," she'd said gently, the day she found me on the front porch with my left thumb in my mouth and my right hand inside my shorts.

In the morning, Dad shook me awake and told me to hurry or I would be late for church. I grabbed my clothes and ran to the bathroom grateful it was empty. When I came out, I picked up Ginger and ran to the door. "Leave the dog," Dad said. "There's no time. Let's go." As though she understood, Ginger squirmed out of my arms and ran away, leaving me grasping air.

Neither Dad nor I said anything the whole way to the church. I was growing agitated like the Hulk, and not just about Ginger. Dad had sent Billie away from me in the night, and he wanted to leave her. When he stopped the car to let me out in front of the church, he said, "I'll see you next Sunday again. Remember? To celebrate your birthday." He reached for me, but I leaned away, jumped out of the car, and slammed the door without saying goodbye. I raced for the church but couldn't outrun my thoughts: I hate you. I hate you. I wish you were dead.

Dad was right. It was late. The organist had started to play, and Mom and Grandpa stood in their usual pew singing the opening hymn. "What's wrong?" Mom whispered.

"Nothing," I said, trying to slow my breathing, shocked at what I'd wished, but not sorry for being mad at Dad.

After two more verses, I calmed down a bit, but got worked up again. There were scripture readings to come, like the one about being mad at your brother. It probably applied to your father too. If you were angry with someone, you were supposed to reconcile with him before you approached the altar. Otherwise, God would throw you into the fires of Gehenna. Ruminating about that, I didn't hear the readings, the homily, or anything else.

During the recessional hymn, I resolved to call Dad and apologize for acting like a jerk, but after church Mom and I went out for brunch with Grandpa and my aunts, and when we got home, I shot hoops for a while and did my homework. Then we had supper and I watched some TV before I went to bed. In the morning, when I realized I'd forgotten to call Dad, an apology no longer seemed urgent. He wasn't one to hold a grudge, and we'd be together again in a week.

I shouldn't have, but I let it go.

CHAPTER FIFTEEN

THEY SAY WHEN TRAGEDY STRIKES, TIME STANDS STILL, but it doesn't. It ticks right along. It's the person hit with the life-altering loss who falls out of sync with time until he makes sense of the misfortune or accepts his fate. At least that's how it was for me early that next Sunday morning.

Lying in bed on my stomach with my face toward the wall, I strained to make out the words that crept up the stairs. From the somber sound and the groan of my door, it was bad news and it was coming for me. Mom's slippers scuffed the floor, and the mattress sagged as she sat down on the edge of my bed.

"Finn, honey, are you awake?" she asked, sniffling as she rubbed my back. "I have to tell you something." She paused, and when she spoke again, her voice cracked. "I'm so sorry. Your daddy's dead."

Dead. Ping. Dead. Ping. Dead. The word bounced around in my brain like a silver sphere in one of the arcade's pinball machines.

"But it's my birthday." Yes, that's what I said when I sat up and saw Mom's sorrowful expression, her red eyes. What was I thinking? That it was my day, that I shouldn't have to share it? Maybe I wasn't thinking. I could have been in shock. Regardless, every year I grow older while Dad stays thirty-six. If I'm an old man someday, will it seem like he was my son instead of my father?

"Oh, your birthday," Mom said, as though her forgetting that detail was as tragic as the news she'd just delivered. After a pause she added, "He died in his sleep. We don't know why."

I wish you were dead.

I shuddered at the recollection and at what had been my plan for the day, celebrating my birthday with Dad and—oh no, Billie.

Mom put her arm around me. "Come downstairs," she said. "Grandpa and Pete are here."

I didn't go right away. I lay down on my back and stared at the clouds on my ceiling. If only I could ride out on the horse, sail away on the boat, lift off in the spaceship. When I finally got up and went into the bathroom—

You got your wish.

I grabbed the edge of the sink to steel myself against the wave of shame.

In the kitchen, Grandpa motioned me over, hugged me tight, and let out a wild animal cry like we sometimes heard coming from the woods behind his house. He sobbed so hard I was afraid he wouldn't be able to catch his breath. Embarrassed for him, I patted his back the way he'd patted mine when I'd cried as a kid. Mom's face crumpled, and she covered her mouth with her hand. When I felt I couldn't support Grandpa for another second, he stopped crying, released me, and reached into his back pocket for his handkerchief. He wiped his eyes, blew his nose, and set his mouth in a grim straight line.

Mom poured more coffee for him and Pete and set a glass

of juice in front of me. She turned on the radio and tuned in the classical music station like she did every Sunday before church, but when it was time, we didn't get ready. We didn't go. We sat in the kitchen where the details of Dad's death lingered as though waiting for us to absorb and accept them. The ambulance driver, a friend of Pete's, had called him from the hospital at four in the morning but told him not to rush to get there. It was too late. After Pete left the hospital, he went home for Grandpa and they were at our house by six. Nobody said, but it would have been Billie who called for the ambulance, Billie who was with Dad when he'd died.

That sparked the notion that his death was somehow her fault, not mine. If she'd never come to Danton, if Dad and I had never gotten into her car, if she hadn't winked at me and danced with me and let me see her naked and made me like her more than I loved Dad, I never would have wished for him to die. But then I faulted Dad for falling for Billie and Mom for making Dad leave. I couldn't blame Billie. I wasn't sorry she'd come.

After my aunts arrived and cried, they took charge. It was strange to see them so confident, and I marveled at how they knew what to do without asking Mom. Rachele was all business as she answered the phone, briskly thanked callers for their concern, and told them to check the *Monitor* for visiting hours at the funeral home. Aunt Rina responded graciously to the bell at the front door, the knocks at the back. Neighbors and friends presented her with foil-covered casseroles, bread from the bakery, bottles of wine and whiskey from the liquor store. What did they think we were celebrating? When she invited them inside, though, they shook their heads, said they didn't want to bother us, and made a quick get-away. It was like they thought we had a communicable disease.

Except for the firemen, elderly parishioners, and my grandmother, I'd known of only one other person who'd died, a girl two grades behind me in school who drowned in the river one summer. Tragedy was incompatible with the joys of vacation, so by the time school started in September, I questioned whether she was dead after all. For all I knew she might have moved away. In a similar way, I dissociated myself from Dad's death. Mom wasn't explaining everything, and I didn't have an instruction sheet like the one that had come with my Millennium Falcon.

The household activity didn't involve me until late afternoon when Mom said she didn't have anything to wear because Dad thought black was depressing, and I didn't have a suit. My aunts said they would take care of everything, and, with a flurry of phone calls, they did. In minutes, as though they'd been waiting to be summoned for service, women neighbors and friends appeared with three dark suits for me and three black dresses for Mom. There was a problem with each of the suits, though. If the pants fit me, the coat sleeves were too long or too short, and if the jacket was okay, there was something wrong with the pants. Five women tugged at the clothes I tried on until they paired the pants from one suit with the coat from another and agreed that together they'd do.

After everyone left that night, after I'd gone upstairs, Mom came into my room and sat on my bed as she had in the morning. "I'm sorry," she said again. Instead of consoling me, her words pricked. I was the one who should have been sorry.

When I woke the next morning to a pattering on the leaves outside my window, I imagined the drizzle washing away the previous day's events or absolving me, but then a heavier rain drummed the roof, demanding answers. Where are you, Finn? What have you done? I burrowed under the covers until Mom came into my room.

She said Grandpa was downstairs again and would stay with me while she went to the funeral home and church. Making arrangements—that's what she called it. I thought Grandpa would be all cried out, but after the paper was delivered and he checked the death record on the front page, his eyes filled with tears again, and he dabbed at them with his handkerchief. When he turned to the obituary page, he caught his breath, and said, "Look, Finn." Along with a photo, the *Monitor* editors had given Dad a glory obit that ran over two columns halfway down the page. For once, Grandpa didn't complain about the special coverage. The obituary listed Mom and me as Dad's survivors. It didn't say anything about Billie, and the paper didn't specify the location of his death despite being a stickler for every who, what, when, where, and why. That was a huge concession to Mom. I wondered whether she'd notice.

That evening when Grandpa drove us under the funeral home portico, the car door opened before Mom could reach for the handle. A sober-looking man greeted her with a slight bow as though she were royalty. He led us up the steps of a house like ours, but inside, I understood why Grandpa had called it a funeral parlor. In a room to our left, ornate old-fashioned sofas and chairs sat stiffly around the perimeter waiting to receive callers. Formal drapes and coordinated shades covered the windows, walling off the world outside.

Straight ahead past that room was a larger one filled like the flower shop with arrangements in baskets and vases set atop tables and tall pillars. The strong smell of lilies overwhelmed the scent of more delicate blooms. A few steps into the room, I stopped. When Mom asked if I was all right, her voice came from a distance and her face was a blob of light.

"Water. We need water," she said. I sank onto a padded folding chair and bent over, putting my head between my knees like she told me. After a few minutes I sat up, sipped some water from a funnel-shaped paper cup, and stared at the floor trying to process what I'd seen before things went all wobbly. It was Dad lying in the casket in his suit, looking spent, not just asleep, as though he'd battled Death before he lost the fight.

Mom helped me up and walked me over to the casket. She touched Dad's hand while I stared at his fused-looking fingers. That occurred in some mammals he'd told me once. There was a funny word for it. Syncro or syndica something. No, syndactyly. It was a rare condition in humans, though.

Then I turned to Dad's face.

"He looks good, Monica," Grandpa said behind me, and I whirled around. Grandpa seemed serious, but how could he be? Dad didn't look good to me. He didn't even look real. His skin was waxy, and his features barely stood out. His mouth was too soft and too pink, like a girl's. I shuddered. What had they done to him? Why did Mom let them?

Dad's head rested on a small pale pink satin pillow, his cowlick sticking up the way it always did. It was the one aspect of his appearance he would have wanted changed, but the only one they'd left untouched. Someone should smooth down that tuft of hair. But, hey, don't look at me. I can't do it. I can't touch him. I stayed at arm's length from the casket, the way Billie had held me the first time we'd danced. Billie. What was she doing? Had she stocked her freezer with ice cream, her cupboard with sundae toppings for a party? Had she bought me a present for my birthday? How would I get it now?

Misreading my preoccupation as hesitation, Mom said, "I know you feel bad, Finn, but you can do this." She positioned me next to her to one side of the casket. People approached us from a long line that backed out the door of the room at times, and then sat on the folding chairs and whispered among themselves like an audience awaiting the start of a performance. I wished I were sitting among them instead of standing up in front. I didn't know my lines, my blocking. I hadn't had any rehearsal.

"I'm sorry," most people said to Mom and me, but some said,

"You have my deepest sympathy." When they uttered that more formal phrase, I almost expected women to curtsy and men to bow and kiss Mom's hand. It made Dad sound important, but I was confused by the sentiment.

"Why do people say they're sorry?" I asked Mom. "It's not their fault."

"No, of course not," she said. "But they feel bad for us because we're sad."

Sad? Sad was how I'd felt when Grandpa got hurt in the storm, when friends moved away, when I learned Dad wanted to leave Billie and come back home. But sad about Dad dying? Ow. Oh. There it was, the sudden pain in my chest forcing me to breathe twice as hard to get half as much air.

Toward the end of the evening, people talked more loudly and every so often someone laughed. I wormed my way into a circle of men and listened to Mullaney from the pub describe how wakes in Ireland involved drinking and singing and pranks like tossing the corpse in the air. When the pack of people howled, I squeezed out of the ring, looked for Grandpa, and sat with him on a settee next to the casket.

"Why are they laughing?" I asked him. "Aren't they sad anymore?"

"Oh, they're sad," he said, releasing a weary breath. "Almost too sad to bear it. Laughing eases the pain. At least for a little while."

The next afternoon, Mr. Weiss came to the funeral home with some of the kids from my previous year's sixth-grade class. Jeff walked up to Mom, who hugged him, and then motioned for me to follow him outside. He threw his arm across my shoulders as we walked. "How are you holding up?" he asked, sounding like the adults who addressed Mom or Grandpa or Pete. I told him how Dad didn't look like I'd remembered him. "It's the stuff they pump in to keep him from rotting," he said. So, Dad wasn't himself on the inside either.

We'd walked almost all around the block when I saw the red Camaro. For the first time since getting the news about Dad, I brightened. I crossed the street and when I reached her car, Billie got out. Her eyes were red-rimmed, not made up, and she cleared her throat. "I'm so sorry about your dad, Finn. There was nothing I could do."

"I know," I said. I didn't know, of course, not for sure, but it seemed like the thing to say to try to make her feel better. She tried but couldn't quite manage a smile.

Then, just when I thought things couldn't get any worse, they did. Billie said one more thing before getting back into her car and pulling away. Glued to the spot, I waited for Jeff to cross the street.

"What'd she say?" he asked.

Saying the words out loud would give them a finality I didn't want to accept. I swallowed hard before answering him. "She said she's moving back to Florida."

But what I'd heard as the last word, Jeff regarded as a hiccup. I should have known and not despaired. "Ask her to stay," he said, as though that was the obvious solution.

I'd just have to work out how and when to do it.

That night before we left the funeral home, I knelt at the casket with Mom, as my eyes flicked from the flowers to the lampstand to the crucifix to Dad. Something was wrong, different from the afternoon, and then I saw it. His features were blending, maybe even melting. Nobody else said anything. Maybe they hadn't noticed, but it was a good thing Dad was going to be buried the next day. If we waited much longer, he might not have any eyes or nose or mouth at all. He'd be the Man Without a Face.

At home, Mom tried to prepare me for the funeral the next

day. "It will be the last time we see your dad," she said. "If you want to, you can put something in the casket, something special like one of your lucky pennies." So, she'd noticed me collecting them. Dad probably would like to have one of the coins. I took one of the pennies from my box, fingered it for a while, then put it in the pocket of my suit pants.

When I dressed in that suit the next morning, it still felt different from my everyday clothes, but not as strange as when I'd first tried it on. For once Mom would have been right to think I'd grown overnight. I felt older, taller even. Working deliberately like he was trying to slow time, Grandpa tied the tie for me, draping, wrapping, looping, tucking, snugging it up at my neck. Girding me.

Later, kneeling beside me at the casket in the funeral home, Mom took a small envelope from her purse and slipped it between the satiny lining of the casket and the satiny cover over Dad's body. Was it a card, a letter, a note? What did it say? Why would she leave it? It wasn't like Dad could read it.

I fingered the penny in my pocket but couldn't make myself take it out. I couldn't even say I was sorry for keeping it. I'd collected it. It was my memento, no one else's, especially not Dad's. I did do something else for him, though, something I thought he'd appreciate as much as having a reminder of Billie. At first, I wasn't sure I could do it, but I didn't want to wimp out. I reached for Dad's head the way he'd often reached for mine to rub or pat or stroke my hair. I smoothed his cowlick, tucking it down between his head and the pillow. I waited a few seconds for it to pop back up, but for once, it stayed put.

Outside the funeral home, Mom, Grandpa, my aunts, and I got into a long black limousine with the same lush leather interior as Billie's Camaro. I imagined her riding with me as the procession undulated for blocks behind us and traffic stopped at intersections for us like we were a passing parade.

At the church, bells pealed like they rang for Sunday Mass. Uncle Pete and five friends of my dad who'd been riding in a smaller limo in front of us got out and huddled behind the hearse. They pulled the casket from the vehicle, then in one smooth move hoisted it up onto their shoulders. Mom gasped then squared her own. As we followed them into the church, she walked like a queen.

"Why did they do that?" I asked her in our front-row pew as the pallbearers positioned the casket on a bier in the center aisle.

She whispered back, "To show their respect." Then she gave a little laugh. "Or maybe they were showing off."

Stacked flower arrangements from the funeral home formed a garden wall in front of the altar. Although at capacity, the church was quiet. There was no murmuring like on Sundays when people greeted each other and conversed quietly, just an occasional cough or throat clearing until the choir began to sing. The sweet smell of incense wafted from the censer reinforcing the solemnity. Mom motioned to the funeral director to roll the bier closer to where she sat at the end of the first pew. She curled her fingers around the bronze hand rail of the casket and held on all through the service like she was holding onto Dad.

At home after the funeral, I rocked with Grandpa on our porch swing, listening to the crick-creak of the chains, recalling Father Damian's prayer for eternal rest, and the reading about Jesus preparing a dwelling place for Dad.

"Are there really houses for people in heaven?" I asked Grandpa.

"Why not?" he said, after a few seconds' pause. "Mansions for the poor and people who were very good in life."

"Dad wouldn't want a mansion," I said, "and he wouldn't rest."

"You're right about that," Grandpa said, managing a slight

smile.

"Do you think Dad will find Hudson, the boy who disappeared after the storm?" I asked him.

"Then neither one of them would be alone," Grandpa said, his surprise morphing into pride as he patted my back. "It's good of you to remember that boy, Finn."

People who'd followed us home must have run through everything they had to say about Dad. In the snatches of conversation I overheard, they talked about their jobs, the Steelers, and weekend plans, though still in the subdued voices they'd used in the funeral home. Mom and my aunts fussed over the food, dividing it up, packing it in containers to send home with the mourners. Her preoccupation confirmed I'd been left with the practical parent. Mom would see to it that I was fed and clothed, did my homework, went to after-school and weekend activities, and didn't watch too much TV. With Mom, I'd get what I needed, but without Dad, well, it was up to me to get what I wanted.

Straining against the straightjacket-fit of the suit, I shrugged out of the coat, pulled at the tie to loosen it, and took them up to my room where I changed into jeans, a T-shirt, and sneakers. Back downstairs, I grabbed my jacket from the hall closet. As I weaved my way around the people in my path, no one asked where I was going. No one even looked at me. Maybe I'd developed a superhero's power after all. Maybe I was invisible. I slipped out the back door closing it quietly, although I doubted anyone would have noticed if I'd let it slam shut. I went into the garage through the side door, got my bike, and walked it down the driveway.

I'd only ever gone to the apartment in Dad's car, but I could get there on my bike. I pedaled furiously on the straightaways and practically flew while coasting down the hills. The one hazardous spot was the four-lane highway, but since it was mid-afternoon on a weekday, there wasn't much traffic. I crossed to the island in the intersection, waited for the light to change, and then walked my bike across the last two lanes and up the steep hill.

By the time I reached the apartment, I was breathing heavily and ruminating, "Why me?" and "It's not fair." I propped my bike against the storage box that held my baseball gear and grabbed my bat. Imagining myself on deck in a game, I swung it once, twice, three times, thrilled to finally feel in control of something. Glinting in the sun, one of the headlights on Dad's car caught my eye. Was it a ball sitting on a tee or a pitch coming straight at me? Whatever. I assumed a hitter's stance and struck it with a level swing. The impact jarred my hands, and the headlight shattered, sending splinters flying. Power surged through my arms and I slammed the bat against the hood, a fender, the driver's-side door. The smooth metal surfaces crumpled like the balled-up pieces of paper I shot into Dad's wastebasket at work.

"Finn!" When Billie yelled and ran down the steps, I went limp, dropped the bat, and stared at the battered car, shocked to see so much damage. "Oh, no, you're bleeding," she said when she reached me. There was a cut I hadn't felt on the back of my hand. Billie rolled the cuff of her white shirt down over her wrist, pressed it against my hand, and led me up the stairs. In the bathroom, she said the cut was just a scratch and covered it with a bandage. The warm washcloth she gave me to wipe my face absorbed the last of my fury, and I mumbled my plea into it.

"What did you say?" Billie asked.

I removed the washcloth from my face and repeated, "Don't go." Since Jeff's suggestion, I'd focused only on making the request, not on how Billie would respond.

"Oh, Finn," she said. "I don't see how I can stay." She spoke the words whisper-soft, but they cut like the shards from the car's shattered headlight. Embarrassed, I hid my face again.

There was a scratching at the bedroom door, and when Billie

told me I could go get Ginger, the dog jumped into my arms and I slid to the floor. She licked my face and I pressed it into her fur. I wanted to hide under the bed or lock myself in the bathroom so I could stay, but I couldn't even hold onto Ginger let alone Billie. Breaking free, the dog dashed into the kitchen, the nails of her paws tap, tap, tapping the linoleum floor.

Billie made a phone call, and when my uncle showed up, Pete told her he would have Dad's car towed away. "Are you okay?" he asked, and when she didn't answer, he said, "Let me know if you need anything." She looked at him like she was seeing Dad, and my heart nosedived. No, Billie, don't. Not Pete. Devastated, I followed him out of the apartment on autopilot.

Pete hoisted my bike into the bed of his truck and opened the passenger door for me. When he climbed in behind the wheel, he gave my thigh a couple of awkward pats, but I didn't want his sympathy, not when it felt like I'd lost Billie and he might win her. I hugged the door. I couldn't help myself. I'm sure he was as startled as I was when I wailed and the words tumbled out.

"I'll never see Billie again."

CHAPTER SIXTEEN

By the time Pete pulled his truck up in front of our house, I'd stopped snuffling but started worrying that he'd tell Mom what I'd said about Billie. I should have said Dad. I'll never see Dad again. And I shouldn't have gone to Billie's in the first place.

"Keep it," Pete said, when I tried to hand back his tears-and-snot-soaked handkerchief. I shoved it in my jacket pocket.

My voice wavered when I asked him, "Am I in trouble?"

"Guess you'll find out," he said, pointing me toward the porch with a noncommittal lift of his chin.

The steps rose like bleachers, and drained of the emotion that had overtaken me at Billie's, I climbed wearily, pausing on each tread before launching myself onto the next. I braced for the questions Mom would surely ask: Why did you go there, Finn? What were you thinking?

I don't know why. I wasn't thinking. I'm sorry. Don't be mad.

The living room was dark and empty. Lights and low voices drew me to the kitchen where Grandpa and my aunts sat at the table in a sort of tableau. With sheepish smiles, they looked sorry, like it was their fault I'd slipped away unnoticed. Standing behind them, Mom studied me as though I were a mystery. I shifted under her scrutiny.

"Are you hungry?" Grandpa asked. "How about a sandwich or some meatballs?"

"There's lasagna," said Aunt Rina.

"Or that macaroni and cheese you like," Aunt Rachele added.

On the table was a store-bought half sheet cake with "Happy Birthday" piped in blue icing. We were finally celebrating my birthday, and I was relieved Mom hadn't added candles to the cake. With lit candles, everyone would have coaxed me to make a wish, but even if I blew out the flames on all thirteen, I'd never see Dad again, and I couldn't imagine how I'd ever get to be with Billie. Everyone sang to me, and after we ate the cake and ice cream, I unwrapped the present Mom handed me and gaped at a video game console and two cartridges.

"It was your dad's idea," she said. "He bought them when you were in the hospital and wanted to give them to you when you got home, but I told him to wait until your birthday. I'm sorry about that, Finn."

"Well, open it," Pete said, nudging me. "Let's get it set up." My aunts dragged chairs from the kitchen, and everyone gathered around the TV in the living room while I attached the game cable and Pete connected it to the TV's cable jack. I showed them how to play Space Invaders, firing at the advancing rows of aliens.

"Now you won't be playing this all the time," Mom said. "And you'll have to do your homework first."

"Blah, blah, blah. Can it, Monica," Pete said as he fumbled with his controller. "He knows. He's not a kid." She smacked the back of Pete's head, and everyone laughed at his exaggerated, "Ow," and the way he hunkered down. They went crazy over

Pac-Man.

"Watch out," and "Get 'em," they shouted as I gobbled dots and outraced ghosts. We got lost in the games until ten when Mom looked at the clock and chased everyone home with a hurried "oh-my-gosh-look-at-the-time" and "Finn's-got-to-go-to-bed." She was sending me to school in the morning so I could be with my friends and get back into a routine.

After everyone left, I was afraid Mom would ask why I'd gone to Billie's. Instead, she focused on what Billie must have reported over the phone about what I'd done to Dad's car. "It's okay to be mad that your dad died," Mom said. She said some other things, too, like, "I want you to remember you're not the man of the house. It's my job to take care of you, not the other way around." And, "I'll try to take good care of myself, but, God forbid, if anything happens to me, Grandpa and Pete and your aunts will take care of you." It must have eased her anxiety to express the worst of her worries, but then they gnawed at me. I didn't want to think about being an orphan. The last thing she said was, "I know it's been a long hard day, and I'm sorry there will be more of them, but we'll get through them together, and after we do, we'll be even stronger."

It was her teacher's voice striving to convince me—or both of us, and it might have worked if I hadn't woken after midnight to the sound of her sobbing. I rolled onto my side and pressed my pillow to my ears, but I couldn't fall back asleep even after Mom stopped crying. I lay on my back, and then my stomach. I rolled from one side to the other. The numerals on my clock flipped as the minutes ticked by. One thirty-two, one thirty-three, one thirty-four. I punched my pillow to fluff it up. I tried to do what Mom had told me when I was little and couldn't sleep: "Lie still. Just rest your body." I even got up out of bed, sat in my chair, and read for a while. Nothing helped. I was wide awake. Then I remembered Billie's trick. I crept past Mom's room and down the stairs to the kitchen where I poured milk into a mug and gave it a minute on high in the microwave.

I was sitting at the kitchen table—imagining Billie there with me—when the squeak of a step signaled Mom would be joining me. She asked what I was drinking, then how I knew to try it, but she must have guessed. "Never mind," she said. "Does it work?" When I nodded, she heated a cup of milk for herself and sat down to drink it at the table.

When we'd finished Mom finally let me have it as though she'd read my mind and knew exactly what I was thinking. Her voice was calm but she slammed the door on the prospect of my returning to Billie's apartment. "Don't even think about going back there again," she said.

In the morning, the bus squealed to a stop in front of our house, and the noise inside died. As I walked down the aisle, kids looked up, then away—at their books, at the floor, out the windows—anywhere but at me. The ones who sat alone slid over toward the aisle to keep me from sitting with them. I took the only empty seat and moved close to the window, but everyone who boarded after me sat elsewhere. Some of them sat three abreast, crowded into one seat to avoid sitting with me in mine. A lump lodged in my throat, and my eyes watered, blurring the scenery like heat haze in summer. The driver kept glancing at our reflections in his mirror, but he didn't once have to yell at us to keep it down. No one made a sound.

The walk to my locker in the high school's seventh-grade wing was as long and lonely as the bus ride. When kids looked at me and then away, I imagined them whispering, "That's the kid whose dad died." I might have done that myself had it been anyone else in my position. I wasn't mad, just sad and feeling sorry for myself. I was different now, and in junior high, different was the one thing you didn't want to be.

At lunch, Jeff gobbled his ground beef and macaroni and finished half of mine. I didn't get it. Before lunch I'd been famished, but standing in the cafeteria line, I lost my appetite. I might have gone to the nurse's office to tell her I was sick so she'd call Mom to come and take me home, but Jeff had another idea.

"C'mon," he said when the bell rang signaling it was time for our next class. At the cafeteria doors, he turned away from the main hall and headed toward the exit to the student parking lot. Outside, we zigzagged as we ran among the cars, ducking alongside and behind them, and although it was fun, like playing cops and robbers when we were kids, it wasn't necessary. No one tried to stop us. No one even saw us.

I followed Jeff across the road beyond the parking lot and slid behind him down a steep grassy bank to a winding gurgling creek. Dragonflies hovered and water striders skimmed the surface. A frog's glug-glug sounded almost human. Stirred by the breeze, trembling leaves on tall trees scattered sunlight and shadow on every shade of green below. I didn't expect to find a memory of Dad, but there he was pointing to a cluster of mayapples, saying, "Look, Finn, fairy umbrellas."

"How'd you know this was here?" I asked Jeff.

"Saw it from the bus," he said, pointing to the road over a culvert ahead of us.

For a while Jeff and I tossed leaves and twigs into the creek and watched them float downstream or get snagged and stuck along the bank. Then we waded in, gathered flat stones, and built a dam. When the icy water numbed our feet, we dried off in the grass, put on our socks and shoes, and walked all the way downstream to where the creek petered out in a marsh and scores of cattails rose higher than our heads. With his pocket knife, Jeff cut down two of the cattails and handed one to me. It looked like a hot dog stuck the long way on a stick for roasting over a fire.

"On guard," Jeff shouted, assuming a fencer's stance, poking my chest with the tip of the stalk. I lunged, he parried, and we beat the stalks against each other until the catkins burst and disintegrated into clumps of filmy white fluff.

Revived by our fight, I yelled, "Let's get the rest of them," and after Jeff cut them down, we carried the canes to a clearing where we divided them into two piles. Solemnly, we each picked up a new weapon, faced off in proper form, then laughed and hollered as we flailed our foils. We worked our way through the stack of cattails until we'd destroyed every stalk. Ankle deep in the feather-light remains, I tossed armfuls overhead, then fell to my knees and rolled onto my back, moving my arms and legs like I was making a snow angel.

The sky was a blinding bright blue and white, not pale like the ceiling of my room, and I covered my eyes with my arm to shield them. "Nobody talked to me today," I said. Jeez. I was back to being a wuss. When Jeff cast his shadow over me, I raised my hand to grasp the one he extended and he yanked me up.

"Screw 'em." That's all he said, but it was enough. As we walked back and then climbed the bank, grabbing fistfuls of grass to pull ourselves up, I felt lighter, like I'd left the weight of the morning behind. We ran back to the school in time for dismissal.

"See you tomorrow—in the office," Jeff said, laughing as we separated. Shoot. I'd be in big trouble when Mom found out I'd cut my afternoon classes. She'd warned me often enough that I'd be punished at home for doing anything wrong at school.

"If you misbehave," she said, "it makes me look bad, too."

If I could convince her I'd been upset about Dad, she might let me off the hook for skipping. Then again, maybe she wouldn't find out. If the school sent a notice, I could intercept it because I got home from school before she did now and I checked the mail. I decided to take my chances and not say anything, but I knew what would happen. "Should I" or "shouldn't I" would sprout cartoon thought-bubble legs and chase each other around in my head for the rest of the day and into the night. I wished I were more like Jeff. He never let anything bother him.

In the morning when we were summoned via intercom to the office, I was relieved to see Jeff waiting for me. "Don't say anything," he said.

"You," the assistant principal said, pointing at Jeff, "I would expect this of you," then, turning to me, "but you, Finn, what would your mother say?" Had I been summoned alone, I might have cowered and caved, but with Jeff beside me, I just shrugged. The assistant principal gave up and said he wouldn't say anything to my mother, not this time, because she had enough to deal with right now, but there'd better not be a next time. He gave Jeff detention.

CHAPTER SEVENTEEN

MOM HAD BEEN BUSY WHILE I WAS IN SCHOOL. SHE'D moved Dad back in with us—in the photo on the buffet and the collage snapshots on the stairway wall. Too bad it was too late.

"I'm sorry. I never should have put them away," she said behind me as I studied the pictures like a visitor in a gallery. In that moment, though, it wasn't Dad or photos of him on my mind. Billie didn't have any pictures of me to display or put away. How would she remember me? My next thought was even worse. Without any pictures to remind me of Billie, would I forget her?

When I'd finished my homework, Mom knocked on the door of my room. She said she had more pictures I might like to see, and she spread her yearbooks and photo albums from college on my bed. "You'll find your dad in every photo, even the ones taken after he had to drop out and get a job. That's when he started to study on his own," Mom said with a slight smile. "He read my texts and asked me to borrow books from the library for him. He liked to quiz me and his friends and often, he stumped us. He was as smart as any of us who stayed in school."

"Who's this?" I asked, pointing to a photo of a guy looking at Mom while she gazed at Dad.

"Oh, John," she said. She tapped another photo of the man, a headshot, then walked to the door, turned back, and gave me a mischievous wink. "That man could have been your father." My mouth dropped like a marionette's and I stared at the door she closed behind her. What a thing for her to say. I studied the guy's closely cropped hair, the horn-rimmed glasses, his serious expression. He looked like a nerd.

Saturday morning, while Mom was in the shower, I ran to Grandpa's with that photo. He asked where I'd gotten the picture and what Mom had said. When I told him, he cackled, but stopped when I didn't laugh with him.

"That's John Wasser, your mother's boyfriend until he introduced her to your dad. Nice guy, but he couldn't compete with Aidan." That was all I needed to hear, but Grandpa kept talking as I tried to leave. "We heard he did all right for himself. Started his own company. Made a lot of money."

"I have to go," I said. "We're getting Dad's things from the office."

Later that morning, Mom pressed the buzzer at the newspaper's entrance and Walt, Dad's boss, came to the door.

"Hey. You didn't have to come, Monica. I would hav—"

"I wanted to," she said, stepping inside, looking around. "You've rearranged."

"Oh, right. You haven't been here in a while," he said.

He led her to Dad's desk, then walked away muttering something about how revenue was going to take a hit. I sank into Dad's chair. Besides the blotter with its calendar insert, his desk held only the phone, a pad of paper, and the pen and pencil holder I'd knocked on the floor the second time I saw Billie in the office. Mom picked up the holder we'd made from a recycled frozen juice container, examined it, and set it inside the cardboard box she'd brought from home.

As Mom had said it would, the bottom drawer of Dad's desk held hanging file folders. In the top side drawer, we found his coffee mug and some books. I looked for the one Billie had given him at Christmas, but it wasn't there. From the shallow center drawer Mom retrieved the silver letter opener she'd given Dad and frowned when she discovered our framed family photo face down in the drawer. When she set it on the desk, I realized I hadn't seen it there in months, although I couldn't remember when Dad had put it away.

"We can leave these," Mom said of his sales manuals as she added to the box Dad's book of famous quotations, the letter opener, his mug, and his appointment book.

In contrast to Dad's desktop, Billie's was cluttered and colorful. She'd doodled on her calendar with fuchsia, chartreuse, and purple markers, and beside her gold nameplate, she'd placed matching pen and paper holders and a lamp with a flowery-print shade. A conch shell from Florida sat atop a stack of newspapers.

Mom studied Billie's desk for a moment then placed the box in my arms. I'd taken only a couple of steps when a scraping sound cut through me and I turned. Mom held a sharp corner of the picture frame above a long, jagged scratch on the top of Billie's desk. Shocked, I stared at the gash as Mom tossed the frame into the box and headed for the exit like she was turning her back on Dad all over again. I had to leave with her, but before I did, set the box on Billie's chair and moved her stack of newspapers to hide the gouge.

I struggled to square the damage Mom had done with her lectures about respecting other people's property and controlling my impulses. When I'd defaced a wall or book as a kid, she'd said, "I love you Finn, but I don't like what you did." I wondered whether she'd been honest about that, though. I didn't like what

Mom had done to Billie's desk, and in the moment, I didn't like her either for doing it. But then I remembered what I'd done to Dad's car. I was no better than Mom.

In the afternoon, I rode with Pete in his buddy's tow truck to get Dad's car. "She won't be there," he'd told Mom. Still, as we approached the apartment, I looked for Billie and imagined her waiting on the landing, and then running down the steps to greet me.

"Do you think your friend can fix it?" I asked Pete as he inspected the car.

He huffed. "I don't know. You really did a number on it."

I couldn't imagine the strength I'd summoned to bash the car when at the time I'd felt so helpless.

Pete backed the truck up to the rear of the car, anchored the big hook under the back bumper, and climbed back into the truck. When Billie drove up, I thought maybe Pete had known she would be there after all and brought me with him so I'd get to see her again, but then he told me to wait for him in the truck. How dare he tell me what to do?

"Hi, Finn," Billie said in her whisp of a voice as she passed my open window. In the side mirror, I watched her walk up the steps with Pete following, carrying her grocery bags.

"Be right back," he'd said, except he wasn't. What was he doing? Putting the groceries away for her? Or something else? I stewed, turned around to check if he was coming, and then turned back to stare scowling straight ahead. If anyone should have been spending time with Billie, it was me. When Pete finally came out, he set a big cardboard box on the seat between us. It was filled with Dad's clothes.

"Wait," Billie called, running down the steps. This time, I got out of the truck. "Here, Finn. You'll want these," she said, holding out my bat, ball, and glove she'd retrieved from the storage box. I couldn't take them. It would be like Billie was disposing of me too.

I didn't cry, not in front of her, but my raspy voice betrayed me. "I don't need them," I said as I turned away, blinked back tears, and walked to the truck. In the cab, I wiped my eyes on the bottom of my T-shirt. In a minute or so, Pete opened the door, stowed my equipment behind his seat, climbed into the cab, but didn't say anything. I stared out the window.

When Pete dropped me off at home, I carried the box of Dad's clothes into the house and down to the basement where Mom was washing clothes. From Dad's long-sleeved flannel shirt on top of the pile, I inhaled the scent of Billie's perfume. If I could keep the shirt in my closet, maybe I could conjure Billie the way I'd thought she conjured the storm.

"Sure," Mom said, when I asked if I could have Dad's shirt, but before I could grab it, she sniffed it, frowned, and tossed it into the washer.

Nooooo, doooooon't.

"Let me wash it first," she said.

CHAPTER EIGHTEEN

Another mother, alarmed at how I'd trashed Dad's car, might have taken me to a shrink, but Mom sent me to Gus's Gym with Uncle Pete.

The brick-and-block interior was lit by low-hanging bare bulbs and one grimy window as big as our garage door. The wood floors creaked and groaned. A couple of punching bags sagged from the ceiling in one corner, and a canvas for sparring squatted in another. The equipment wasn't dirty, just worn. An elderly attendant regularly wiped everything down, layering antiseptic over the odors of leather, liniment, and sweat. Except for a bell that clanged at the end of a practice round, sound was deadened, voices subdued.

It was a wonderland.

I sat on a nicked wooden bench beneath a rack of gloves and headgear while Pete wrapped my knuckles with strips of cotton, helped me slip on a pair of the smaller-sized gloves, and laced them. "Your hands are your protection. Hold them up in front of you. Feel the leather on your face," he said, gesturing for me to tap the gloves on my cheeks just below my eyes.

First, he showed me the jab. "Keep your left hand up by your shoulder and hit my left with your right. Good. Again. Now your left." Because of how he'd muscled in on Billie at her apartment, I hit him as hard as I could, but I didn't hurt him. Pete was as rock solid as his name. He showed me the hook and the uppercut, and when he positioned himself behind one of those hanging bags, I pummeled it like it was his body.

When a couple of guys ducked under the ropes of the makeshift ring, Pete led me over to watch them spar. "See how they move? Light on their feet? Try it," he said. "Shift your weight to your left foot. And now the right." The boxers sidestepped, moved in and out, and held onto each other in a clinch. They transformed into Billie and me gliding around the ring, and then gliding around her kitchen, just the two of us with no one to cut in on me anymore, until Pete snapped his fingers in front of my face and laughed, snatching me out of my daydream.

"Is that Aidan's kid?" one of the boxers asked. He reached a gloved hand through the ropes and touched my head like he was bestowing a blessing. When he said, "Loved your old man, kid," love for Dad and for that boxer surged inside me. I could have hugged him, hugged the whole building.

For three years, I went to the gym with Pete on Saturday afternoons, and Jeff met us there when I asked if he could come too. With his broad shoulders, narrow hips, and long reach, Jeff had a boxer's build, and he mastered a boxer's stance and blows. "Hands up. Elbows in. Step in. Step back," the trainers called out, but it was as though they were broadcasting a play-by-play rather than telling Jeff what to do. He was way ahead of them. When I switched to lifting weights, I marveled that my arms developed the definition of Dad's, but mostly I went to the gym to be around guys who remembered him. If they'd loved Dad, maybe they'd love—or at least like—me too.

CHAPTER NINETEEN

Dad died of a ruptured aneurysm that bled into his brain.

Mom waited until after his funeral to call our family doctor's office, but said we had to see him right away. In the waiting room the next day, she picked up a magazine, flipped the pages one at a time, back to front with her thumb, and put it down. Then she picked up another magazine and did the same thing. Her fiddling made me fidgety too. Could Dad have gotten that bulge that burst because he was always reading, researching something new? Expanding your mind with knowledge sounded like a good thing, but what if it gave you a brain aneurysm?

When a nurse opened the waiting room door and called my name, Mom startled, and when the doctor greeted her, in his book-filled study scented with lemony polish, not betadine like the exam rooms, she didn't sit where he gestured or even say hello.

"Could Finn have an aneurysm too?" she asked hurriedly, like she couldn't wait another second for an answer.

Peering over the half-moon lenses of his glasses, Dr. Walker said, "It's unlikely in a person as young as Finn. We usually associate aneurysm with a history of high blood pressure."

"Is there a test to find out for sure?" Mom asked.

"There's an X-ray," the doctor said, hesitantly, "after injecting dye into the blood vessels in the brain."

At my wild-eyed expression, Dr. Walker flashed me a not-to-worry gesture and continued talking to Mom. "I wouldn't advise it, though. It's an invasive procedure with its own risks. Would you want to put Finn through that, Monica?"

"Well," she said. "Not if you think it's unnecessary."

"I do," he said. "How are you doing?" he asked, switching his attention to Mom. "Are you sleeping, eating well? Have you gone back to work?" She nodded absentmindedly, but when he glanced at me, I shook my head, and he focused more intently on Mom. "I wouldn't worry about Finn. The best thing to do is be alert to warning signs like a sudden, intense headache and pain behind the eyes," he said. "I'll have the nurse give you a pamphlet."

Good. Something to read. That would reassure her. Finally, Mom sank into the chair in front of the doctor's desk and shifted her thoughts to Dad. "What was it like? For Aidan?"

Dr. Walker took off his glasses and rubbed a hand over his eyes. "Survivors say it's like being hit over the head with a board or having the worst headache of their lives," he said. "But if Aidan died suddenly, he wouldn't have suffered. Let's try to think that was the case."

On our way out of the office, Mom brightened, said we had to celebrate because I was most likely okay, and stopped at a Friendly's on the drive home. She ordered us ice cream sundaes topped with crumbled Oreos. By then she was downright giddy.

"Two large, please," she told the waitress. "We're going to spoil our supper."

"Lucky you," the waitress said, smiling at me.

"Lucky us," Mom said, smiling back.

Her mood held until we walked past another booth on our way out of the restaurant. A woman sat on one side with her back toward us. On the other side was a man with his arm around a boy a few years younger than me. Mom glanced at the two of them, then away, and covered her mouth with her hand. In the car, she sat for a few minutes staring at the dash.

"Mom?" I asked. She moved her seat back a few inches then forward again. She adjusted the rearview mirror, started the car, and backed out of the parking space. At the "ding, ding, ding" when she pulled forward, she put her foot on the brake, buckled her seat belt, and then grasped the steering wheel again. She drove, her eyes fixed on the road, but I worried she couldn't see. Twice I had to shout at her: "Red light, Mom" and "Watch out for that car."

"I see it," she said sharply after the second incident, but she shook her head like people do to rouse themselves after they've dozed off. Pete would have said her mind was slipping gears.

I had to keep her alert, and since I'd been wondering about the whole afterlife thing anyway, I asked her, "Does Dad know what we're thinking now?"

She straightened in her seat looking consumed by the thought as she composed her answer. "Well, it's not like he can read our minds," she said. "But if there's something we want him to know, I think it gets through to him."

"How?" I asked.

"I don't know how," she said, "and I don't know that it does, but I feel better thinking it's possible." After a pause, she asked, "What would you want your dad to know?"

"Oh, nothing," I said with a shrug, relieved that Dad wouldn't know about Billie and me as long as I didn't telegraph my thoughts.

CHAPTER TWENTY

The next morning as I left the house to catch the bus, Mom packed her briefcase for her return to school. With two days remaining in the week, she said she'd ease back in, but when I got home in the afternoon, her car was still in the same spot in the driveway and, sitting at the kitchen table, she gave me a lost look. "What are you doing home?" she asked.

"It's three o'clock, Mom," I said.

"Oh," she said, straightening up. "I don't know what came over me. I couldn't move all morning, not even when the phone rang and rang. The principal sent Mr. Weiss at lunch time to check on me. He brought these." She scooped up a handful of half sheets of colored construction paper decorated by her pupils with stick figure drawings and printed good wishes.

When he came back after school, Mr. Weiss—who said I could call him Tim now that I was out of his class and in the high school building—made tomato soup and grilled cheese sandwiches and stayed to eat with Mom and me. We could have been a family if Tim weren't younger than Mom—and gay.

"How are you doing?" he asked me while he washed and I dried the dishes. Although he didn't show it, I'm sure my answer surprised him.

"I miss Billie," I said with a big sigh. He dried his hands, looked me in the eye, and nodded.

"Yes, I guess you would," he said. "What is it you like about her?"

That was an easy one. "She's pretty."

"You're right about that," he said chuckling.

"How do you know Billie?" I asked.

"I've seen her around," he said. "Her hair's an unusual color, isn't it?"

"Like a brand-new penny," I said.

"Oh," he said, like a light had dawned. "That's why you collect pennies. They remind you of Billie."

"How did you—"

"Your mother mentioned your collection once," he said. Then, lowering his voice as though he were sharing a secret, he added, "I have a collection too. Pieces of sea glass like a pair of ice-blue eyes."

"To remind you of your friend?" I asked. "From the beach? In the summer?"

"What?" I'd caught him off guard, but just for a moment. "Oh. Did your mom tell you about David?" he asked.

I nodded. "Why doesn't he ever come to Danton?"

"Oh," Tim said, looking away. "I'm afraid that wouldn't be a good idea."

"Tim," I said tentatively, trying out his first name for the first time. "I didn't think you were afraid of anything."

He opened, then closed his mouth a couple of times, like he wanted to say something but didn't know what. He settled on, "That's what your mom said."

Talking with Tim like that must have triggered an incident

that night. "Hey, bud." At the sudden familiar greeting, I sat bolt upright in bed. "Dad?" I didn't hear anything else, and he vanished as soon as I'd sensed his presence, but he'd been in my room. I was sure of it.

As the goose-pimply, hair-standing-on-end sensation subsided, I lay back down, but after a few minutes, I drifted up and out of my body. Oh, I was still lying in bed, but at the same time I was hovering above myself. Then, I felt myself expanding, filling the whole of space, floating in a black void. It was a peaceful vacuum, not scary, and I lay basking in a reassuring warmth until I fell asleep.

On other nights, I re-created the experience, but not by forcing it. I had to lie still, untether my mind, and wait for the sensation to overtake me. I never told anyone about it. I knew I wasn't crazy, but I didn't want anyone questioning or discounting what had occurred. I was sure it meant I was special, like I'd discovered a secret of the universe.

Or maybe I was stuck.

Other weird stuff happened. Mom cried for no good reason, like when the sink got stopped up or a cake failed to rise.

In a dream, I visualized a pair of Dad's shoes on the garage floor positioned one ahead of the other as though he'd been walking and walked right out of them.

At dinner on Thanksgiving, instead of saying what we were thankful for, everyone said something nice about Dad. Mom astonished me, though, when she said, "Remember how Aidan followed up with his accounts on the weekend? He was so conscientious about his job." I couldn't believe it. She was idolizing him for those Saturday morning trips that used to infuriate her.

Like I said, weird stuff happened.

With carols on the radio and wreaths on the lampposts downtown, Christmas crowded in even before Thanksgiving. "It's too soon," Mom said. I understood. If Pete could have hooked me up to a dynamometer, he'd have detected my own lack of oomph. After Grandpa told Mom not to spoil the holiday for me, she asked what I wanted for Christmas.

"More video games and clothes, I guess," I said with a shrug. I hadn't played with the Millennium Falcon for months. Oh, on a good day, I'd take it down from the shelf and remember how excited I'd been to open the package and assemble the model. It reminded me of Billie. On a bad day, I'd try not to look at it, because it reminded me of Billie. I wondered whether she was happy or sad about Christmas coming and whether she missed me. And Dad.

When Pete offered to get us a tree, Mom said, "Maybe we shouldn't bother."

"What? You have to," Pete said, and he badgered her for two weeks until she sent me with him to the tree farm to cut down a good one—a tree with a straight trunk and no bare spots among the branches unless there was only one empty space that could be hidden against the wall in the corner of the living room. Oh, and the tree had to be tall.

"What's the point of having a nine-foot ceiling if you settle for a six-foot tree?" Dad used to say.

"This one," I said to Pete when I spied a stately fir with the blue-green needles Mom liked. Riding home, I was certain the people we passed envied our prize. Secure in the bed of his truck, the tree extended a whole three feet beyond the tailgate. At home, Pete hauled the tree onto our front porch, and then into the house where he anchored it in the stand.

After church the next day, the tree's branches had fallen and the room smelled like the outdoors. I fed Pete the strings of lights the way I'd held and handed them to Dad, but unlike Dad who just draped the strands, Pete took his time wrapping the green wires around the branches so skillfully that the wires nearly disappeared. When he was done, the tree glowed as though lit from within by the hundreds of tiny white lights, and a bulb went off for me: Pete could show me a lot of things—if I'd let him.

I hung only two stockings from the mantle. It wasn't like we were expecting Dad, and I thought it might make Mom sad to see his, but I didn't want her to think I'd forgotten him either, so I laid his stocking on his desk in the living room. When she noticed it, Mom sat down and traced Dad's embroidered first initial with her finger. It didn't seem to make her any sadder than she already was, so I figured I'd done the right thing or, at least, I hadn't done wrong. It was hard to know sometimes.

We missed Dad the most at Christmas Eve dinner when Grandpa, missing Grandma, sank into a pit of sadness, his head in his hands. Had he been present, Dad would have sung offkey and mixed up the words on purpose to get Grandpa to correct him and come around to lead the caroling. Without Dad, we didn't sing at all, and when we opened presents, we just got it over with instead of taking our time and exclaiming over every gift.

In church at midnight, I raised my eyes to the window I'd avoided since the whole God-make-Billie-stay episode. I suppose I should have begged forgiveness, but I got all worked up over my hateful wish to be rid of Dad—and how God had responded. I looked him right in his all-seeing, all-knowing eye and rebuked him for listening to me and letting Dad die: You should have known I didn't mean it.

After the holidays, flu flattened Mom the way Pete had felled our tree at Christmas. She came home from school on a Friday with a sore throat and woke up Saturday with chills and a fever. When she took some pills and went back to bed, I called Grandpa. In the afternoon, he made her soup, gave her juice and more medicine, and she went back to sleep. Sunday was the same. She ate soup, drank juice, took medicine, and slept.

When she called Dr. Walker's office on Monday, his nurse was surprised Mom was so ill. She said there wasn't anything going around. Grandpa, Pete, my aunts, and I—none of us got sick. Curled up on the couch when I got home from school, Mom lifted a limp hand to acknowledge me and Tim, who brought get-well cards from her students and the other teachers. She missed a week of school and, weakened, dragged around for another week after she went back.

Once she recovered, she switched to doing the grocery shopping on Saturdays and strolled the aisles instead of hurrying through the store. She spoke with people she knew, said hello to those she didn't, and stopped to talk to parents who asked about their children's progress in her class. I almost didn't recognize her. It was as though the fever had cauterized her prickly nerve endings and the chills had chased away her sense of superiority. Like the latest model car, she was new and improved. I liked her better that way.

CHAPTER TWENTY-ONE

In the spring, Mom bugged Uncle Pete to take me to work with him.

"Nope. We're too busy," Pete said.

"Then Finn could help you," Mom countered, but Pete didn't buy it.

"You mean get in the way," he said.

"He's not a kid," Mom said. "He's thirteen." Then she wheedled. "You know a lot about cars, Pete. You could teach him about cars."

"Maybe when he's older. Not now." Case closed. Pete didn't say that, but he may as well have. Well, if he didn't want me hanging around, maybe I didn't want to be around him either. Except that wasn't true. I liked being with Pete as long as I didn't think about him maybe wanting to be with Billie.

Mom was undeterred. One Saturday morning, she drove to Simpson's and marched me past the open garage doors. When Pete looked up from under the hood of a car, I raised my hand in greeting, but he went back to work without acknowledging me.

The excitement I'd felt at the prospect of joining him dwindled. Inside the showroom, the salesmen gathered around us.

"Oh, we're doing all right," Mom said in answer to a question. "But Finn needs some more good men in his life. I thought you all could help." They straightened as one and said they would do whatever she wanted. Even Mr. Simpson came out of his office, buttoned his suit jacket, smoothed the flyaway strands on his balding head, and shook Mom's hand. "Pete thinks Finn will be in the way," she said.

"Nonsense," Mr. Simpson said. "It's the least we can do."

"Well, if you think it will be all right," she said, as though letting him talk her into an arrangement that was his idea, not hers. "Do what they tell you," Mom said to me before leaving with a triumphant stride.

Mr. Simpson huddled with his employees and then put me to work. First, I stood alongside the salesmen who greeted people as they came in the door. Then I carried papers from the salesmen to the manager to the billing office. When I passed by the open door to the service department, one of the other mechanics called me into the garage. "Hey, kid, we could use some help out here," he said, adding with a laugh, "You afraid of getting your hands dirty?"

Instead of giving me a job, though, he motioned me into a car and raised it on the lift. I was too old for a stunt like that, but he got a kick out of it. When the mechanic lowered the car and let me out, Pete called me over to where he was working. For the rest of the morning, I handed him each wrench, ratchet, or socket he requested and listened with his mechanic's stethoscope to engines whine, tap, click, or knock. From the sounds, Pete diagnosed problems like worn gears, faulty valves, or defective bearings, and then operated on the vehicles to fix them.

As far as I could tell, we'd had fun, so I was disappointed that Pete battled Mom again over whether I could return to the garage. Grandpa got caught in the middle.

"Is it so bad, Pete?" he asked my uncle, who grunted and walked away. "Monica, don't you think you're overstepping?"

"Mr. Simpson doesn't mind," she said. "Why should Pete?"

On Saturday mornings, Mom had to drop me off at the dealership because Pete wouldn't take me. Once I was there, though, he let me help him, and he brought me home after he punched out at noon. Compared to Dad, Pete didn't talk much either with customers or with his coworkers, and instead of manuals, he relied on his experience and instinct to make repairs. It was another way for a man to be.

As was Tim. Once or twice a month on Sunday afternoons he took Mom to a theater in the city that showed independent and foreign films. She bragged that the films with subtitles and serious or quirky themes were movies that most people wouldn't choose to see and wouldn't understand if they did.

While Mom made us supper after their return one evening, I asked Tim how he'd managed to have Jeff transferred to his class in the middle of sixth grade. "What makes you think it was me?" he asked. I followed his gaze toward the kitchen. Mom. Of course. It was exactly the sort of solution she would have engineered.

That night before he left, Tim gave me a journal and suggested I write in it what I remembered about Dad—and Billie too—if I wanted. "But be honest," he said. "Nobody's perfect, not even a hero. Write about his mistakes."

"Was Billie a mistake?" I asked.

"Oh, I didn't mean that," Tim said hurriedly, then, "It's not for me to say."

Who would have a say then? Mom? God? If it was wrong for Dad to get involved with Billie, was it a mistake for me to be preoccupied with her too? Or was Billie a mistake for Dad because of Mom, but not for me? I didn't want to give Billie up, and even if I'd wanted to, I didn't think I could. Whenever I saw her car or we drove by the office or near her apartment, she popped into my head like she was coming around to say hi. As far as I knew, she hadn't left Danton, though that may have been because of Pete, not me.

I smoothed my hand over the soft, supple cover of the journal, opened the book from the back, and fanned the pages. They were unlined, intimidating. I'd have to think first, write later.

"I wish Tim was my uncle," I told Grandpa when I showed him the journal.

"You have an uncle," he said.

"I know, but—"

"But what?" Grandpa asked.

"Nothing. Never mind." He wouldn't want to hear that Pete didn't care about me, that he only spent time with me because Mom nagged him to. And I couldn't tell him it looked like Pete had become my new rival for Billie.

That evening, I was surprised to get a phone call from Pete and even more surprised when he said he would take me fishing.

CHAPTER TWENTY-TWO

Fishing was Pete's solitary pursuit, his Sunday morning ritual like the Mass but celebrated in nature where he said he would spend all his time if he were God. He took a Saturday off work and had Grandpa with him when he picked me up in his truck. He drove us an hour from Danton to a river stocked with all kinds of fish like walleye and perch, bass and catfish.

When we reached the river, Pete pulled off the road and parked in a field as quiet as an empty church except for the bird that sang, stopped, and then sounded his notes again like a cantor leading a congregation through a new and unfamiliar psalm response. I carried Pete's net like a vessel and wore Grandpa's creel strap across my chest like a vestment. The basket bounced against my hip as I hurried, eager to get to the river. I knew Grandpa had to go slow, but I didn't understand why Pete was lagging.

"Hold up," he called to me. "Take some time to look around." I gazed where he pointed, up at birds flitting in the branches of budding trees, down at yellow-green shoots poking through dead leaves that rustled from a scurrying underneath.

The world is waking up. When the words came to me, I imagined writing them in my journal, but wondered whether the thought was mine to record. It was something Dad might have said, and I followed my memory of him down the narrow dirt path through hip-high brush. At the river's edge, I squinted at the sun's reflection on the water and teetered on the rocks under my feet. I picked up three flat stones, selected one, flicked my wrist the way Dad had taught me, and let the stone fly. It skipped the surface of the river five times.

"Hey," Pete said. "Don't disturb the water. Did you come to fish or fool around?"

I gripped the two remaining stones in my left hand. I wasn't fooling around. Skipping stones was an art and a science. Angle, speed, and rotation determined how far a stone would travel and how many times it would skim the water. According to Dad, physicists had shown a stone could go on skipping indefinitely if the right speed were maintained, but Pete wouldn't be interested in any of that. I relaxed my hold and let the stones fall.

Grandpa called me over to where he'd set up his short-legged stool and told me to rub my hands in the dirt like he did and then rub them together, to hide my scent from the fish. I held his rod as he attached a hook, sinker, and bobber to his line. He opened a small cooler, sifted through the compost for a worm, and took the hook in his other hand. Holding them close to my face so I could see how he did it, he pierced the worm about half an inch from one end and slid it up the hook.

"Now you do it with the other end," he said, coaching me to leave some slack so the worm would be able to wiggle and attract fish.

Then, straightening up, he drew back his pole. With the same side-arm motion I'd used to skip my stone, he swung his rod in a half circle until it was pointing in front of him out over the water. The line whizzed out. After it hit the surface and the sinker pulled the line down, Grandpa pressed the reel lock with his thumb, handed me the rod, and told me to watch the bobber and wait for a fish to tug the line.

I watched and waited, but didn't see or feel any movement. I checked out fishermen on the opposite bank and a couple of squirrels doing gymnastics in a tree. When Grandpa sighed and told me to reel in the line, I discovered I'd been outsmarted. The worm was gone. Grandpa said to try again. After I baited the hook, he put his hand on mine to guide me as I cast the line. This time I concentrated on the bobber as I imagined fish circling the bait. Surprised by a sudden tug, I jerked the pole.

"Have you got one?" Grandpa asked. I nodded, wound the reel rapidly, and when I pulled the line up out of the water, my first fish dangled in front of me.

"Good job, Finn. I knew you could do it," Grandpa said before telling me I'd have to return the fish to the river.

"What? Why?" I demanded.

"It's too small. It has to be at least six inches to keep." Grandpa removed the hook from the fish's mouth and bent down to put it back in the water. It wriggled away and I said fishing was stupid.

Pete snorted and shot Grandpa an I-told-you-so look. "If you're going to fish, you have to follow the law," Pete said. "Besides, where's the challenge in landing a minnow like that?"

I turned my attention to how Pete was fishing. He pulled his rod back until it was almost resting on his shoulder then thrust it overhead and out in front of him like he was cracking a whip. The line sliced the air once, twice, three times then kissed the surface of the water when he let it go. It was one of the most elegant movements I'd ever seen a man make, especially a rough-around-the-edges guy like Pete. It was expansive. He commanded the river. It was how I wanted to fish.

When Pete reeled in his line, he showed me the feathery yellow plastic attached to it.

Surprised, I said, "It looks like a bug."

"Guess that's why they call this fly-fishing," Pete said, having a good laugh with himself.

"But it's fake," I said.

"Looks real enough to the fish. That's what matters." Pete cast his line again, and as though confirming his assertion, the tip of his rod vibrated and the line unraveled. Pete let it go for a few seconds then wound the reel with a click, click, click, paused to let the line go, and then wound it again. They played back and forth for a bit, the fish trying to swim away, Pete pulling it back. When the end of his rod bent sharply toward the water, Pete gave the rod a strong tug and reeled in the line.

"Grab my net, Finn," he said, as he walked to the water's edge. I watched as he lifted the line, pulling up a prize that twisted in the air, still trying to break free. He wouldn't throw that fish back. It was about a foot long.

Pete handed the rod to me, grabbed hold of the line, and scooped the fish in his net. He extracted the hook and held the smallmouth bass for me to admire before slipping it into the creel.

After casting again, he placed the rod in my hand, resting it on the tip of my index finger so I could feel the tension when a fish mouthed the lure. A minute or so later, I felt it—the almost imperceptible pressing against my finger. Pete came closer and simulated a complete turn of the reel. I imitated him, and then stopped when he held up his hand. After a few seconds, when I detected another slight tug, I followed Pete's lead and wound the line some more. When I paused for a third time, the pressure was strong, and I grasped the rod tightly to keep hold of it.

"Now," Pete said, pulling back on his imaginary rod and reeling as I did the same with the real one. I frowned when Pete called my fish crappie, but he laughed, said that was the species; the fish was long enough to keep, and it was one of the best-tasting freshwater fish. Besides my fish and Pete's, we headed for home with a bluegill for Grandpa, and two more bass for Pete packed on ice blocks in a cooler. I was the last one, not the first, to leave the river, straggling up the path behind Grandpa. When I looked back, light streamed from a cloud as though God were taking Pete's advice and checking out his creation.

Mom had said she'd cook any fish I caught, but not clean them, so after I showed her my fish, I took it back to Grandpa's. Whistling in his kitchen, Grandpa worked while I sat on the back porch steps with Pete examining his lures, learning about the fish-fooling feature of each. If I wanted to be a fisherman, Pete said, I'd have to develop patience, but I'd shown promise, and if I mastered fishing, it would give me the confidence to try and succeed at other pursuits. He sounded like a teacher. Or a parent.

"How come my dad never went fishing?" I asked.

Pete snorted and Grandpa did too, loud enough for us to hear him from inside the house.

"Your dad couldn't be still to save himself," Pete said. "I took him fishing once. Let him use a new rod and reel. When he propped it up and went wandering off, a damn fish pulled the whole thing in." Pete wasn't mad, though. He laughed and then said, "God, I miss him."

I'd miss Dad too, I realized in all the new things I'd try but wouldn't be able to share with him. The thought gutted me like Grandpa's fish knife, and I set down Pete's lures to wipe my eyes.

"What's wrong?" Pete asked.

I didn't want him to regret having me around, so I forced myself to get out two words: "I'm okay."

"Hey," Pete said. He waited until I looked up at him to add, "It's okay if you're not."

CHAPTER TWENTY-THREE

Whether someone gave Mom the idea or she came up with it on her own, she let me get a dog, a shelter dog like Billie's. Surprised when she asked if I wanted a pet, I said, "But we won't be home to take care of it."

"I talked to Grandpa about that," she said. "He'll keep the dog during the day, but you'll have to feed and walk him after school."

"But Ginger," I said, still hesitating.

"I know that accident must have frightened you," Mom said, "but it taught you better than any warning I could give. You'll be careful. I know you'll take good care of a dog."

The animal shelter was a cement block building not much bigger than a classroom. As soon as we stepped inside, barking erupted, as though all the dogs were saying, "Pick me! Pick me!" I scanned the rows of cages stacked two high, then walked past, examining the dog in each one. Most of them jumped. Some even growled. Then in the last cage on the left in the bottom row was the textbook illustration of a friendly dog. He pressed his wriggling mottled brown, black, and white body up against the front of his cage and wagged his tail loopily and low. His mouth was open in a doggie grin. Dark fur around one of his eyes made me think of a pirate.

"Patch. Hello, boy," I said as I sank to my knees and hooked my fingers into the cage wiring. The dog licked them.

"That's a good name," said a worker who opened the cage and let the dog out. "We've been calling him Bandit." When the dog danced around and licked my face, I hugged him.

"Looks like he's stolen a heart," Mom said. "Hello, Patch." When she stroked the top of the dog's head and scratched him under his chin, he made Ginger's bell-like whining sound.

Mom said Patch would have to sleep in the basement, but when I took him down that night, he bounded up the steps, scratched at the door, and whimpered until she said he could stay in the pantry alcove. In the morning when she found me on the floor next to him in his doggie bed, she gave in and said Patch could sleep in my room—on the floor. That night, I pulled him up onto the foot of my new double bed, and he worked his way up next to me onto what became his side.

We were inseparable except when I was in school, and then he was Grandpa's shadow. Grandpa described their walks around the neighborhood, how Patch pressed up against the hands of passersby who stopped to pet him. "That dog's a real people person," Grandpa said. Mom and I laughed at his use of an anthropomorphism, but we knew what he meant.

"You made a good choice, Finn," Mom said. "I couldn't imagine a better dog."

The weekend we got Patch, the *Monitor* ran a feature story about pets who resembled their owners. The photos were hilarious—the scowling man with jowls like his bulldog's, the pointy-nosed woman in a white fur like her collie. I studied Patch's wiry body, his tilted head, the tuft of hair that stood up like a cowlick, and compared him to the photo on the buffet. How had we missed it? Patch looked like Dad. Calling Patch to follow, I went upstairs to my room, closed the door, and scooped him up on the bed beside me. I smoothed that bit of whorled fur on his head.

Dad? I didn't say it. I knew my father hadn't been reincarnated. I wasn't that gullible. Still, if I could telegraph my thoughts to Dad, like Mom said, maybe Dad had sent Patch to stay in touch with me. People talked to their dogs all the time, so no one suspected when I said, "What do you think, boy?" that I was really asking Dad, trying to figure out what he would say about whatever was on my mind. Patch did his part whenever he accepted a hug from me—he soaked up some of my remaining sadness.

Our other outing that weekend was to the cemetery to view Dad's headstone. Grandpa had seen it because he visited Grandma's grave at least once a week. "I wish I could plant some flowers for Aidan," Grandpa said, but Dad was buried in the new section of the cemetery at the top of the hill where the headstones had to be flat, their tops level with the ground so caretakers could easily cut the grass. In the vaselike cone-shaped holders mounted on the grave markers, families could leave only phony-looking artificial flowers that faded in the sun. If that was the best we could do, I thought it better not to bother.

At least Dad was buried in an orderly grid-like space. The original cemetery had spread chaotically. Monuments and mausoleums of all shapes and sizes sat randomly on the hillside, and obelisks and other old memorials leaned as though they'd been pushed from below, inspiring spooky stories about people buried alive trying in vain to claw their way out of the ground.

Mom and I walked past headstones of gray and black and pink granite glinting in the sun. Small American flags rippled at veterans' graves. Clouds rolled out a runner of shade over Dad's marker, but stopped short of covering Mom's engraved name and birthdate. I hadn't expected to see the beginning of a memorial to her too. When she bent down to brush away bits of dried grass and touched the inevitability of her mortality, I had to look away.

"I don't find cemeteries particularly comforting," Mom said, "but I'll bring you anytime you want to come."

"That's okay," I said. I didn't think I'd want to visit either. I wouldn't want to be reminded that she'd leave me too someday.

CHAPTER TWENTY-FOUR

On my fourteenth birthday, a year after Dad's death, I received what I believed was a message from Billie. The passage in the *Monitor*, in an ad on the obituary page under Dad's photo, sounded like those in the book she'd given Dad that Christmas: "Death leaves a heartache no one can heal. Love leaves a memory no one can steal."

I was surprised Mom had tucked the folded newspaper page under the edge of my plate at breakfast and smiled when I looked at it. Usually, she ridiculed the tributes people ran in memory of their loved ones. She'd groan and read them aloud, exaggerating the singsong nature of lines like, "While he lies in peaceful sleep, his memory we shall always keep." Even worse were the messages in survivors' own words. "I'm saving the pieces of my broken heart so you can mend it when we meet again," wrote one bereaved husband to his deceased wife. Mom shuddered when she read that one. "Much too personal," she said.

After that first message, there were more ads in the paper.

They appeared on my birthday, on Dad's birthday, and on St. Patrick's Day, always an Irish blessing or saying, always, I was sure, from Billie and the book she must have taken back after Dad died. My stack of clippings grew. This was my favorite:

"Death is nothing at all

I have only slipped away to the next room.

I am I, and you are you.

Whatever we were to each other, That, we still are."

Oh, I knew the ads were meant to memorialize Dad, to try to keep him alive for me, but I focused less on that and more on the certainty that whenever she selected and submitted one of those messages, Billie was thinking about me.

CHAPTER TWENTY-FIVE

It's ironic that in a small town you can go years without seeing someone who was once a big part of your life. After the day Pete towed Dad's car, I saw Billie only three times, all within about a year of Dad's death.

My first glimpse was on a winter Saturday in the grocery store. Billie's hair was longer, curly, and puffed up on top but still the same coppery color. She wore leggings, a jacket, and a headband—all in different sherbert colors. Mom and I were still going up and down the aisles, but Billie had checked out. She was a blur of orange, lime, and raspberry as she exited the store.

I saw her a second time in Mullaney's Pub on St. Patrick's Day. It took some convincing to get Mom to go. Grandpa tried first. "It's been five months, Monica. No one will fault you for stepping out. We'll all go."

Pete succeeded when he told Mom, "They'll have something to say about Aidan. You should be there."

The pub rang with fiddling and drumming and voices straining to be heard over the music. The hostess showed us to a table near the bandstand and the waitress who took our drink orders was back in a flash with a pitcher of Guinness, three glasses, and my Coke.

"Slainte," Mom said, surprising me when she tapped the rim of her glass against mine. I'd never heard her give the Irish toast before, but she pronounced it as perfectly as Dad always had. "Your dad and I used to come here before you were born," she said, sitting back in her chair and looking around. Dancers wearing floppy felt green-and-white-striped stovepipe hats bobbed and bumped into each other, and Pete was right. Every few songs, the band leader raised his hand toward the ceiling and called out, "This one's for you, Aidan."

Mom smiled and clapped, her eyes glistening. When guys who'd been drinking staggered over and bent down to talk to her, she didn't pull away. She whispered to them and patted their backs as though comforting them. As one of them stumbled away, she said, "That man asked whether I thought your dad was watching over us. Isn't that nice, Finn? His friends haven't forgotten him."

I saw Billie on my way to the restroom. She sat alone in a booth in one of the whitewashed stone alcoves that ringed a secondary room of the pub. Waning light through the small arched window lit her face and drew me to her, but surprised to see her, I was tongue-tied. When she asked if I was having a good time, her voice did a jig in my head and I nodded. I wanted to sit with her, but I didn't get the chance.

"Come on, Finn. Let's not bother the pretty lady," Uncle Pete said behind me.

"Oh, it's no bother," Billie said, smiling up at him.

"Well then," he said, grinning as he sat down across from her. "Weren't you on your way to the john?" he said to me.

I didn't want to leave, not with Pete sitting there with Billie, but I had to pee. A long line of guys trailed down the hallway from the men's room, and it seemed like an hour instead of minutes until I got in, out, and back to the table where Billie and Pete were—correction—*had been* sitting. I scanned the crowd, but didn't see them dancing or standing around talking with anyone else. I shouldn't have left her alone with Pete, but I'd assumed Billie would wait for me. She had to know I was coming back. Crushed like her crumpled napkin with the lipstick blot, I slid onto her still-warm seat in the booth and looked out the window. It was too dark to see anything, but she was out there with Pete in her car or his truck, and my mind wandered after them. Pete wasn't such a bad guy, and it wasn't like I could drive Billie anywhere. If she was going to be with Pete, maybe that's how I'd get to see her again.

"Sorry, hon. I need this table," a waitress said. In the bin where she tossed them, Pete's beer bottle and Billie's glass clinked like they were toasting. No. Forget it. I didn't want to share Billie with anyone anymore. I didn't want to take a back seat.

At our table, I had to shout over Mom's clapping and singing along with the band. "Oh, don't worry about Pete," she said with a laugh and a wave. "He knows his way home." I wasn't worried that he'd left, only that he'd taken Billie with him.

With Mom preoccupied by the band, it was easy to slip out of the bar. I didn't see Billie's car, but Pete's truck was where he'd parked it. I didn't have the proper tool for what I was contemplating, but a fork would work as well, so I went back into the bar and swiped one from the servers' station. I could have crouched next to the front tire on the driver's side, out of sight of anyone entering or exiting the bar, pressed one of the fork's tines into the tire valve, and held it there until the tire flattened. But as I stood next to the driver's-side door, the fork rose in my hand as though it was bewitched, pressed itself against the door, and scraped the width of the panel. At the nails-on-the-blackboard screech, I shuddered, dropped the fork, and stared at the scratch, trying to separate myself from the act of having made it. It wasn't just wrong. It was mean. I was as bad as Mom when she'd scratched Billie's desk with the photo frame. It was pointless too because Pete wouldn't know it was me trying to get back at him for taking Billie away. I slunk back inside the bar ready to go home.

I paid for my misdeed anyway. When he discovered the damage to his truck, Pete groused to Grandpa about punk kids vandalizing property, ruining the town. With a scowl twisting his face, Pete gestured to the scratch and referenced Jeff. "You and that pal of yours," he said to me, "you'd better never do anything like this." Then he made me help him sand, prime, sand, paint, and wax his truck door until the scratch was gone.

The third and final time I saw Billie was after my fourteenth birthday. Jeff and I were at a newsstand near his house when he ogled a *Playboy* and shoved it in my face. "I don't need to look at that," I said, pushing him away. "I've seen a real woman naked." As soon as I said it, I was sorry. I didn't want to tell Jeff about Billie. I wanted to keep her to myself.

"Ha. You wish," he said, fake-slapping my face. "Who? When?"

I flailed my arms at him. "Billie. Now quit it." He backed off and for once didn't demand details.

"Shoot," he said, sounding intrigued. "You like her. When did you see her last?" When I told him, he said it was time for me to check her out again. "Halloween," he said. "We'll watch her hand out treats. Hey, we can dress up and go to her door."

"We're too old for that," I said, though I wondered whether we could.

"We don't have to take the candy," he said.

Jeff convinced Mom to let me go home with him on the bus, and at dusk, dressed all in black and wearing ghoulish masks, we trailed a group of kids from his neighborhood.

"What did you get?" Jeff asked them after they'd visited a few houses. When a boy opened his bag for us to see, Jeff grabbed a handful of his treats. "Too much candy is bad for you," he said to the boy with a villainous laugh. I didn't raid any of the kids' bags. I didn't want to be mean and I wasn't interested in candy.

At Billie's apartment, we watched from behind a tree across the street. When she opened her door to a pirate, a princess, and a pint-sized Frankenstein, my pulse quickened the way it had every time I saw Billie waiting for me on the landing. After handing out the candy, she told the kids to be careful going down the steps and waved to them when they turned around at the bottom.

That glimpse was enough for me, but Jeff said, "C'mon," and raced across the street toward the apartment.

"Wait, no. Don't, Jeff," I called. When I caught up with him, he pushed me up the stairs and pounded on the door. Billie parted the curtains, but then, with a frightened look, pushed them back. She flicked off the kitchen light and clicked the door lock. My excitement fizzled as I saw Jeff's brilliant plan for what it really was—a bad idea.

"Hey. Trick or treat," he shouted, rattling the doorknob and beating the door.

"Go home," Billie said. "You boys are too old for trick or treat."

Jeff laughed and kept pummeling the door as though he was in the boxing ring. I pulled on his sweatshirt to try to get him to leave. "I'm just kidding," he said. "Don't you want to talk to your girlfriend?"

"No. I want to go," I said, panicked when Billie asked, "Finn? Is that you?"

I didn't hear the car pull up alongside the house, but there was no mistaking the revolving red light of the police cruiser on patrol in the neighborhood to protect trick-or-treaters.

"Beat it," Jeff said as he ran down the steps ahead of me, leapt over the railing, and raced off in the direction of his house. The cop caught me at the bottom of the stairs, peeled off my mask, and shone his flashlight in my face. I squinted and raised my arms to try to cover my eyes.

"Finn Maguire. All alone and far from home. Some friend you've got there," he said, flicking his flashlight toward the path Jeff had taken. The cop was Jerry, one of Pete's friends. I was in big trouble. When Billie opened the apartment door, I turned away.

"Don't worry, Billie," Jerry called up to her. "This one won't give you any more trouble."

"Don't hurt him," Billie called back before she closed the door.

As though I was too disgusting for Jerry to touch, he grabbed a fistful of my sweatshirt and propelled me toward the cruiser. When he pushed me into the back seat, he put his hand on my head like cops do with a perp. I felt like a criminal.

From the front seat, Jerry radioed the dispatcher. "Call Monica Maguire," he said. "Tell her I'm bringing her kid home. I don't want her to worry when I drive up." Then he laughed, the sound deep within his throat like he was relishing the situation. "Oh, boy," he said, catching my eye in the rearview mirror. "I wouldn't want to be in your shoes, kid."

I didn't want to be in my shoes either. I almost asked him to take me to jail.

When Jerry pulled into our driveway, Mom was waiting on the porch. I wanted to get my punishment over with, but he prolonged my agony. "Wait here," he said before getting out of the car. The radio's static and his boots scraping the concrete obscured what he said to Mom. When he came back and let me out of the car, he didn't say anything, but I got the message.

It was the same one the assistant principal had delivered the afternoon I'd skipped classes with Jeff: there'd better not be a next time.

Mom's eyes bored into me as she asked, "What were you doing, Finn? I thought I told you not to go there." I looked away and shrugged. I didn't want the blame, but it would be worse to try to pin it on Jeff. After an exasperated sigh, she said, "Get in the car. I'll deal with you later."

"Where are we going?" I asked.

She shut me up with, "Never you mind," and drove to Jeff's. When he appeared in the doorway, Mom got out of the car, and I rolled down the window. Her words stung. "Bring me Finn's stuff. He won't be coming over anymore," she called to Jeff.

When he reappeared with my backpack and brought it to Mom, he mumbled something I couldn't make out, but I was relieved to hear her reply, "Yes, you can still come to our house."

My punishment was to write and send a letter, but it was to Billie and it said I wouldn't bother her anymore. Later, when I heard the expression, I knew I'd written that letter with a heavy heart.

CHAPTER TWENTY-SIX

I stayed away from Billie's after that, but I didn't forget her. I couldn't forget. I'd hear a song that we'd danced to or I'd catch an episode of a TV show we'd watched together and I'd long for her. Once, Mom triggered the yearning herself when she brought home Chinese takeout, tried to eat with chopsticks, and fussed over the fortunes in our cookies: "The best things in life are free" and "Big journeys start with a single step." They were lame compared to the fortune I'd saved for three years waiting for that dream to come true.

Billie only took a back seat when I started to drive, but then everything took a back seat when I started to drive. Driving promised power and freedom. It was all I could think about as I studied the driver training manual. If Dad had been alive, Mom would have had him teach me, but when Grandpa offered, she said she'd do it. As far as I knew, Pete didn't want to get involved.

Before letting me venture out on streets or the highway, Mom made me drive the perimeter of the empty high school parking lot, stopping at every corner as though at a stop sign.

She had a litany: Come to a complete stop. Easy on the gas. Check the rearview mirror. Now the side. Watch your speed. Use your turn signals. Don't touch the radio.

She taught me how to parallel park and how to do the dreaded three-point turn without bumping the log barrier that simulated a curb at the testing center. She showed me how to negotiate curves by easing off the gas while heading into one, then picking up speed halfway through. She didn't say why. Dad would have gone into detail about inertia and centrifugal force, or was it centripetal?

I passed the test on my first try and once I had my license, I had the means to go where I wanted. Billie's apartment was out of the way and technically still off limits, but I got my chance late one night when Mom discovered we were almost out of milk. The grocery store was closed, but there was an all-night convenience store on the west side of town at the foot of the hill below Billie's apartment. After I bought the milk, I drove past the house picturing Billie on the landing waving me over and up to the second floor.

"I'll go," I offered after that whenever the car's gas gauge was nearing empty or Mom noticed that we needed bread or milk. The errands took longer than they should have, so while driving home I dreamed up explanations for my delay: There were a lot of people in the store. I ran into a classmate and talked for a while. The car was making an odd noise, so I drove around to make sure it was okay. I never needed those excuses, though, because Mom never asked what kept me.

The more I drove by Billie's, the more I wanted to go back and the more time I spent scheming about how and when to get there. I was out of control. One night I poured almost a whole half-gallon of milk down the kitchen sink so I could make the trip.

"I thought I just bought milk," Mom said looking confused

when I told her I'd better go to the store.

Instead of just driving by Billie's that night, I parked on the side street across from the apartment and her Camaro in the driveway. I turned off the engine, leaned back in the seat, and flipped through memories of my visits until a final image flashed: Billie's naked body. Flushed, I sat up and looked around. The street was dark. I was all alone. Staring at the house, thinking of Billie inside, I pushed the seat back as far as it would go. No. Don't do it, Finn. Not here. I wrestled with myself but not for long. Resistance is futile. Wasn't that what Dad had said about beautiful women? I unsnapped and unzipped my jeans.

Leaning back again, I closed my eyes and pictured Billie running down the steps to meet me, then dancing with me, then—Oh, God, that's it—kneeling on the floor beside me where I lay on the couch. My touch turned urgent as she whispered, "Hush, Finn. We don't want to wake your dad, do we?"

"No, oh, no," I groaned, imagining it was Billie's hand, not mine, making me come.

I gasped then panted, wondering whether I'd called her name, grateful the windows were closed. When a car breezed by me to the stop sign ahead, I sat up and quickly covered myself. But I was safe, still shrouded in darkness. I took a few deep breaths to calm down, and when I was breathing normally again, I put myself back together, started the car, and gave myself a talking to on the way home. Okay. So, you slipped up. One time. Just don't let it happen again.

I held off for a week.

Getting away with what I'd done coupled with my desire drove me back. I told myself I'd just drive by, but then I stopped the car. Okay, I'll stay just a minute, but then I pictured Billie and got carried away again. Well, so what, nobody knows. No one even suspects. It's harmless, a way to console myself for being cut off from her. It's not something I—we—would ever do.

When I started the car to drive home, a vehicle behind me flashed its bright lights, and before I could pull away, the driver was at my door. My heart in my throat, I lowered the window.

"What are you doing here, Finn?" It was too dark to see his face, but there was no mistaking Pete's voice.

"Nothing," I said, struggling to keep my cool.

"Thought this place was off limits to you." How did he know that? Did Mom tell him about that Halloween incident? Or did Billie?

"I'm going," I said.

"Good," Pete replied. He stepped back and I pulled out. He never mentioned the incident to me or, as far as I knew, to Mom. Rattled, I just wanted to get out of there. It unnerved me to think what he might have observed if he'd approached me any earlier, but on my drive home, I seethed for failing to confront Pete about Billie. He didn't just happen to show up. He was on his way to see her.

Through the winter, I stopped driving to Billie's apartment, but not because of Pete or because it was cold. I was to be confirmed in the spring, and in classes to prepare us for the sacrament, I kept hearing about gifts the Holy Spirit would bestow like wisdom and knowledge and right judgment, qualities to help us order our lives and respond when tempted by doing the right thing, not because we had to but because we wanted to please God. They weren't gifts to be put on a shelf like the Millennium Falcon. They were attributes we'd have to develop so they would strengthen and shield us. It sounded like a path toward becoming a hero, but I balked.

"Father Damian is shrewd," I told Tim as I described the classes to him. "He chose attractive young couples to teach us, and in class I think I want to be like those guys with their perfect lives and pretty wives, but after class, I'm not so sure. When they tell us to put everything in God's hands, it feels like they're indoctrinating us."

"There can be a fine line between indoctrination and education," Tim acknowledged.

I continued with my complaint. "Like do you really have to pray over every decision whether you're trying to decide which college to attend or whether to go to a party? Couldn't you weigh the pros and cons or go with your gut at least on some things, the minor decisions? Wouldn't God want you to? Why else would he give you a brain and instinct?" I took offense at Tim's sudden grin. "Are you laughing at me?" I challenged him.

"No," he said, contracting his smile. "I'm empathizing with you. Questioning anything you're taught is a sign you're growing. You can decide what to believe, what to integrate into your life and what to discard."

When I said, "Good," Tim presented the flip side. Of course there was a catch.

"Once you choose," he said, "you're responsible for your choices."

During the ceremony in late April, the bishop said being anointed with oil would help us give the devil the slip. It didn't take for me, though. A week later, I was back to driving to Billie's again. It was Jeff who got me to stop.

"Where've you been, man?" he demanded when I was late picking him up one night. I didn't tell him what I'd been doing. I just said I'd stopped for a while across from Billie's. He smacked the back of my head and laughed. "Dude," he said, "you've got to get over her."

Then he fixed me up with Francine.

CHAPTER TWENTY-SEVEN

I'D PLAYED WITH FRANCINE IN PRESCHOOL AND KINDER-garten even after guys said girls had cooties, and I'd partnered with her on class projects in elementary school. Smart but not bossy, she agreed to use my design for the sixth-grade science class egg drop and didn't blame me when our raw egg smashed in the carrier meant to cushion it.

"Oh, well. We tried," she'd said with a shrug and a smile. The big valentine she'd given me that year was still in my box of treasures.

But on the first day of school in seventh grade, a gulf opened between us. Francine stood on the other side, comfortable and confident in the sweater and short skirt that hugged her body, accenting the curves she'd developed over the summer. The ninth-grade guys noticed.

"Out of my way, dork," one of them said as he shoved me aside. He planted his hand on the locker above Francine's head, made her laugh at what he said, and left me as hapless as Dad had when he intervened with Billie on the newspaper tour.

The prospect of attending our sprawling junior-senior high school had excited me, even though I'd be the small fish in a big pond, as Dad would have put it, but that first day I discovered Francine had a manual for navigating high school. I didn't. She would sail smoothly, tacking expertly to stay on course, while I got swamped or stuck in a choppy crosscurrent.

She was always in the middle of a group of girlfriends. The one time she approached me alone, though, I got cold feet, ducked into a nearby restroom, and then kicked myself for the rest of the day. All I would have had to say was, "Hey, Francine," or "How's it going?" or even "'Sup?" I'm pretty sure she would have responded. It was too late, but all that afternoon, I reimagined our hallway meeting with a more satisfactory result: "Hey, Francine."

"Oh, hi, Finn."

"'Sup?"

"What?"

"What's up?"

I could only converse with her in my head. If we'd been partners again, I might have relaxed and been able to talk to her, but we were never in the same class until one Indian summer day in eighth grade when our fourth-period gym classes combined for a coed volleyball game. When we counted off by twos, Francine and I were on the same team. The yelling started even before the first serve and gave me cover and the courage to address her.

"C'mon, Francine, you can do it," I hollered before the heel of her hand met the ball, but she was short and not particularly athletic, so the ball didn't even reach the net. Everyone moaned as the serve went to the other side. "Shake it off," I told her. "You'll get it next time." When our team got the ball back, she was at the net in front of me and I set up a shot for her, but startled her when I yelled at her again. She hit the ball into the net, not over. I reacted with a frustrated "Jeez," and smacked my hand against my forehead. When she glared at me, I poked her, playfully, I thought, but she shoved me so hard I staggered back.

"Cut it out, you two," our male teacher hollered. "This isn't a contact sport." My heart sank and I slipped back into my shell for the rest of the class.

"Why were you so hard on Francine?" one of the guys asked me when the teachers blew their whistles and sent us to the showers. The situation was dire if he'd picked up on it. I hadn't meant to fault or make fun of Francine. I'd only dared to speak, to touch her, because I liked her. Couldn't she see that? Again, it was too late, but as I hurried to change, I reimagined my interaction with Francine, giving myself new lines that wouldn't antagonize her. I waited for her outside the girls' locker room, but before I had a chance to say I was sorry, she brushed past me, then turned, hot with an anger that left me cold.

"How could you embarrass me like that, Finn? Stay away from me," she ordered.

I did. For two agonizing years.

In our sophomore year, something changed. Maybe Francine forgot about the volleyball game or forgave me for acting like a jerk. Maybe, because I'd grown six whole inches, I was harder to ignore. Whatever the reason, she smiled shyly when we passed in the halls. Neither of us spoke, though. It was like we were strangers waiting for an introduction before we could interact.

"Leave it to me," Jeff said at lunch. "Come by their lockers at the end of the day." He meant Francine and her best friend, Angela. Jeff had a thing for Angie because of her big tits, his words not mine. I didn't like that girl. She'd been misnamed. Loud and rude, there was nothing angelic about her. It was a mystery why Francine was her friend, but then, people didn't understand why I hung around with Jeff. That afternoon as I headed to meet Francine, my stomach tumbled like it was stuck in my morning phys ed class.

Kids yelled and slammed their lockers, but the end-of-the-school-day din diminished when I turned the corner. Francine's gaze locked on mine and pulled me toward her like a tractor beam. I docked in her heavy-lidded brown eyes, eyes that made her look like she was just waking up no matter the time of day. She wasn't beautiful like Billie, but she was definitely cute. She had shiny pink lips and bright white teeth and curly chin-length hair. Was it brown? Was it black? I couldn't tell. The color changed with the light. She was right in style with her slouchy, sweatshirt-like top and so petite I was sure I could lift her a foot in the air where we would be eye to eye.

Later, when I heard that sappy adage about how a young man's fancy turns to thoughts of love, I remembered that spring day with Francine. Her smile set off a new sensation. It was my heart fluttering, not my stomach churning. I wasn't nervous and I didn't need an introduction. Francine said "Hi," I said "Hey," and the space and time between us dissolved. We grinned like we'd come to the end of one journey and would set off on another. Together. Forever.

Outside the school, I stepped into a Disney world, squinting at the intense greens and blues, stirred by the soundtrack of cheeps and whirs. I was the robin bobbing in freshly cut grass that smelled of summer fun. I could have walked for hours with Francine, but had to settle for walking her to her idling bus, then walking the length of it until she reached an empty seat and opened the window so we could say goodbye.

"Down, boy," Jeff said, laughing beside me.

We ran to the student parking lot, and as the buses snaked away from the school, Jeff nudged his car in line behind Francine's. At the first stop, he blew his horn until Francine and Angie appeared in the rear bus window and chased some younger boys out of the last two seats. Angie took one seat, Francine the other and they sat sideways, looking down at us. My gaze traveled from Francine's face to her hiked skirt and bare legs then back to her face again. I grinned and waved while Jeff laughed at me. When the bus stopped at the intersection near Francine's house and a bunch of kids got off, Francine and Angie walked back to Jeff's car and talked with us until Francine's mother appeared on their porch to shake out a rug.

Shielding her eyes from the sun and looking in our direction, she called, "Francine, time to come home now."

When I got home, Francine crowded out thoughts of anything or anyone else. Mom had to remind me to go get Patch at Grandpa's. Then she had to tell me to feed him. And take him for a walk. That annoyed her. "What's wrong with you, Finn? Where's your head?" she said.

It took twice as long as usual to finish my homework because I couldn't stop thinking about Francine, and after I was done, instead of going downstairs to watch TV, I lay on my bed staring at the ceiling. Over the years when Mom had asked if I wanted to paint over the clouds, I'd said no. I liked gazing up at them while daydreaming. All evening and into the night before I fell asleep, I relived the afternoon's events. My cheeks ached from grinning.

In the morning, eager to see Francine again, I hustled to her locker before homeroom. Crouched on the floor beside her, a seventh grader sorted his books until a junior walking by kicked the stack and sent them flying.

Instantly, Francine ran after him, yelling, "Hey, get back here. Pick up these books."

"Oooo. I'm so afraid," the upperclassman said, raising his hands defensively as he walked backward, "but no." Sneering, he turned and sauntered down the hall.

"You jerk," Francine shouted. Then she walked back and stooped down to help the younger boy pick up his books.

"What?" she said, still irritated when she stood up and saw me staring.

I flinched at that eighth-grade anger of hers flaring up again and tried to defuse it. "That's telling him," I said, trying a teasing touch like Dad might have, but that was a mistake.

Francine glared. "Are you mocking me?" she said.

"No," I said automatically. While her reaction seemed out of proportion to the incident, I didn't want to express that thought and have her turn on me. "That was good of you," I said. "To stand up for that kid. To help him."

"I hate bullies," she said, slamming her locker.

"Me too," I said automatically, but her vehemence resurrected the distress I'd felt witnessing confrontations between Mom and Dad. For a split second, I considered bolting to keep from getting sucked into a similar situation with Francine, but then she smiled.

"I'm sorry," she said.

I can't say my fears dissipated, but they diminished. I didn't want to run. Aside from her temper, Francine was nice as well as pretty. And then there was her voice. It didn't grate on me like Angie's and she didn't speak in a monotone like the girls who acted bored with life. Francine's bubbled like the fizzy first pour of a bottle of Grandpa's sparkling wine. I could get drunk on the sound.

Next morning, I stopped beside one of the three-foot-high concrete planters outside the school's main entrance and made a show of looking around. "I think I'll hang out here for a while," I told Jeff. "It's too nice to go in." The sun was out but hadn't yet warmed the chilly air.

"Right," Jeff said, laughing. "Tell the girls I said hello."

Leaning against the edge of the planter, I pulled out my math homework and pretended to check it. My heart palpitated as buses pulled up and I scanned them for Francine's. When her bus rolled to a stop, I stuck the paper back in my math book and strolled alongside the bus, hoping it would look like I'd just happened by. "Oh, Fin-ley, were you waiting for us?" I cringed at Angie's taunt.

"Don't mind her," Francine said when she caught up with me. She smiled as she swung her backpack from one arm to the other and stumbled into me. When I reached out to steady her, we clasped hands. Francine's was soft and cool, but then a surge of heat fused it to mine and we held hands all the way to her locker. That's when I started thinking of her as my girlfriend. Finn. Francine. Even our names went together.

"Are you going with Francine?" a classmate asked, as we left homeroom for our first-period classes. If he was going to razz me, I didn't care, but his response, when I said yes, surprised and pleased me. "Cool," he said.

At the end of the day, I asked Francine if she wanted to go to the school dance with me that night. She said she would meet me there. I couldn't pick her up and drive her because she wasn't allowed to date until September, the start of our junior year. When Mom got home from school and I told her about Francine and the dance, she set her briefcase on the floor and busied herself with hanging up her coat. We hadn't discussed dating in any detail. "It's good to start with school activities," she said.

Jeff was late picking me up that night, and impatient to meet Francine, I hurried ahead of him into the school to where the girls waited outside the gym entrance. "It's about time," Angie said, her arms crossed, one foot tapping the floor.

"Later," Jeff said to me, as he grinned and headed back down the hall to the parking lot. Hands in his pockets, he didn't take Angie's hand. She grabbed his arm, then linked hers through his.

Francine frowned as they left. "I told Angie she should

stay, but she doesn't listen to me. Jeff has too much influence over her," she said. I had a feeling Jeff wasn't making Angie do anything she didn't want to do, but I didn't want to argue with Francine. I paid for both of us and we walked hand in hand into the gym. Inside, I flashed back to dances in seventh and eighth grade when my friends and I ran up and down the bleachers and around on the floor.

"Walk, don't run," teacher chaperones scolded as they chased us back up into the stands. We went to dances back then because there wasn't anything else to do and our parents, well, mothers anyway, thought we ought to. We pointed and snickered at the few couples who dared to take the floor while girls in our grade sat glumly on the sidelines. We didn't know, didn't care, that they desperately wanted to dance. In ninth grade, I'd stopped running around long enough to notice that if you danced, you got to press yourself against a girl's body while you rocked from side to side. That was more than I'd done with Billie. I thought I might like it.

When I took Francine's right hand in my left and put my other hand around her back at her waist, her sleepy eyes widened, but she followed me with ease.

"Who taught you to dance like this? Your mother?" she asked.

"No," I said, considering how to answer. "It was a friend of my dad's."

"Oh. You mean that woman he lived with? Before he died?"

I winced at the self-consciousness that struck me, but of course people would have talked about my parents' separation and the other woman involved. That's what people did.

"Yes. Her name was Billie. Is Billie," I said.

Saying Billie's name transported me back to the apartment. I was a kid again and she was guiding me through the box step. For a moment, the recollection of her flowery scent overpowered the fruity essence of Francine's hair. I closed my eyes and drew Francine closer, a bit guilty that it was the memory of Billie prompting the action, but then sort of sorry that while I'd been falling for Francine, I'd forgotten about Billie.

Francine. Billie. Billie. Francine. They kept cutting in on each other, and I wondered whether it was like that for Dad. When he left Mom for Billie, did he still care about Mom, and when he said he wanted to come home to Mom, was he sorry to leave Billie? Mom. Billie. Billie. Mom. Was it possible to love two women at the same time? How would you do it? Would you wall them off from each other in the separate chambers of your heart? Could you?

When I opened my eyes, our English teacher Mrs. Harmon tapped Francine on her shoulder. "Would you mind, dear? I haven't danced with anyone since my husband died," she said, "and Finn is such a good dancer." Francine looked at Mrs. Harmon, and then up at me. I regretted having made a spectacle of myself. I wanted to keep dancing with Francine, but I didn't think I could refuse Mrs. Harmon. Her expression was so hopeful.

"Sorry," I mouthed to Francine as she backed away. Mrs. Harmon put a hand on my shoulder, held up the other for me to take, and then followed me gracefully, her curly gray hair tickling my chin. I tensed when another guy approached Francine, but relaxed when she shook her head and he walked away. Once we were reunited, Francine and I danced to every remaining slow song until the last one when she dropped my hand and ran off the gym floor.

"Where are they?" she said outside the gym, searching the hallway until Angie ran toward us and Jeff strolled behind her.

"C'mon, Francine. Don't keep your dad waiting," Angie said, grabbing Francine's hand and pulling her out the door before we had a chance to say goodbye.

On our way home, Jeff said he and Angie had driven to what

had become the preferred parking spot after the storm-ravaged trees were cleared from the hillside. "Man, she was all over me, even before I stopped the car," he said. Angie let him fish his hand up under her skirt, but wouldn't let him touch her hair. He laughed as he imitated her in a high-pitched voice: "'Don't. You'll mess it up.'" While I was sure Francine wouldn't be as free with her body, she might let me run my fingers through her curls. That would be something.

Being one half of a couple—like the quarterback and the featured twirler, the captain of the basketball team and the head cheerleader—conferred a status individual students lacked on their own, and with Francine, I'd achieved it. Women teachers smiled and nodded when we walked past, but they glared at Jeff and Angie.

"Unhand that girl," old Mrs. Entwhistle shouted when Jeff cupped Angie's butt as they walked past her classroom. Usually, Jeff defied teachers, but he must have been caught off guard because he removed his hand. After that he avoided Mrs. Entwhistle's room and put his hand wherever he wanted on Angie. Another time, he was thrown out of an assembly when a teacher noticed Angie's hand moving around in his lap. I would have ejected her.

In the last weeks of school, the coming summer offered all the time in the world to spend with Francine, until she told me she had a job as a camp counselor in the Poconos almost three hundred miles away. She'd leave right after school was out and wouldn't return until the end of August. The camp had one computer and one phone for office and emergency use only. We'd have to write letters to keep in touch. She may as well have been taking off for another galaxy.

CHAPTER TWENTY-EIGHT

The day after Francine left for camp, a red sports coupe streaked through an intersection in front of me. It could have been Billie's car. She was back, competing with Francine for my attention, and, while Francine was my girlfriend, I had many more memories of Billie. It wasn't my fault I wavered. If Francine hadn't gone away, I wouldn't be conflicted. I would be consumed with thoughts of her.

I teetered between the two of them until Francine's first letter arrived. As I pulled the cream-colored parchment-like envelope from the mailbox and read my name on the front, my pulse quickened. I tossed the rest of the mail on the dining room table and ripped open the envelope as I took the stairs two at a time. In my room, I pulled out three sheets of folded paper that matched the envelope and gazed at the swoops and swirls. It was a delicate handwriting, feminine like Francine, but with a slant that drove the words forward, compelling them to deliver their message. I sped through her description of the camp to the end: "I miss you, Finn." Heart pounding, I began my reply on the spot: "I miss you too, Francine."

"Francine says families and friends can visit on the weekends," I told Mom, but she dismissed my hope of making a trip.

"That's too far away," she said.

After a few days, as Francine had written about the camp, I wrote to her about Danton, the way Dad had described it to Billie, the way people reacted to Grandpa. You're a good writer, Finn, Francine wrote in her second letter. I want to be a writer, I wrote back. She said she wanted to be a teacher like Mom. Her closings were the best part. She drew hearts or X's and O's. She said she missed me, wished she hadn't had to go away, and was counting the days until her return.

Midway through the summer, I opened an envelope that held the left side of three pages torn in half from top to bottom. In a note at the top of the first page, Francine wrote that she'd mailed Angie the right-side pages of the letter, and I would have to get together with her to read it. That was clever of Francine, but I wished she'd sent the other half of her letter to anyone but Angie. I dreaded calling that girl. When we met at the drugstore's soda fountain, she wouldn't shut up and let me read.

"There's a boys' camp on the other side of the lake," Angie said, drilling me with a look. "Francine was in love with one of the counselors there last year. I wonder if he's back."

"She hasn't said," I answered, striving for a feigned indifference, but Angie snickered.

Unnerved, I took her pages and left. Over the next few days, that guy, whoever he was, pushed me out of every picture I tried to imagine with Francine. Desperate to see her, I told Mom I was going fishing on Saturday. Late in the day after arriving at the camp, I'd call home, and while Mom might be angry, she'd likely tell me to stay over somewhere and drive back the next day. I packed clothes in my gym bag and stashed the bag in the trunk Friday night. Early on Saturday, I crept past Mom's room to the kitchen, but she was already at the table. She'd even packed me a lunch. Smiling over her coffee mug, she said, "Catch us something for supper." I winced and made my getaway.

In the car I turned on the radio and upped the volume. In seventy miles, I'd reach the university my parents had attended. After that, I'd be in new and unfamiliar territory, but I'd highlighted the route on the state map with a neon yellow marker. With Dad's excited shout of "Road trip" in mind, I stuck my elbow out the rolled-down window and tapped the steering wheel in time to the beat of songs on the radio. I checked the rearview mirror as much for my expression as for the traffic behind me and rehearsed my greeting: "Hey, Francine, surprise!"

When I reached the university, I took a brief detour past the ivy-covered redbrick buildings, the grove of giant oaks, and the flagstone amphitheater set in a lush lawn. Guys tossed Frisbees over girls who lay sunning themselves, books pushed to the fringes of their blankets on the grass. On the hand-holding couples walking well-worn paths, I superimposed images of Francine and me.

Several miles on the other side of the campus, the terrain turned brown and dreary. It was the stretch with the abandoned coal mines and the fire hall where Mom as a student had tutored kids from families trapped and forgotten in the hollows. My mood faded to match the landscape.

When I spied a rough wooden sign citing chapter and verse on the side of the road, I slowed the car to read the scripture passage: "Enter not into the path of the wicked." It wasn't unusual to see signs like that along the backroads of what my parents called the Bible Belt. Mom had bristled at the proselytizing and the judgment implied, but Dad had laughed. They were harmless, he said, like the *Monitor*'s horoscopes, generic messages that could apply to anyone in any situation.

Farther down the road a second sign unnerved me: "Repent,

then, of this evil plan of yours." Huh? What? Who, me? A third even larger sign loomed in the distance. Curiosity drove me forward but dread rode along. When I reached the sign, I pulled off the road and put the car in park to contemplate it: "Avoid it, do not pass by it. Turn away from it and pass on."

Spooked, I shook my head to clear it, shifted the car into drive, and hit the gas to pull back onto the road. The car stuttered and stopped. Shoot. I shouldn't have let it idle, but that's no big deal unless—Zzzit. Crackle. As though someone had pulled the plug on me, I flatlined. The car was out of gas.

Now what? There was no traffic and there weren't any houses where I could ask for help or make a phone call. I was miles out of town and had no idea how far it was to the next. I got out of the car, slammed the door, kicked the front tire, and then kicked it again. Stupid, stupid, stupid.

"Well, no one's coming to get you." Yeah, I said it. Out loud. I opened the door, grabbed the bottle of water Mom had packed with my lunch, and locked the car. Looking ahead, then back down the road I'd traveled, I tried to remember where and when I'd passed the last service station. How long would it take me to get gas for the car? Would I still be able to make it to Francine?

I'd walked back toward the campus for almost an hour, growing hot in the sun, when a sports car whined and downshifted behind me. I turned and waved to flag down the driver, and a black Ferrari convertible slowed and, thankfully, stopped beside me. And I'd thought Billie's car was rad. Behind the wheel was the typical old-guy driver of convertibles, a stocky man with gray at his temples, but on second glance, he wasn't that old. He looked about Mom's age. "Was that your car I passed back there?" he asked, and when I nodded, "What's the trouble?"

Boy, I hated to admit it. "I just need some gas."

He laughed, but in a friendly way. "It happens," he said. "Hop in."

Relieved to be rescued, I blabbed about how stupid I felt for not filling the tank. I hadn't learned anything from Dad's lecturing Mom and warning me, "Let this be a lesson to you."

"Oh, you have now. Look at it this way, you'll always be checking," the driver said, tapping his car's fuel gauge, "so it'll never happen again. And you picked the right direction to walk. There's nothing back there for twenty miles." He gassed the car and we zipped along. "So where are you headed?" he asked.

Again, I rattled on, telling him about Francine and Angie and the letter and my plan. When we reached a service station on the edge of the campus, I filled a five-gallon can at the pump while a couple of guys came out of the garage to admire his car.

"Do you live around here?" I asked him when we got back on the road.

"No, I have a meeting at the university," he said.

"Did you go there?" I asked.

"I did," he said.

"So did my parents," I told him.

He cocked his head and asked, "What's your name?" After I told him, we rode in silence the rest of the way back to Mom's car. When he let me out, I reached for my wallet, but he said he didn't want my money. "Just help out the next guy, Finn Maguire," he said, as he waved and took off. It was weird how he said my name, with familiarity, as though it wasn't the first time. While filling the tank with gas from the can, I wondered whether he'd known Mom and Dad in college.

Back at the gas station, I returned the can and topped off the tank at the pump debating whether I should push on to the camp. After I ate the lunch Mom packed, I put away the map and said a silent goodbye to Francine.

By the time I found a pay phone and called home, I had my excuse. "I tried a new fishing spot and lost track of time," I said when Mom answered on the first ring. "And I didn't catch any fish."

"Maybe you want to try another explanation," she said in her no-nonsense tone, before breaking into a laugh. "Considering you left your pole and tackle on the back porch."

When I got home and confessed where I'd really been headed, she said, "I thought so."

"Angie said there was a guy there last year—"

"So, you went to check up on Francine?" Mom interrupted.

"Well, Angie said—"

Again, she interrupted. "And you believed her? Oh, Finn, think about it. Angie's jealous of you and Francine. She'll say anything to undermine your relationship."

Then she humbled me. "Maybe you should ask yourself whether you're worthy of Francine."

CHAPTER TWENTY-NINE

AS I APPROACHED FRANCINE'S HOUSE AT THE END OF SUM-mer, my heart beat like it would burst from my chest and outrace me to her. I parked, Francine ran down her porch steps, and I jumped out of the car.

"I missed you," we said simultaneously as I lifted her in the street, whirled her around, and kissed her. Any concern about a previous boyfriend, real or imagined, vanished. As we walked to her front porch, Francine said her parents had okayed a double date with Angie and Jeff before the start of school. Settled beside her on the porch swing, I pushed off with my foot and imagined us soaring. We wouldn't need a starship.

When I shared the news with Mom, she said, "Your first real date. What will you do?"

"Probably go out for pizza," I said.

"And after that?"

I hadn't thought beyond the meal. "I don't know."

"You could come here," Mom suggested, a little too eagerly.

Whoa. No way. "Jeff will think of something," I said.

"Yes, I'm sure he will." I let it pass when she added, "But it's high time you start thinking for yourself, Finn Maguire."

When our date night arrived, Jeff drove us to Francine's where we were picking up the girls and groaned when I made him go to the door with me as Mom had instructed. At the Pizza Hut outside town, we claimed a corner booth. When I asked Francine what toppings she liked, she didn't hesitate. "All of them."

"Even anchovies?" I asked, sure she'd say no.

"Especially anchovies," she said, smiling broadly as she bumped up against me.

"Ewww, swimmers," Angie said, scrunching her face as the rest of us laughed and Francine squeezed my hand under the table.

Half cheese, half pepperoni was agreeable to all of us, but then we had to select thin or thick crust. Angie didn't want too much bread, so we settled on hand tossed. Again, I was sure I was with the better girl. Angie made an issue of everything while easygoing Francine went along. After dinner, she played miniature golf with Jeff and me at the course down the highway and laughed when the rotating arm of a windmill batted back the ball she tried to hit through. Angie stomped behind us, complaining it was a stupid game.

"Hey," Jeff said, when we piled back into his car. "Want to see where the tornado hit the hill?"

"It wasn't a tornado," I said.

"How will we see anything?" Francine asked. "It's getting dark."

But Angie said, "Sure, let's go." Had she told Francine she'd been there before and what she'd done there with Jeff? Did girls talk about things like that the way guys did?

In the clearing, we sat on the hood of Jeff's car and watched vehicles crawl or careen on the four-lane highway below. Francine and I would be together for the two more years of high school ahead of us, but Jeff and Angie were transferring to the vo-tech school where she was enrolled in cosmetology and he would take auto mechanics—his ticket out of town. He said he wasn't about to get stuck in Danton for the rest of his life.

"What's wrong with Danton?" Francine asked. "Don't you like it here?"

"Too small," Jeff said. He'd told Mom and me it wasn't that he wanted to live in a city with a lot of people. He yearned for a place with different people, people who hadn't made up their minds about him, people who would give him a chance. "People have cars everywhere. I can get a job as a mechanic anywhere," he said with confidence. "Day after graduation? I'm heading out. I'll see where the road takes me."

"Yeah. Yeah. Sure, you will," Angie taunted him.

"You think I won't? Watch me," he said, his tone so cold I almost felt bad for her. I'd asked Jeff during the summer if he really liked Angie.

"Not like you like Francine," he said. What he liked were all the things Angie did with him when they were alone. "Don't look so shocked. Why should I care about her? She doesn't care about me. You see how she looks at other guys." He was right. I'd noticed.

When we got back into the car, I put my arm around Francine and pulled her close to me in a corner of the back seat. In seconds we were kissing. From that point, I was oblivious to what was going on in the front, but when Francine stiffened, I knew something was up.

"We should go home now, Angie," Francine said.

Angie's voice was muffled but her annoyance was clear. "Jeez, Francine, sometimes you're such a baby." But, after a zipping sound, Jeff sat up, then Angie sat up, and Jeff started the car.

When Jeff parked in front of Francine's house, Francine

and I walked with Angie toward the front porch until Francine pulled me around the side of her house to the darkness in back.

"Let's not go out with them anymore," she said. Steadying herself with her hands on my chest, she raised up on tiptoe, pressed her lips against mine, and parted them for a long French kiss. That did it. I'd stood up for Jeff when Mom questioned whether he was a problem and dismissed her admonition that I should think for myself. Jeff had been my best friend for a long time, but versus Francine, he didn't stand a chance.

In the car when I told him there'd be no more double dates, Jeff wasn't offended. He jabbed me. "Hey, maybe if you're alone, she'll put out." It was a crude comment, but I didn't slug him. He was just mouthing off. And, hey, maybe he was right. Maybe Francine would do with me what Angie did with him. Not right away, but someday maybe.

Francine was allowed to go out once a week either Friday or Saturday night and to school activities like games and plays, dances and concerts. Neither her parents nor my mom wanted us spending too much time alone together in a car. They would have been surprised to find that mostly we talked or, rather, I talked and Francine listened.

"I can't imagine it," she said one fall Friday night in Mom's car in the school parking lot. "What was it like to lose your dad when you were just a kid?"

I wasn't surprised that Billie sprang to mind. She was all tangled up in my thoughts and feelings about Dad, but I set her aside. "It might sound heartless," I said, "but in some ways, it wasn't so bad. I still had Mom and Grandpa, Uncle Pete, and Tim, I mean Mr. Weiss, and I was used to Dad not being around every day. But on those every-other Fridays when he would have picked me up and taken me to his apartment? That's when I missed him. I got a pain in my chest."

"You were heartbroken," Francine said.

Huh. I'd never thought of it that way.

"I wanted to tell you I was sorry in the funeral home when Mr. Weiss brought us," Francine said, "but I was at the end of the line and before I could get to you, Jeff took you away."

"Is that why you don't like him?" I teased her.

"No," she said, laughing and elbowing me. "I don't like the way he acts. He's not so tough once you get to know him, but he doesn't think about others. He seems like he doesn't care. He's—"

"Fearless," I said.

That made her laugh again. "I was going to say selfish. He's not like you."

"I know," I said. "That's why I like him."

Giving me that valentine in elementary school was thoughtful, but Francine's invitation to talk was a lifeline, one I hadn't realized I needed until she extended it. Her gentle questions evoked my younger self and encouraged me to examine feelings I hadn't been able to process when Dad died.

"I think the whole funeral home thing threw me," I told her. "Dad looked so strange. I was afraid to touch him until the last minute. I feel bad about that now. I guess I was in shock.

"I know it wasn't his fault he died. It wasn't like he smoked or drank himself to death, but it was like he abandoned me anyway, left me alone with Mom. Oh, she bought my food and clothes and arranged my activities, so I know it might have been worse if she'd died instead of him, but without Dad, there was no more joking around, no more riding around town on Saturday mornings stopping in at businesses where employees made a fuss over me.

"Everyone had a dad except me and, well, Jeff. I guess that was one reason I stuck with him. I didn't like being different."

"Nobody does," Francine said, squeezing my hand.

"I think about all the things Dad didn't get to teach me.

And I have these weird thoughts, like does he miss me? Does he ever think about me? I'm sorry I'll never know him man to man. Sometimes I wonder what he would think of me now. If he were alive, would he still want me hanging around like he did when I was a kid?"

Francine squeezed my hand again, harder. "Of course he would. Don't be silly."

After a couple of months, I got up the nerve to share my most troubling thoughts with Francine, to confess the worst thing in the world about me and hope she'd understand and still like me. Nothing I'd said to that point had shocked her. Again, we were parked in the school lot. To keep us warm, I had to start the car and blast the heat every fifteen minutes or so.

"Remember when you asked how I felt when my dad died?" I asked her. When she nodded, I told her—not about Billie—but how I'd gotten mad at Dad over the incident with Ginger. For the first time, I said the hateful words out loud and recoiled at their cruelty.

Francine paused before she spoke. "Your dad didn't die because you wished it. You know that, don't you? You were a kid. You didn't mean it."

"No, not now. But back then? Yeah, I think I did mean it," I said.

When she didn't speak right away, I worried that I'd said too much, but she put her hand on my chest, leaned her forehead against my cheek, and whispered, "Well, you're going to have to forgive yourself for that. Your dad can't do it."

Walking Francine back to her house that night, I considered how I could exorcise my guilt now that I'd acknowledged it. Maybe I could leave it on her porch and be done with it. Yeah, I liked that idea.

"What are you smiling at?" she asked me.

"Oh, nothing," I said.

"Tell me," she insisted.

I waved her off. "No, I can't."

"Finn," she said, grabbing my arm.

So, I told her. "Silly, right? Or stupid?"

"Neither," she said. "But don't leave your guilt here. You'll just trip over it next time you come. Take it with you. Drive out of your way going home and throw it out the window."

I stared at her.

"What?" she asked.

"That's brilliant," I said, in awe of her solution, in awe of her.

Francine offered a shy smile. "You might have to do it a few times," she said. "I mean imagine yourself doing it. It's a way to manage your worries, to try to minimize them."

"How do you know—"

"I read about it," she said.

How much like Dad. It could be a sign.

I picked the bridge as the place to toss my guilt so it would float away down the river. Slowing down as I drove across the bridge, I lowered the window and waved my arm out the opening. But Francine was right. Remorse recurred when I thought too long or too hard about that last morning with Dad. I had to keep visualizing the act of unburdening myself, throwing my guilt off the bridge, leaving it on the train tracks, burying it in the cemetery.

One winter-into-spring night, when we no longer needed to turn on the heat in the car, I took a chance and told Francine how sometimes I missed Billie as much as I missed Dad. She wasn't shocked. She said she could understand because I'd spent so much time with Billie and she'd been so nice to me. Something told me not to tell her about seeing Billie naked, though, and aside from that there was only one more thing to share with Francine, Dad's obit page ads, the In Memoriams. I produced my collection of clippings for Francine to examine on the first spring day warm enough to rock without jackets on our porch swing.

"They're beautiful," she said. "Your mom really loved your dad."

"What?" I asked, wondering whether I'd heard her correctly.

"Your mother. She placed the ads, right?"

"Mom? I don't think so. She thinks those ads are silly," I said, even as I realized Francine had to be right.

"Who then?" she asked.

"Maybe a friend? It says, 'Sadly missed by family and friends.' He had a lot of friends."

"Well, the words are perfect," she said. "They could be your dad speaking to you."

Or Billie. Honestly? I still wanted it to be Billie.

After I'd talked things over with Francine, I got out the journal from Tim and on the page following words I'd copied from the ads, I wrote some of my own: When my dad died, I was old enough to grasp that death was final and irreversible, but young enough to be distracted. I shed my occasional bouts of sadness like a shrugged-off sweatshirt on a hot afternoon. Now that I'm older, my grief demands to be dealt with in a more adult way. It's the sheet that twists me up on a restless night.

As our junior year ended, I gave Mom a new photo to display and kept a framed copy in my room. It was the picture of Francine and me at the junior-senior prom. In three-inch heels with her soft curls piled high on her head, Francine was almost as tall as me, and she glowed in a long gauzy buttery-yellow gown. All night at the dance, she was the sun that wouldn't go to bed.

Instead of going back to the camp, Francine stayed in town for the summer working to make money for the car she'd need to commute to the community college. After two years there, she would transfer to join me at the university my parents had attended. At Mom's and Tim's urging, I'd applied early and had secured a place in the prestigious honors college founded and funded by an alum. It seemed a long way off, though. Francine and I had another whole year together.

CHAPTER THIRTY

But that year? Our senior year? It whizzed right by. Again, Francine and I went to games and dances, concerts and plays, but each was bittersweet because it was the last. When we talked about our future, we reassured each other it wouldn't be like when she was at camp. We'd be only seventy miles apart, not three hundred. I'd come home from the university on weekends or Francine would visit me on campus. Weeknights, we'd talk on the phone—after 11 when the rates went down.

In the spring, when we'd been together for two years, Francine and I made a big decision. By then it wasn't just Jeff and Angie who'd gone all the way. Plenty of couples were having sex—or said they were. And we were ready. We loved each other. We'd even said it, and not just when we were necking in Mom's car or at a party.

"Not in your car. Not at a party," Francine said. "And you'll have to take precautions." I didn't dare smile at the formality of the expression. I had to be serious.

"I will," I said, making the cross-my-heart sign.

"About time," Jeff said, laughing and slapping me on the back when I confided in him. "You know what to do? Need any pointers?"

I elbowed him away. No, I wouldn't need his input. Mom, who turned every incident into a teachable moment, had long ago told me what to expect. When she'd observed me playing with a neighbor girl in a way that must have concerned her, she hadn't stopped or scolded us. Instead, she'd come out of the house with milk and cookies for us, then sent my playmate home.

"What were you doing?" she asked me.

"Touching tongues," I said, surprised that Mom had asked. It was new to me, but when the girl had proposed it, she made it sound like a game everyone played.

"That kind of kissing isn't for kids," Mom said. "That's the way grown-ups kiss." Then she described another kind of touching that at the time sounded gross, but I figured I didn't have to worry about it since it was for a man and a woman who were married and wanted to have a baby.

But from Jeff I'd learned that if we were careful, Francine and I wouldn't have to worry and wouldn't have to wait. I'd been with him a few times when he'd bought condoms. He'd slapped the package down on the counter as though calling attention to his purchase and daring the clerk to question him or make a wisecrack. I didn't have the nerve to buy them at the drugstore in town where I was known. I drove to a store in the strip mall.

The aisle with the family planning sign was crowded with women examining boxes of feminine hygiene products and packages of panty hose. As I kept doubling back, I half expected an employee to confront me for casing the store. When the aisle was empty, I whipped by the display, grabbed the box I'd seen Jeff buy, and hid it under a bag of chips when I placed it on the counter. I pretended to read the headlines on the rack of tabloids and thanked God the cashier didn't have to call for a price check and get anyone else involved in the transaction. When she gave me my change, I noticed the newly minted penny in my palm, remembered the ones I'd collected when I was stuck on Billie, and dropped it in the take-one-leave-one paper cup on the counter.

"What we talked about?" I whispered to Francine in school on a Friday two weeks before our senior prom. "We're all set for Sunday afternoon. Mom has tickets to a play in the city."

Francine's wide-eyed expression threw me. I'd thought we'd agreed to go ahead, but she looked like she was reconsidering sex in practice vs. sex in theory. Maybe I should have asked if she still wanted to go through with our plans, but if she'd changed her mind, I didn't want to know. I wouldn't force her to do anything she didn't want to do. That would be wrong, but I didn't want to offer her an easy out.

"So, what are you two going to do today?" Francine's mother asked after letting me into her kitchen Sunday at noon.

She was so absorbed with scrubbing her sink that I questioned whether she'd hear if I said what was on my mind: "We're going to have sex. All afternoon in my room. How about that?" At that moment, though, she stopped working and looked at me, waiting for an answer. "Uh, I'll let Francine decide," I said, in case she'd come up with a cover story without cluing me in.

Francine had never made me wait for her before, and when she finally appeared, she stalled. "Do you want a piece of pie, Finn? It's blueberry. Still warm."

Trying not to sound overly eager, I said, "No, I'm good. Ready to go?"

In the car Francine was quiet, twisting then smoothing, twisting and smoothing the strap of her purse. To try to help her relax, I took her hand. "What a great day, huh?" I said, then realized the weather hardly mattered if we would spend the day inside. I tried again. "You look nice." With her jeans, she wore a scoop-neck yellow T-shirt I hadn't seen before, and I throbbed in my own jeans as I wondered what she was wearing under her shirt.

True, Francine had never been in my room, but she acted a little too preoccupied by it. "Oh, look at the clouds," she said, glued to the doorjamb as she gazed at the ceiling.

I had to say, "Come in," to get her to enter. Then she examined my Falcon model and studied the spines of the books on the shelves above my desk. Was she going to read every title?

And how to go about getting us into my bed? In the car, while we'd have been cramped, we could have progressed naturally from positions we'd already assumed. I stepped behind her and put my hands at her waist. When she relaxed and leaned back against me, I nuzzled her neck, and when she turned around, I wrapped my arms around her. As we kissed, her soft moans emboldened me and I popped the snap on her jeans. When she unsnapped mine, giving me the go-ahead, I groaned.

A sudden shout from below stopped us cold.

"Finn, where are you?" Grandpa called up the stairs. Immediately, Francine pushed me away and snapped her jeans. Crap. In my excitement over being with her, I'd forgotten Grandpa's TV wasn't working and he'd planned to come over to watch the game.

"Wait," I whispered, holding up my hands to try to freeze Francine in place. "Let me see if I can get rid of him." Out in the hall, though, I cursed myself. I couldn't do it. If by some miracle I convinced Grandpa I had to stay in my room and do homework, he'd call up to me like an announcer after each run or out. He might even come upstairs to try to lure me down. I wanted to blame him, but I was the one who'd screwed up. When I returned to Francine and reached for her, I said, "I'm sorry. This sucks."

She batted my hands away and said, "Get me out of here."

"Okay," I said, trying to calm her. "We can sneak out the back door."

"What do you mean 'we'?" she asked.

"I'll take you home."

"How? Your mother has the car," she said. "I'll walk."

I protested that idea. "It's too far."

"Then I'll go to Angie's," she said.

No, not Angie. I didn't want her involved, but what could I do? Boy, I'd really screwed up. I went downstairs with Francine behind me, peeked around the corner to make sure Grandpa was settled in the living room, and then led her to the back door.

"I'm sorry," I said again.

"Maybe it's a sign. Maybe we're not supposed to do this," Francine said, sounding a little too relieved as she left the house.

"No, don't say that," I said from the porch as I watched her leave. Jeez, I'd screwed up royally.

Monday in school, Francine was still shaken. She wouldn't talk about the incident until Friday. By then the prom was a week away and she was excited. She thrilled me too when she leaned into me and whispered, "Maybe we'll have another chance."

CHAPTER THIRTY-ONE

When I got home from Francine's that Friday night, Jeff's car was parked in front of our house. The glow of his cigarette tip drew me to the darkened corner of the porch where he sat. Something was wrong if he was smoking again with Mom in her reading chair on the other side of the screen door. He'd given up the habit when she said she didn't want him to get hooked and asked him to quit.

"Hey," I said, my curiosity building.

Jeff mashed his cigarette against the sole of his shoe, pitched the butt over the railing, stood up, and spat out the words. "Angie's pregnant."

Stunned, I stared at him. "But you used condoms."

"Not every time," he said, sounding more resigned than angry, as though confronting too late consequences he hadn't considered. He took a few steps and turned, stepped, and turned again like he was bumping up against invisible walls desperate to find a door. It was strange to see him acting trapped, and he caught me off guard when he said, "Well, I'm outta here."

"Wait. What?" I said, hoping I'd misheard.

"I'm leaving," he said again, this time like he'd found a door.

Deep down, had I been like Angie, convinced his plans were all talk? "No. Don't go, Jeff. Talk to Mom," I said.

He brushed me off. "I already did. You were right not to get in so deep with Francine. Sorry I ragged on you."

Reeling, I asked, "Where are you going?"

He waved me off. "It's better if you don't know."

Mom came to the door then and stepped out onto the porch. Jeff wrapped his arms around her, buried his face in her neck, and murmured something I couldn't make out. When he let her go, she gave him a sad-eyed smile. "Of course, I won't forget you, Jeff," she said. "You be careful in the ring. I know Pete says you're a natural, but I don't want you to get hurt."

Without another word, he ran past me down the steps to his car, revved the engine, and peeled out. Dumbfounded, I watched until the taillights disappeared, listened until the rumbling faded. That wasn't his way home. It was the fastest way out of town. He was really going. I didn't want it to be like this, a final scene with no promise of another.

"Why didn't you tell him to stay, Mom?" I asked her. "He listens to you."

"That Angie. I told you she was trouble." The disdain in her voice made me think she'd encouraged Jeff to go. When she turned to me, she softened her tone. "This town is good for you, Finn, but it would suffocate Jeff."

Boy, I hated the way she thought she had me pegged, the way I had to follow norms that never applied to Jeff. I rolled every annoyance and every grievance she'd ever inspired into a sphere of fury and let her have it like a fastball: "You ruin everything. You send everyone away."

She recoiled, and, shocked at what I'd said, I braced for a retort, maybe even a slap, but she just said, "Don't stay up too late," as she went back into the house.

"I'm not staying here," I shouted, then lobbed a last insult, "First Dad. Now Jeff." I bounded down the steps, ran to Grandpa's house, and stopped, bent over on the sidewalk.

"Little late for a run, isn't it?" Pete said from the darkened porch.

I climbed the steps, plopped beside him in the other wicker chair, and said, "I don't want to talk."

"Fine by me. I'm going to bed," Pete said, getting up. He caught the screen door before it banged shut and closed the front door behind him.

I got up and paced like Jeff, turning after bumping up against my own invisible walls. I didn't want Jeff to be trapped, but if Angie was pregnant, didn't that change things? Wasn't a guy supposed to stick around to at least be a father to his kid? I assumed that's what Mom would think. How could she let him go? I moved to the glider, sat slumped for a while, then lay down.

Roused hours later by an early bird, I shifted under an afghan and pulled it to my chin, wondering who'd covered me and when. The rocker creaked and I looked over, expecting to see Grandpa waiting for the paper and enough daylight to read by, but it was Mom.

"You're right," she said. "I sent your dad away. He didn't want to go. He said he was sorry, that he would break off the affair, but I refused to listen." She paused. "Then, later, when he asked to come home, I put him off." She stood up, walked to the top of the steps, then looked back at me. "Don't be like me, Finn," she said.

When I woke again, it was to sunshine and the sound of traffic. I turned down Grandpa's offer of eggs and bacon and went home. When I opened our kitchen door, Mom greeted me as though I'd just come down from my room.

"Pancakes?" she asked.

"Mom, I'm sor—" I began, but she shushed me with a wave of the spatula.

"I know," she said.

I spread the butter, poured the syrup. Of course, Mom was right about Jeff and me, the difference between us. I was bound by Danton's borders. Jeff wanted what lay beyond. I was rooted. He was ready to fly. At least he'd left me his stride, his swagger, but I lost that too when I had to face Francine.

She came to our house after breakfast straight from Angie's, spewed the news before I could open the screen door, and ranted about how selfish and irresponsible Jeff was. When she stopped for a moment and noticed my expression, she stepped back and voiced her surprise. "You already know."

Taking a deep breath, recalling Jeff's agony, I said, "He was here last night."

"He told you he was leaving?" she asked. I nodded. "And you didn't try to stop him? How could you do that to Angie?" Francine asked, pounding each question into my still-waking-up brain.

"I tried," I said, but even to me, it didn't sound like I'd made much of an effort.

If only Francine had gotten mad, she might have worked through her anger and forgiven me, maybe even apologized for blaming me, but she didn't get mad. Instead, she gave me a withering look that reassessed and found me lacking. She held up her hand, silencing me, keeping me from following her to her car, and left.

I flashed back to the disastrous volleyball game in eighth grade. Again, she was rejecting me, but this time I didn't deserve it and I didn't stay away. I couldn't get past the girlfriends who surrounded her at school, but for five days straight, I called and went to her house. When her mother answered the phone or came to the door to tell me Francine was out or busy or didn't want to see me, she was never brusque. Instead, she sounded like she was on my side. "I'm sorry, Finn. I've tried to talk to her," she said, "but Francine's a stubborn girl when she thinks she's right."

Finally, after school on Thursday, Francine appeared behind her locked screen door. Her voice was flat, unfeeling when she said she couldn't go to the prom with me Friday night because she wouldn't have a good time with Angie so miserable.

"But—"

She cut me off as she turned away, stepped behind the front door, and shut it solidly. Confounded, I stared at the door. I didn't understand. I thought I meant more to Francine than Angie did. Francine meant more to me than Jeff. I knocked and rang the doorbell. I called her name, but she didn't reappear. I'd never hurt so badly, not even when I was cut off from Billie. Billie had never rejected me.

Mom said she thought Francine would come around in time. She said I should go to the prom anyway. I was a senior. I was entitled. But after our two years together, there was no way I'd present myself without Francine. She was the half that made me whole. When the delivery boy brought the corsage I'd ordered for her, he may as well have stuck me with the pin that came with it.

At graduation a week after the prom, speakers talked about the exciting opportunities ahead of us. If I were still with Francine, I might have envisioned them, but without her, the screen in my head had gone dark. I began to wonder whether it was more than Jeff and Angie, whether Angie's situation was an excuse. Maybe there was something about me Francine didn't like. I was being irrational, but I couldn't help it. I questioned everything.

I reread Francine's letters and wrote her one more. In it, I apologized and offered to try to track Jeff down and bring him back to town though I had no idea how I would do that. I begged her not to break up with me. I told her I loved her and hoped the words would be more persuasive in writing. When I was done, I was drained. The letter weighed ounces, but strained me like a twenty-pound plate from Gus's Gym.

"I need to see Francine," I said when her mother answered the door, but she told me Francine was gone. She'd left that morning for the camp to fill in for a counselor who'd quit at the last minute.

"Is that a letter for Francine? Shall I send it for you?" her mother asked, twisting a dish towel in her hands.

"No, I'll do it," I said. Had I snatched that towel from her and flailed it, slapping the siding, whipping the porch post, it might have relieved some of my frustration.

By the time I got home, I was fuming. I took Francine's letters from the top drawer of my chest, threw them on the bed, grabbed a handful, and hurled them against the wall. I couldn't trash the letters or burn them. I wanted to believe Francine's words hadn't lost their meaning. I had to do something with them, though, and remembered the letter Francine had mailed in two pieces to Angie and me. I grabbed one of the envelopes, ripped it in half, and threw it back on the bed. It felt so good I picked up another letter, then another, and tore them too. I had a slew of letters because Francine had written me almost every day she was away, and I tore at least half of them before I ran out of steam. I pushed the letters aside, lay down on my bed, and stared at the ceiling. Once I'd calmed down, I gathered the letters, buried them in the bottom dresser drawer under my out-of-season clothes, and shoved the drawer shut with my foot. If not out of mind, at least they'd be out of sight.

I was surprised Mom left me alone as long as she did to stay up past midnight with Carson or Letterman and sleep in until noon. She didn't suggest I go fishing and she ran errands herself. I had no desire to drive anywhere. She took over feeding and exercising Patch, reassuring him with a pat after their walks around the block, "I know, boy. You miss Finn, but I'm here. I haven't forgotten you." The dig didn't shame me. I couldn't get any lower.

After two weeks, Mom had had it. She came into my room one morning, threw back my comforter, and yanked open my curtains, blinding me with the sun. "Enough of this," she said. "I know you feel bad, but you won't feel any better just lying around." Although that was how she'd said I could spend my last summer before college, she'd suddenly changed her mind. "Get up. Get out. Go find yourself a job," she said.

When I went to the paper, Dad's old boss Walt told me that without sales experience, there wasn't anything I could do in advertising, but I could try circulation where they always needed help. As I approached the department, I learned why.

"I quit," shouted a guy who'd been a year ahead of me in school. He brushed past me as he left, knocking me back a step. I peered into the office he'd stormed out of.

"What can I do for you?" asked the man behind the Rob Walker nameplate. When I told him I wanted a job, he snorted. "Well, maybe you heard. I have an opening. Question is, do you have a thick skin?"

"Pardon?" I asked.

"When customers call circulation," he said, "they're mad because their papers weren't delivered or got soaked by the rain. We let them complain 'til they cool down. Then, we tell them we're sorry and ask what we can do to make it up to them. Some people will take a credit. Others want a copy of the paper, and, even if it's late in the day, we'll deliver a copy."

People want to be heard. I try to listen. Recalling Dad's words and manner, I told Rob I could do it.

On my first day, Rob treated me to lunch at Jake's. That

morning and then again before lunch, I'd walked through the ad department where Walt read my mind.

"If you're looking for Billie," he said on my second trip, "she's in the North Danton office now."

Francine. Billie. Billie. Francine. But Francine didn't want to be with me anymore.

One afternoon after delivering a customer's missed paper, I passed the small satellite office where Walt had said Billie was working. At a ramshackle general store down the road, I stopped to get a cold drink and build up my nerve to drive back, go into the office, and face Billie after almost five years. The store wasn't much bigger than Sam's barbershop, and it was crammed like the paper's ad department but with worn shelves of cartons and cans that stretched to the ceiling. A rickety ladder and an old wooden grabber kept items within reach. The only thing that could be described as new was the refrigerated soft drink case. I opened the door and helped myself to a Coke, then wondered who or how I should pay.

"Hello?" I called toward the back of the store.

"Hold on." The two words told me I'd roused an old woman. When she emerged, she shuffled toward me in fuzzy slippers on the creaky wood floor. She wore baggy white cotton pants and a pale blue denim work shirt with the sleeves rolled up to her elbows. Her hair was a gray mound of cotton candy with loose strands that waved like whisps of spun sugar. She stopped, stared, and asked, "Are you the ghost of Aidan Maguire?"

What did she say? I shivered as she resumed her shamble. "Did you know my dad?" I asked when she reached me.

"Who didn't?" she said, looking up, inspecting me. "But you're taller."

I spoke without thinking: "He told me I would be—back when I was worried about not growing."

"Let me guess. He never lived to see," she said.

"No," I said, mystified. "How did you know my da—"

She gestured for me to sit down on a bench. "When he came here the first time, I told him I couldn't afford to buy any advertising. He said it didn't matter. After that, he stopped in once a month or so just to talk. Tell me, did he get back together with your mother?"

Who was this woman? Dad's shrink? "He wanted to," I said.

"Well, that's something," she said.

When another customer came in and the woman disappeared into what must have been the stockroom, I left money for my drink on the counter and ducked out. It was rude to leave so abruptly, but she'd given me the willies. I dismissed the idea of going to Billie's office and headed straight for home.

"The crone," Tim said when I described the storekeeper to him.

Surprised, I asked, "You know her?"

"I know the archetype," he said. "A wise old woman, maybe a little scary. She can block your path—"

"She knew my dad," I interjected.

"Or show you the way," he said.

Time passed more quickly once I was working, and before I knew it, it was time for my farewell picnic in Grandpa's backyard.

"Guess this is it, college boy," Pete said with just a touch of his usual sarcasm.

Aunt Rina looked like she was going to cry. "I'll miss you, Finn," she said.

"*We'll* miss you," Rachele said, glaring at her sister.

"For goodness' sake. It's not like he's going to the moon," Mom said, irritability masking what must have been her own mixed feelings.

Grandpa poured me some of his grappa, clinked his glass

against mine, and said, "Your dad would be proud."

Francine was like Dad, a presence because of her absence. If they missed her like I did, though, no one slipped up and said so, thank God. It was hard enough to think about her, let alone speak about her, in the past tense.

Just when I was sure there was nothing that could cheer me, Pete surprised me with a present parked in front of the house—Dad's old car looking like new.

Mom huffed at him. "I don't know why you bothered. He doesn't need a car at school."

"I thought you sold it," I said to Pete, walking around the car, examining it the way Dad had inspected Billie's first Camaro years before.

"Bought it back," Pete said, brimming with satisfaction. Damn. I never expected such a gift from him. Maybe he deserved Billie.

The upperclassman who helped unload my packed boxes from Mom's car said I was lucky it wasn't raining. It usually did on move-in days. Rain would have suited my mood. Later, my roommate listened politely to Mom's chatter about all the changes since her days on campus, like coed dorms and no curfew. His parents were already gone, so I told Mom I'd unpack later, and before she could embarrass me further, I hustled her out of the dorm to the honors college orientation.

Toward the end of the presentation, the university president introduced the college's founder—and funder. Square jaw, short hair, but without the nerdy glasses, he was John Wasser, the guy Mom knew in college, the one pictured in her photo album, the driver who'd come to my aid when I'd run out of gas on my ill-fated trip to Francine's summer camp.

I wondered if he'd remember me and whether he still had a thing for Mom, and when she said, "Let's go introduce ourselves," I found out.

"Monica," he said, lighting up as she approached and wrapping her in a bear hug. "So, this is your son?" he asked, shaking my hand as though it was our first meeting, but winking at me when Mom looked away to let me know he remembered rescuing me on the road. Scanning the crowd behind us, he asked, "Where's Aidan?" and when Mom told him Dad had died, he looked stricken. "No, not Aidan," he said, as though he didn't believe her, as though waiting for one of us to say, "Hey, sorry. Just kidding. He's all right." When John asked Mom to wait for him so they could catch up, she said I could go back to my room.

Earlier, I'd been eager for her to leave, but suddenly as I kissed her goodbye, I was sad and empty. Oh, I'd already dealt with enough change in my life to know I'd eventually fill my days with classes, my head with new ideas until I had a full tank again. The sidewalks and beaten-path shortcuts radiating from my dorm would become as familiar as the walkway from our house to Grandpa's. It would just take time.

But later, when my roommate and a couple of guys from down the hall asked if I wanted to go out and explore the campus, check out the girls, I stayed in my room with memories of Francine. God, I'll never get over her.

And then, the next morning, in my first class, I did.

CHAPTER THIRTY-TWO

When the professor called my name, I raised my hand to acknowledge my presence and caught a self-satisfied expression that tugged his smile off center. "Cassandra or is it Cassiopeia?" he asked, his voice caressing each syllable of the exotic names.

The reply came firm and flat behind me. "Just Cassie."

Chastened, he looked down, cleared his throat, and repeated, "Just Cassie then."

I turned and the vision took my breath away. So that's what they mean by a heart-shaped face and cupid's bow lips. The girl in the center of the room was gorgeous. Her straight blond hair fell over her shoulders from a center part, and I pictured her turning her head, tossing that hair. Her cool blue-gray gaze fixed me with a what-are-you-looking-at stare, so I turned around, but the image stuck. The lecture? I never tuned in, and after class, I waited for her outside the classroom door.

"Everyone knows the Big Dipper but not Cassiopeia," I said, stupidly parroting Dad. At least I didn't go on about how the constellation spends part of the year upside down as punishment for its namesake's vanity. I braced myself for a wisecrack that didn't come.

"It's just Cassie," she said again, more irked than angry, and then, "Would you like me to call you Phineas?"

My initial reaction was a cheesy line: You can call me anything you want. Instead, I raised my hands and said, "Sorry." And then she did it. She shook her head, tossed her hair, snagged, and reeled me in. I was hooked.

"He's so full of himself," she said of our composition professor. "They all are. Founts of knowledge. They'll dole out bits and pieces of their wisdom, always checking to make sure we're hanging on every word. Well, I won't do it." She stamped her foot, and her ire vaporized as quickly as it had flared. She turned to me as we left the building. "So, Finn Maguire, what's your story?"

Surprised—and pleased—that she'd caught my full name, I soon learned Cassie noticed, and had an opinion on, everything. Sororities were silly, Prince should be crowned the greatest recording artist of all time, and the Capital Restaurant's dinner plate–sized cinnamon roll was preferrable to pizza for a late-night snack. She seldom revised her initial assessment of anything. It was the one way in which she reminded me of Mom.

"All over." That's where Cassie was from. "Military brat. Born in Germany. Raised in Japan. High school in Iowa City and Brooklyn. How's that for contrast?" she said, laughing, leaning into me. Her touch was electric. I'd follow her anywhere. That first day it was to the union for coffee and, later, to the dining hall for lunch. My description of Danton confounded her.

"You lived there your whole life?" she asked. "Same town? Same house? Didn't your parents ever want to live anywhere else?"

"Not that I'm aware," I said.

Confusion creased her forehead. "Why not?"

I shrugged. "Well, my parents had their jobs, and my mom's family was there."

Cassie tried another tack. "Where did you travel?"

"We didn't. I'm not sure why," I said, never having considered the question. "You'd think we would have. Mom's a teacher and my dad was a history buff. I guess they must have been content."

If I'd missed out on something, so had Cassie. "I don't know what it's like to have a hometown," she mused.

After lunch, she directed me to her suite of rooms on the third floor of a large Victorian six blocks from campus. She'd enrolled too late to secure a dorm room, but it was just as well, she said. An only child like me, she'd never shared living space with another girl and didn't think she could or would want to.

We climbed two flights of weathered outdoor stairs like the ones that led to Billie's apartment, but the interior of Cassie's place couldn't have been more different. Sophisticated vintage ad and travel posters toned down the canary-colored main room, and fabrics printed with Oriental designs draped the tall windows and bedroom doorway.

"What a great place," I said, doing a three-sixty.

"Glad you like it," Cassie said, as cheery as the room. "Come back again anytime."

"Really?" I asked.

"If you want to," she said with a shrug.

Who wouldn't want to? For the first time since Francine had turned away from me, I stopped dragging my ass around feeling sorry for myself. Crowding out any other thought, Cassie was in my head the rest of the day, in my afternoon math class and biology lab, in the dining hall at dinner. In my room at night, I was sure I wouldn't be able to sleep unless I took a cold shower, but what the hell. I turned on the hot water and took care of myself in the stall.

The next day I had two classes with four hours between them. I suppose I could have gone to the library or back to my dorm, but I headed straight for Cassie's place. When she opened the door, I was stoked and she could tell.

"Well, hello there," she said in a sexy growl.

I tried to control my shaking. "You said I could come back."

"I did," she said, stepping aside so I could enter. "Are you done for the day?"

A head rush overwhelmed me. "Yes. No."

She closed the door, backed me against it, ratcheting me up even more, and in that same guttural growl asked, "How much time do we have then?" She didn't wait for my answer. She pressed her body against mine and kissed me. Weirdly, I thought about Pete and an alignment because we were a perfect fit. I didn't have to bend my knees, and Cassie didn't have to raise up on her toes like Francine. I groaned when she ground herself against me. Immediately, we fumbled at undressing each other, then switched to freeing ourselves from our own clothes and underwear. Kissing again, we staggered to her bedroom as though we were bound together for a three-legged race.

She pushed me down on the bed and straddled me. I reached for her hips, and then slid my hands up her slim torso to breasts that made her just the right degree of top-heavy. What luck. I'd only known Cassie for twenty-four hours and already I'd gotten further with her than I had in two years with Francine.

"Wait," I said, panicked. "I don't have a condom."

She dismissed my concern. "You won't need one."

For a second, I froze remembering Jeff and Angie, but whether I figured I could trust Cassie or was too far gone, I plunged ahead, trembling. Oh, God, this is it. I'd heard about how a guy should try to hold back, but I couldn't do it that first time. I was surprised that I wasn't embarrassed, and I hoped my enthusiasm would make up for my lack of experience.

"Can we do that again?" I asked once my breathing returned to normal. Cassie laughed, but not like she was making fun.

"Whenever you're ready," she said, waggling her eyebrows. She rolled to one side, picked up a Nikon camera from the nightstand, and peered at me through the viewfinder.

"What are you doing?" I asked, clutching the covers to my chin.

Click. "Relax," she said. "I'm only shooting your face. Your chiseled features."

"You're the one who should be photographed," I breathed. "You're gorgeous."

"Been there. Done that," she said with a dismissive wave. "I'd rather be behind the camera. The photographer has the control."

"Sometimes it's chance. Being in the right place at the right time," I said, thinking about the *Monitor*'s photographers at a game or a fire.

"Not if you position yourself to wait for the image with impact," Cassie said. She had me there.

"Are you going to join the newspaper staff?" I asked.

"I don't think so," Cassie said. She already had a freelance assignment from a magazine in New York City. If she got a good picture for a planned photo essay on college students, the editor had said he might use it and give her a shot at a summer internship.

"You're not thinking of me for the photo?" I asked.

"Maybe," she said, again in that teasing tone.

I took the camera from her and put it back on the bedside table. When I straddled her, she raised her eyebrows, I waggled mine, and we laughed together. Our second time was less a tutorial and more mutual discovery. I lasted longer and afterward she seemed satisfied too. I pictured us on the cover of one of Billie's romance novels and laughed out loud.

"What?" Cassie asked.

"Nothing. I love this," I said.

When she woke me hours later, she told me I'd have to leave. Her landlady was adamant about no overnight visitors.

"Does she think you wouldn't do it in the daytime?" I whispered. She giggled and pulled me close for one more encounter. This time I was confident, cocky even, but Cassie met my every thrust with a squeeze. She giggled when I groaned, "I hope your landlady's hard of hearing."

Walking back to campus, I was ravenous, but I didn't want to eat in a loud and crowded dining hall. I veered toward Hoagie Haven, ordered a meatball sub, and ate it in a window booth communing with my reflection in the empty hole-in-the-wall sandwich shop. Sex with Francine would have been a culmination, but with Cassie it was a kickoff. Anticipating the excitement of a rematch, I grinned at the idea of a bout with two winners, no losers, but then checked my enthusiasm. Will she want to see me again? What if it was a one-time thing? I dared to reassure myself by channeling Jeff: "Are you kidding, man? Trust me. She wants you. Go for it."

The next morning dawned bright and clear as though revealing to the world what I'd done, and I sauntered to our second comp class shouting in my head to everyone I passed: Yeah, I did it. And it was fan-FUCKING-tastic! Boy was I lit. I couldn't concentrate on anything but Cassie sitting behind me, and when class ended, we ran to her MG two-seater and raced to her apartment. We got right into bed and were rolling around when she stopped.

"What?" I asked, raising my head from the pillow, expecting her to say something, but she slid under the covers. When her mouth reached its target, I gasped, reached down, and tangled my fingers in the silky strands of her hair, then groaned when she finished me off.

"I can't believe you did that," I said between ragged breaths when she emerged unembarrassed from under the covers. I pulled her close, and when I recovered, I repaid her in kind.

Later, as we dressed to return to campus, I hopped on one foot, halfway into my jeans and grinned. "That does it. I'm changing my major to sex." Cassie shrieked with laughter.

The next sex-every-day two weeks were the best of my life, followed by one of the worst days ever.

When Professor Hadley, the composition professor, handed back our first papers, I grabbed mine by the top right corner to hide the big fat F. My mouth went dry and my face burned, probably turning as red as the grade on my paper. How humiliating. I'd never failed anything in high school. English majors like me were expected to ace this writing course required of all freshmen and earn exemption from Comp II in our second semester. I thought Professor Hadley liked me. How could he do this? The throbbing in my head drummed out his entire lecture.

"What'd you get?" Cassie asked after class. I hesitated, but showed her my paper.

"Yikes. What happened?" she asked.

I shrugged, still shaken. Other than the grade, there wasn't a mark on the paper. I went straight to Hadley's office to ask him about it. "Professor?" When he invited me in, I was too agitated to sit. "I don't understand," I said, handing him my paper.

He looked at it, harrumphed, and handed it back. "This is a personal essay. The class is expository writing. You didn't fulfill the assignment," he said, eyeing me as he leaned back in his chair. Dejected, I sank into the chair across from his desk and, thankfully, moved him to pity. "Tell you what," he said as he studied me. "Rewrite and resubmit it. I can't promise I'll change the grade, but I'd like to see what you can do."

When I returned to Cassie who was waiting in the hallway,

I couldn't resist a rueful observation. "Maybe I should change my major."

"To sex?" she whispered, her eyes lighting up.

"No," I said with a wry snort. "To anything but English."

"Oh, come on," she said, laughing lightly. "What did he say?" When I told her, she said, "See? It's not so bad. You can redo it."

"But I'll still have an F," I said, annoyed at the whine in my voice.

"Didn't he say he'd change the grade?" Cassie asked.

Didn't she hear what I'd said? "No. He said he couldn't promise."

"Well, then, look on the bright side," she said. "He didn't say he wouldn't."

"That's not what I heard," I said, wishing I could share her optimism.

"Finn," she said, as she playfully punched my arm. "You're overreacting. Get off the ledge."

I straightened up after that. I didn't want to flunk out and have to admit it was because I was a sex addict. I still saw Cassie in classes or between them, at the library or in the union. If we went to her place during the week, it was for a quickie. We saved our marathon lovemaking for weekends.

Before our long-weekend break in mid-October, though, we made an exception and spent all day Thursday together. I was going home, but Cassie was going to New York to meet with the editor of that magazine about the internship. "Brilliant," he'd said of the photo she submitted for his spread. There was a young woman student in the picture, but she was in the background gazing with longing at the focus of the photo, a Patrick Swayze look-alike "townie" wiping down a cafeteria table.

I couldn't imagine a whole summer with Cassie away in New York. It would be hard enough to get through the next four days without her.

CHAPTER THIRTY-THREE

At home on Saturday afternoon, I lazed on the porch swing trying to concentrate on a Classical Lit assignment. I'd been distracted since reading the obituary page ad for my eighteenth birthday: "Why should I be out of mind because I am out of sight? I am but waiting for you, for an interval, somewhere very near, just around the corner. One brief moment and all will be as it was before. How we shall laugh at the trouble of parting, when we meet again."

While I'd accepted Francine's conviction that Mom was responsible for the ads about Dad, if Billie had placed this one, it would have been the best yet. She wasn't just referencing Dad, and she wasn't just thinking about me. She was waiting for me.

When a car pulled into the driveway and up alongside the house, I dismissed the driver as a visitor for Mom, but moments later, Mom stepped onto the porch, held the screen door open, and said, "Look who's here, Finn." I stopped the sluggish motion of the swing and stared. "I'll bring you two some iced tea," Mom said, disappearing back inside the house.

From beneath their hooded lids, Francine's eyes sought mine and her shy smile stirred me the way it always had. My heart opened wide like the drawer in which I'd stashed her letters months before, and I stood up and moved over so she could sit beside me on the swing. By the time Mom brought the pitcher and two glasses, we were done with the how've-you-been, how's-school-going small talk.

"I've heard different stories but nothing from Angie," Francine said, looking away from me. "I don't know whether she had an abortion or whether she was never pregnant. She could have lied to try to make Jeff stay. Remember how mad she got whenever he talked about leaving town?" She turned toward me, but kept her eyes on her clasped hands in her lap. "I'm sorry I blamed you, Finn. It's good Jeff got away."

It was the apology I'd longed for, but it fell flat.

"Why didn't you listen to me, Francine? Why didn't you believe me? I thought you loved me." I had to say it, but I didn't mean to make her cry. When her tears welled, I put my arm around her without considering what it might communicate. "I'm sorry. Don't feel bad. I'm over it," I said, pulling her into a one-armed hug. She wiped her eyes with her hands and leaned into me.

We rocked for a while without speaking until she whispered, "Do you think we can get back together?" My heart skipped.

"Tonight?" I asked instinctively, caught up in the possibility of being with her again. Nuzzling my neck, Francine assented, but my thrill was short-lived. If only she'd come around before I'd left for school, I would have forgiven and forgotten everything. We'd have been back together again. Forever.

But now? How could I give up the good thing I had going with Cassie? Could I be with Cassie at school and Francine when I came home? "Go for it," Jeff would say. Of course he would. Stringing along two wouldn't bother him, but I doubted

I could pull it off, and if Cassie and Francine found out about each other, I could end up with neither. I took a deep breath. "I have a girlfriend," I said. "At school." Afraid Francine would start crying again or be mad that I'd led her on for even a moment, I braced for a sad or angry reaction, but she was calm, composed.

"Oh, I didn't think of that," she said, pulling away from me. "Tell your mom goodbye for me, okay?" I followed her to the edge of the porch and watched her run down the steps and around the house to her car. There wasn't any other way for things to go, but I was surprised that turning her down hurt just as much as having been rejected.

While I was standing there, looking out toward the route Francine had taken, Mom appeared in the doorway. "What happened?" she asked. "I thought you two would patch things up."

My reply was wistful. "She wanted to."

"And you?" Mom asked.

Turning to face her, I said, "I met someone else."

"At school," she said. It was a statement, not a question. She didn't act surprised. Perhaps she'd expected it. Mom stepped to the swing and when I settled beside her, I rocked us slowly rolling the ball of my foot on the floorboards. She didn't say anything right away. Maybe she had to get used to the idea of me with another girl, a different girl. Finally, she asked, "What's she like?"

"Amazing," I breathed. Mom laughed, but it was a lighthearted sound, like she was happy for me. "She's smart," I added, because that would impress Mom, "and gorgeous," because that couldn't be denied.

"Well, you'll have to bring her home sometime," Mom said.

Would Cassie want to come?

After a few minutes, Mom left me on the porch, but not alone. Cassie. Francine. Billie. Three women, all wanting or waiting for me.

Tuesday morning at school, I feigned surprise when I saw Cassie. "You came back," I said.

"Why wouldn't I?" she asked, looking puzzled.

"Oh, I don't know," I said, rolling my eyes. "Look around. We're in the middle of nowhere here. You've lived on three continents and you were in New York City for four days. How did it go, by the way?"

She grabbed my arm. "It's mine if I want it."

"The internship? Wow. Congratulations," I said, wondering whether I sounded happy enough when I didn't want her to go.

"You'll have to come too," she said, startling me with an excitement that grew as she continued. "New York. For the summer. It'll be awesome. You'll love the city."

I hadn't considered anything other than returning to the *Monitor*. "What would I do?" I asked her.

"Get a job. Live. Write," she said as though anything was possible. "Whatever you do, you'll make more money than you will at home."

And we'd be together.

When I invited her home for Thanksgiving, Cassie said she'd love to come.

"I hope you won't be disappointed. It's a sad old town," I said, sorry to dis Danton, but concerned about how it might reflect on me.

"What do you think I am? A snob?" Cassie asked.

"No," I said. "I want to prepare you. That's all."

When she drove us into town the day before the holiday, she said, "I don't understand what you're ashamed of. These old houses are grand." I'd purposely chosen a round-about route to avoid what I remembered as the dilapidated downtown, but Cassie's reaction made me reconsider my assessment. Had there been a rebirth? For someone who wanted to be a reporter, I'd been oblivious.

I'd also tried to prepare Cassie for my in-control, no-non-sense mother, but Mom blathered on about holiday grade school lunches when she'd traded her thin slice of turkey to Suzy Conley for her scoop of stuffing, and then all the different kinds of stuffing she'd made over the years. Like cornbread. And sausage. Oh, and oyster, which didn't taste any different than plain old bread, so why bother. Whew. Mom sure sounded nervous.

Our sleeping arrangements made her anxious too. She'd told me in advance that she would make up the guest room for Cassie, and when we arrived with my duffel and Cassie's suitcase, she made a point of telling me to take Cassie's bag up there. Hours later when we went upstairs, she steered Cassie to the guest room and said, "I hope you'll be comfortable here."

During the night, though, Cassie came into my room and climbed on top of me in her night shirt and nothing else. She thrilled me when she whispered, "Let's do it here, Finn, where you grew up. Be my little boy." Half asleep, I swear I heard, "Billie's little boy," and I went crazy making love to Cassie, then Billie, and even Francine.

"You'll have to come again," Mom told Cassie the next day as she piled containers of leftovers in her arms. She kissed me goodbye and I relaxed, relieved that she hadn't heard us in my room. I was halfway to Cassie's car when Mom called me back, gave me a penetrating look, and said, "I hope you know what you're doing, Finn Maguire." Why couldn't she cut me some slack like she'd always done with Jeff? So, I hadn't stopped to consider what I was doing with Cassie. So, I'd rushed headlong into a relationship with her. So what? It was my life.

Every weekend all winter, Cassie's room was a refuge, a cozy destination worth the bitter walk from campus. The sex was outstanding, but we talked too. I made a mistake, though, when I told her about Billie.

"Finn," Cassie said, lying next to me one afternoon, her head propped on her hand. "How many women did you have before me?"

"What?" I was floored. Couldn't she tell she'd been the first? Why did I have to admit it? I batted my eyelashes like she did whenever I posed a question she didn't want to answer and gave her standard reply, "Why do you ask?"

"Okay, then," she said, laughing. "Who have you wanted to be with? That could be just as interesting." When we'd first gotten together, she'd warned me, "Be honest with me. Don't ever lie or keep something from me. I need to know where I stand."

I didn't want to talk about Francine, though. Cassie had told me about her crushes on older guys on the military bases where she'd lived and asked if it made me jealous to hear about them. No, I'd said. That was before I met you.

I stared at the ceiling. "I guess I've always had a thing for Billie."

Instantly, Cassie was intrigued. "Billie? Who's Billie?"

I'd already told her about my parents' separation. "She was the woman Dad left my mom for."

"Wait," she said. "How old were you?"

"Almost twelve when I met her."

"And how old was Billie?"

I tried to sound nonchalant. "Twenty-five."

"Twice your age!" Cassie sounded shocked.

"But she looked—and acted—like a high school girl," I said in my defense.

Cassie's belly laugh said she didn't buy it.

"What?" I protested. "She did. And she was always nice to me."

I told Cassie about the macaroni and cheese, eating Chinese food with chopsticks, and the Millennium Falcon. Once I got started, I couldn't stop. I blabbed about how Billie taught me to dance and how Dad made me mad when he cut in, how he made me mad too when he horned in on her during the newspaper tour. I described how Billie and I drank warm milk in the middle of the last night we were together, but stopped short of telling Cassie I'd seen Billie naked. I told her how Mom had punished me for going to the apartment with Jeff on Halloween. Only after I stopped talking did I consider I sounded obsessed.

Cassie became a sleuth trying to crack a case. "Why do you think she stayed after your dad died?"

"I don't know," I said. It would be too weird to admit I'd imagined Billie staying for me.

"Don't you want to know?" Cassie pressed me. "Don't you want to see her again?"

I tried to put her off. "Why would I?"

"Because she was a big part of your life and you were suddenly cut off from her." She made it sound so logical.

"I tried once. It didn't work out," I said.

"But that was when you were a kid," she said. "Your mom can't stop you now. Sounds like you've got unfinished business with Billie."

"Let's change the subject," I said, sorry I'd ventured to talk about Billie at all.

"Too late now," Cassie said. "You should go see her. No time like the present. Isn't that what your dad used to say?"

Good God, she remembers everything. "Enough," I said. It wasn't the last word, though.

"Tell me," Cassie said, "on those nights you slept over, did you ever imagine yourself with Billie?"

My murmured denial was unconvincing.

"Omigod," she said. "You did."

"Jeez. No. What do you think I am?"

"You did, you did," she said, shaking me by my shoulders. I had to roll over on top of her and smother her with kisses to get her to stop.

Professor Hadley hadn't changed the grade on my rewrite first semester, but he gave me an A on my final paper, said it was some of the best writing he'd seen from a freshman, and exempted me from Comp II. Cassie said we had to celebrate, so on a Saturday during the spring thaw, she drove me to New York so I could see for myself how alive and electric the city was.

What a shock. Spray-painted words and symbols defiled alley walls and subway tunnels. Storefronts hawked exotic nude girls—live on stage—and peep shows for twenty-five cents. Trash and discarded drug needles sullied the sidewalks. It creeped me out, made my skin crawl.

"You think it's safe to live here?" I asked her.

Cassie laughed. "I wouldn't live in Times Square," she said.

"To walk around then?"

"If you keep moving and don't look at people, no one bothers you," she said.

"That seems rude," I said. "In Danton, people at least nod to each other, even to The Pointer."

She looked at me sideways and laughed again. When a youngish woman looking old in too much makeup called, "How about a date?" Cassie reminded me not to make eye contact.

"I wasn't looking at her eyes," I said turning away from the bare breasts the woman displayed without embarrassment beneath a sheer black top. She'd assaulted, not aroused, me, but no one else seemed to notice, not even the cops in the cruiser the woman leaned against.

"Yes, it's gritty," Cassie said, her arms outstretched as though she was embracing the city. "But it's a photographer's paradise. It's real life."

Somebody else's life, maybe. Not mine.

It might have been that Cassie could put the city into perspective because she'd already seen so much of the world and the beauty in it. I didn't have that frame of reference. In Central Park, I hoped to channel Olmstead because of his connection to Danton, but the patchy fields were more dirt than grass, and there, too, graffiti defaced rocks and bridges and monuments.

If New York was alive like Cassie claimed, it was a beast that would devour me. It wasn't just a too-big pond. It was an ocean, and I would drown in it.

CHAPTER THIRTY-FOUR

The whole family wanted to see Cassie again, so I invited her home for spring break and gave her the grand tour on Saturday afternoon, reliving trips I'd made with Dad or Grandpa as we stopped in to say hello at the bakery, the barbershop, Simpson's Ford, and the newspaper.

"Everybody knows you," Cassie said, sounding surprised. "I thought you were exaggerating."

"I wouldn't do that. I wouldn't have to," I told her. "Danton is a small town. Everybody really does know everybody else."

After a moment's silence, Cassie said, "You'll never leave."

I chafed that, like Mom, Cassie thought she knew me and had me pegged. "What? No. Of course I'll go. There's nothing for me here," I said.

Our last stop was the church for the blessing of holiday food. From home we'd brought a loaf of pane di Pasqua, the sweet anise-flavored Easter bread. Cassie had taken close-ups of the braided ring and a photo of Mom holding it. "It looks like a nest," Cassie said, fascinated by the colored eggs tucked into the twists of dough and baked whole along with the bread.

"Now I didn't make this," Mom clarified. "I just didn't have the energy this year. It's from the bakery." But Cassie's attention delighted her.

At the altar in church, old women parishioners with their own foods peppered us with questions and comments.

"Is this your new girlfriend, Finn?"

"How pretty she is."

"Look at those eyes, her hair."

"Where are you from, dear?"

"How do you like our town? Our church? Our boy here?"

Cassie charmed them by asking to take their photos, and although they protested, they posed for her.

Driving back to the house, she startled me again. "Show me where Billie lives."

"What?" Had she read my mind? We were a block away from Billie's apartment, and, as usual when I was in the area, I'd been thinking about her.

"Show me where Billie lives," Cassie repeated.

I tried to dissuade her. "We've got to get back home."

"How long could it take?" she said. "Danton's a small town."

"Another time. I promise," I said, hoping she'd let it go.

"Why are you doing that?" she asked.

I was stumped. "Doing what?"

"Keeping Billie to yourself," Cassie said.

"I'm keeping her in the past. Where she belongs," I said.

"Are you?" Cassie challenged me, as she drove up to the house.

Everybody but Pete came to Easter dinner, and after we ate, Cassie wowed Mom and Grandpa and my aunts with her photos and news of her internship.

"I keep telling Finn he should come, too," she said. "New York is a mecca for writers." The conversation stopped abruptly, then resumed.

"What would he do there?" Mom asked.

"There are all kinds of jobs," Cassie said.

"And where would he live?"

"People sublet their apartments all the time," Cassie said, although she'd told me I could stay with her.

"I thought you were going to work at the *Monitor* again," Mom said.

"I haven't decided," I said.

As Cassie drove us out of town back to campus that evening, I gave in. "Billie's place is up ahead, to the left," I said. "If she's home, there'll be a red Camaro out front."

Seconds later, Cassie said, "Looks like she has company." She was watching me when I glanced toward the house, so I fought to keep my expression neutral. It was Pete's truck parked in the driveway.

"What did they mean at the church when they asked if I was your new girlfriend?" Cassie asked. "You've never mentioned anyone but Billie, and I doubt they meant her."

I still didn't want to talk about Francine. "I think they just meant girlfriend," I said. Cassie sure was mulling things over, but she let me read or pretend to while I stewed about Pete and Billie until we arrived at Cassie's apartment and I closed my book.

"Is your mother all right?" she asked. "She looked tired and your aunts did all the cooking and clean-up."

Embarrassed to admit I hadn't noticed, I asked to call home on Cassie's phone. I braced myself for bad news, but Mom batted away my concern.

"Oh, Finn, we caught it early. The doctor thinks he can do a lumpectomy." She didn't want me to worry. That's why she didn't tell me she had cancer.

The way her mother tried to protect Pete in Vietnam, I

hoped Mom wasn't offering herself up in a misguided attempt to save me from something. I asked if her doctor was a specialist at one of the Pittsburgh hospitals, an experienced oncologist up-to-date on the latest surgical techniques and most-effective treatments. She changed the subject, asking about my upcoming finals. I said we could talk about them when I got home on the weekend.

"Don't be silly," she said. "You were just here. Stay at school. Study. Finish your paper."

"I can study at home," I said.

"But it's crazy here," she said. "Someone's always dropping in."

I paused. "Don't you want me to come, Mom?"

She caught her breath. "No, it's not that," she said, then, "I can't come get you."

"I'll hitch a ride."

"No, don't do that. It's not safe."

"With another student. They post ride offers all the time." Was she crying? "Mom?"

"I'm sorry I got sick," she said.

I rushed to reassure her. "It's okay. It's not your fault." I wasn't certain enough to add, "I'm not a kid anymore. I can handle it." When I hung up, I stared at the phone, a lump lodged in my throat.

"I could take you home," Cassie said behind me.

I couldn't trust my voice not to break. Instead, I shook my head.

"Okay," she said. "Whatever you want."

It had been six years since Mom had said she'd take care of herself so she wouldn't die and, until now, she'd succeeded. Was this the end? Would she leave me like Dad had? I wasn't a kid anymore and I wouldn't be entirely on my own. Grandpa and Pete, my aunts and Tim would be there for me. And don't forget the girls, Jeff would say. They'll fight each other off to console you. But—

Oh, God, don't let her die.

This time it wouldn't be enough to pray. The situation called for sacrifice, but what could I deny myself to bargain for my mother's survival?

"Come over tomorrow then," Cassie said, behind me as she wrapped her arms around me.

Of course. "Uh, maybe not. I'm going to have to finish my paper." It was a flimsy excuse. I'd worked many times in Cassie's apartment, but she didn't press me to change my mind.

The next day in my room, I looked at my notes, but the words wouldn't gel. I walked down the hall to the empty lounge and absentmindedly punched buttons on the vending machines. I rode the elevator to the empty lobby, racked the balls on the pool table, and took a shot, scattering them.

Again, I wondered about Mom's doctor. Had he told her what to expect or was he treating her the way she suspected the neonatologists had acted after my premature birth, sharing details in carefully measured doses, monitoring the effect of the news? It left her frantic for more information, certain that the doctors had the answers, but fearful she'd never get them because she didn't know how to frame the questions.

"I was wild with worry." That's how she'd described herself then. It was how I felt now. For a moment I thought I would step up, take charge like she did when her mother was sick, go with her to an appointment, but, honestly, I didn't want the responsibility. I still wanted her to handle everything. To let myself off the hook, I reasoned she'd never give up the control.

Back in my room, I put my notecards in order, roughed out an outline, and typed a draft.

"How'd it go with your paper?" Cassie asked the next day.

"Not too well," I said, trying to buy myself time and distance from her. "I'm having trouble concentrating."

"Maybe you need a change of scene. Why don't you come over today?"

"No. I just have to keep at it." Cassie turned away then turned back. She didn't say anything, though, and while I considered trying to explain, I figured she'd scoff at the notion that my choosing abstinence could somehow influence my mother's fate.

By Friday, she'd had it. She exploded in the dining hall. "What the hell is wrong with you, Finn Maguire? Why are you avoiding me? And don't tell me you're not."

Confronted, I confessed.

"Jeez. Why didn't you tell me that in the first place?" Cassie said.

"Because you'd say I was being irrational."

"Well, yeah," she said, "but I thought you were trying to break up with me."

"What? No, never," I rushed to say as I reached out to hug and reassure her.

CHAPTER THIRTY-FIVE

THE GUY WHO GAVE ME A RIDE HOME DROVE A SCRATCHED and dented yellow Pinto. I was his third and final passenger crammed in the back seat with my duffel between my feet. Neither of the two other riders acknowledged me, although they seemed familiar with each other, perhaps from previous trips. When it started to rain, droplets shimmied on the glass, gyrated together, and slid down the window in rivulets.

Umbrellas proliferated on campus, but Cassie never carried one. She flipped up the hood of her sweatshirt or jacket and sometimes didn't even do that if the rain was a drizzle. I liked that she preferred to be unencumbered, that she could turn her perfect face to the sky, pull her hair into a sleek ponytail or bun. She never complained like other girls that the rain made her hair go straight or frizz up, but then, she didn't have to. Her hair was perfect. She was perfect. As soon as I got home, I'd call her and apologize, try to explain. It's not you. It's me.

I wanted to be worldly-wise like Cassie, but I was small-town backward. On each return to campus, it took a few days, a few classes, a few heady discussions to fit in and not feel like a fraud. At home I talked with Pete about cars and Grandpa about his garden, but not the big issues and new ideas I was exposed to at school. "What's the point of filling my head with substance if I'm stuck in a place where I can't share it?" I said to Tim.

He didn't buy it. "You don't have to be stuck anywhere," he said. "And don't sell people short. It's on you to make them understand. Isn't that what your dad did?"

The conversation in the car was about bands. The U2 Joshua Tree tour wouldn't reach Pittsburgh until the third leg in the fall. October 13, one of the guys said. Day after my birthday. Six more months. Would I still have a mother? With a pang, I remembered that haunting spiritual we sang in junior high and pictured a forlorn-looking version of myself. A motherless child.

"How is she?" I asked Pete when he picked me up where I was dropped off outside town. I dreaded his answer.

"She says she's okay, but who knows," he said with a shrug. "She won't talk about it."

It was time, no, past time, to confront Pete about his involvement with, well, the other woman. "So, you and Billie," I said, adopting his sarcastic tone. "How long?"

He stiffened, as though surprised to be challenged, but recovered to answer me evenly. "A while now."

Yeah, I'll bet. I kept at him. "Does Mom know?"

He took a second before answering. "I don't think so."

"Don't you think you ought to tell her?" I pressed him.

"Not now. She's got enough on her mind," Pete said, his expression conveying that I shouldn't tell her either, and then, that he was on to my feelings about Billie in a way that hadn't been clear to Mom or Dad. "What's it to you anyway?" he said. "Don't you have a girlfriend?"

That shut me up and when we walked into the living room, Pete got in another dig. "Here he is," he said to Mom. "Your

Golden Boy."

Grandpa sat in a chair and Mom on the center sofa cushion, a pillow behind her back, her legs stretched out atop the ottoman. Spread out to one side were books and pamphlets about breast cancer. Typical. She would read all the information available the way she researched a new topic to present to her class. Curled up on her other side, Patch raised his head to give me the oh-it's-only-you once-over, then returned his chin to her thigh and closed his eyes. Jeez. Even Patch was more aware than I was.

When I bent down to kiss her cheek, Mom wrapped her arms around my neck and asked me to pull her up. She dislodged Patch, but called him to follow as she shuffled to the kitchen. "People keep bringing food," she said, rattling the glass lids of casserole dishes in the refrigerator. "I do appreciate it. I just don't feel like cooking." Our fridge hadn't been that full since Dad's funeral. Grandpa, Pete, and I filled our plates while Mom ate a meatball and half a slice of bread.

When they left, I thought we'd have a chance to talk, but Mom kept dozing off until she said she'd better go to bed. Watching her climb the stairs with unusual effort, I hoped that after the surgery in another week she'd be able to run up and down them again with an armload of towels fresh from the dryer or sheets for the washer.

Before I turned off the light in the dining room, I noticed a photo missing from the buffet, the one of Dad hugging Mom. In its place was the one of Mom and Dad with John.

Upstairs, I lay on my bed and stared at the ceiling recalling Cassie's fascination at Thanksgiving with the clouds Mom had painted there. "I wouldn't change it either," she'd said, of my decision not to repaint. "What a treat to wake up to and how could you not have sweet dreams under this sky?" I was sorry I hadn't let her drive me home. Now that I'd seen Mom, my self-imposed abstinence seemed like a foolish overreaction.

Downstairs in the morning, I discovered Mom meditating with Tim.

"May I be open," she intoned, sitting cross-legged on the living room rug, her eyes closed, her face serene. Once again Tim had come to her rescue. Maybe the phrase was the sort of thing you were supposed to say, but I worried it didn't go far enough.

Make her be well. That was my thought as I headed for the kitchen hopscotching over the creaky floorboards to keep from disturbing Mom and her guru. Grandpa sat at the table with a box of donuts from the bakery. At my raised eyebrows and head nod toward the living room, he shrugged and said, "She says it helps."

When kids in our class had asked Tim about meditation in sixth grade, he said it calmed his mind, relieved stress, and helped him deal with the day, but when he tried to show us how to do it, intoning "Om Mani Padme Hum," we snickered until he said we'd better get back to work. Too late we realized meditating could get us out of twenty minutes of class, but when we asked to try it again, he said no. He was on to us.

I was glad the practice seemed to work for Mom. Her energy and appetite restored, she bustled around the kitchen making coffee, setting out mugs and milk, then sitting down to eat a whole cream-filled donut. I could have sat there all morning, just the four of us, but soon there were six, then eight, then a houseful. First to arrive were the Jones twins, Rand and Rudd, recipients of my outgrown clothes in elementary school. When I went to the front door to let them in, it was obvious they weren't wearing anybody's cast-off clothing anymore. On their way to work at the men's clothing store in town, they could have been GQ models.

"How nice you boys look," Mom said, relocating everybody

to the living room.

For the first time, I distinguished between the two. Rand was the preppy one in his khaki slacks, pastel blue polo shirt, and loafers on bare feet. In jeans and a black leather aviator jacket, boots and an earring, Rudd was edgier. Rudd handed Mom a brown paper grocery bag like the ones containing my clothes she'd given them in grade school. She opened the bag and pulled out a small afghan, crocheted or knitted—I didn't know which—in shades of blue.

"It's a prayer shawl," the guys said in unison.

"It's beautiful and so soft," Mom said, holding it to one cheek.

"Ladies at our church make them," Rand said.

"They said we could take one," Rudd added.

"They're for anybody, not just the people at our church." That was Rand again.

"How nice, boys," Mom said. "Thank you." She draped the afghan over her shoulders like a cape. Super Girl. Power Girl. Oh God, let it protect her.

My aunts arrived next, fussed over the gift then fussed over me. "How's our fair Finley today?" Aunt Rachele asked, ruffling my hair.

"We brought you the donuts you like," said Aunt Rina. When we all laughed, her face fell, so I thanked her and propelled her into the kitchen. When I plopped her box next to Grandpa's, she laughed, too.

"It's good you came home," Rina said. "Your mom might not let on, but there's no one she'd rather see. You know that, don't you?"

"That's right," Rachele said from the doorway. She was at my side in seconds and the two of them patted my back and rubbed my arms as they gazed up into my face. I resisted the urge to squirm away as I would have as a kid. I figured they were trying to reassure themselves that Mom would be okay. I was the prop for their ministrations.

When the doorbell rang, we trooped back to the living room to greet Mrs. Harmon and Mr. Simpson.

"Ward is my dance partner now," Mrs. Harmon said, after telling everyone how I'd danced with her in high school. That made her remember the pretty girl who'd let her cut in and she asked about Francine. Conversation stopped. Time stopped too while it dragged me down to where I'd wallowed after Francine and I broke up. I roused myself to explain, and Mrs. Harmon shook her head.

"The course of true love never does run smooth," she said. Then she took Mr. Simpson's arm and brightened. "Perhaps you'll get back together again."

Surprised at the fluttering hope in my heart, I almost asked her, "Do you think so?" But I'd made my choice. I'd told Francine. I was with Cassie now.

Mom intervened, inviting everyone to help themselves to food in the kitchen, but Mr. Simpson said he and Mrs. Harmon had plans for lunch and the Jones boys said they had to go to work. Tim left too to help with renovating the old movie theater downtown. Mom was right about people dropping in, but I was surprised to see so many men who'd been Dad's friends: his boss, a couple of reporters, Mullaney from the bar, Mr. Simpson's salesmen, guys from Gus's, and Jerry, the cop.

Mullaney fixed the leaky faucet in the kitchen. One of the gym rats gave her a set of light weights for her rehabilitation. The reporters talked about the class newspaper they were helping her students produce, and everyone promised to attend career day and talk to her class about their jobs.

Clustered around Mom, they acted like kids themselves, like her pupils vying for her attention. If I'd mentioned Dad, I wouldn't have been surprised to hear them ask, "Who?"

After everyone left, I made Mom the cup of tea she asked for and settled opposite her, ready to talk. She gave a little laugh when the doorbell rang again, although with more effort than earlier in the day, and I said I'd turn away whoever it was.

But it was Francine.

"I didn't know you were home, Finn," she said as she took a step back. Drawn as before into her half-hidden eyes, I took the stack of books she was returning to Mom and invited her inside.

"Who is it?" Mom called.

"It's me, Mrs. M.," Francine said as she entered the living room. "Sorry I didn't call ahead." Mom had been nice to Cassie and told me she liked her, but she really lit up when she saw Francine.

"It's good you came, Francine," Mom said. "I was about to send Finn downtown. You can show him around."

"But I thought we'd talk, Mom," I said. "You had company all day."

"Oh, I'll be here when you get back. Go on. Have some fun," she said, with a wave of her hand toward the door. "Get your mind off me." As if I could. Earlier, she'd acted too tired to move, but she got up, walked us to the door, smiled, and shut it in my face. I was stunned, but not sorry to be with Francine. When she asked about Mom, I couldn't admit I'd been unaware she was ill. "She says she'll be okay," I said. "I hope it's not an act."

In Danton's business district, Francine parked her car across from the old movie theater. Vacant for six years, it was the new home of a community theater group that was renovating it for live productions. Weeks before, Mom had clipped a photo from the paper and sent it to me. With scaffolding still surrounding the spare stage on three sides, it looked like there hadn't been much progress.

"What do you think?" Tim asked when Francine and I walked over to where he was working.

"I think you have a way to go," I said gesturing toward the wood and metal structure.

"The scaffolding stays. To hold the seats," he said. "We're going with an industrial look."

"Oh," I said, reassessing. "In that case, it's perfect."

Tim beamed, but not from my compliment. Someone behind me had called, "Hey, Tim," and when I turned, the pair of ice-blue eyes Tim had described dazzled me. Sea glass. Summer guy. "Finn, this is David," Tim said. No one looked twice as they embraced or even when they kissed. It was another way in which times had changed.

A door in the theater lobby led to a small coffee shop whose owner said he couldn't have afforded to establish a business in the city where he used to live. As his wife filled the display case with fancy pastries they didn't sell at Antonelli's, she said they'd purposely scoped out the bakery so they wouldn't compete with it. They refrained from baking sheet cakes and their own bread and instead bought bread from the bakery for their fancy sandwiches.

And, unlike the bakery, they had tables and chairs where customers could linger. Francine and I took the last two seats, drank our coffee, and shared a plate of what she said were eclairs, madeleines, and macarons. In addition to those newcomers, Francine said former residents had returned, like the mayor's daughter, a hairstylist who'd brought her architect husband, and the Danton grad, a teacher at the community college, whose wife ran an independent bookstore.

"Mr. Weiss says it validates the faith of people who never gave up on Danton even when we fell on hard times," Francine said. Driving me home, she said she planned to return after college if she could get a teaching job in town. "What about you, Finn?"

"Can you see me working at a metro?" I asked.

Building me up the way she always did, she said, "I can see you doing anything you want."

"I wish Mom could. Or at least try," I said. "But she says I'm more suited to small-town life."

"You could try a city," Francine said.

"I already did," I said. "I went to New York with Cassie. The crowds were crushing and the subway was suffocating. Believe it or not, there was even a rotting black banana peel on a sidewalk like in a cartoon. When I kicked it into the street so no one would slip on it and fall, Cassie laughed at me."

Francine hesitated, then asked, "Is that your girlfriend?"

"Oh, yeah. Sorry," I said.

We were silent until Francine pulled into our driveway behind the Ferrari. "Wow. Whose car is that?" she asked.

And, more importantly, what's it doing here? "Friend of my mom's," I said, as I told Francine goodbye.

Inside, Mom and John were already in her room, but during the night, I encountered him leaving the bathroom as I was on my way in. Barefoot, in boxers and a T-shirt, he didn't seem embarrassed or uncomfortable running into me. He acted like he belonged.

Finally, on Sunday morning Mom and I were alone. "Go to church with me?" she asked as she bustled around the kitchen.

"What about John?" I replied.

"Oh, we'll let him sleep. He's not much of a churchgoer," she said, before heading upstairs to get ready. I would have preferred to spend the morning sitting with her at the kitchen table, drinking cup after cup of coffee, and reading the paper, circling the stories we each thought the other should read. Neither of us had adopted Dad's habit of interrupting and reading items aloud, although I liked to think we both missed hearing Dad do it. He was still on my mind when we got into the car.

"So, how'd you end up with Dad?" I asked Mom. "Instead of John."

She took a deep breath, and her face took on a lost-in-the-past look. "John asked me to take a book to your dad at the newspaper where he was working. I was going to leave it with the receptionist, but when I heard talking and laughing, I peeked around the divider into the big open office. Your dad was holding court among all the other employees, some of them twice his age.

"I'd been feeling sorry for him because he'd had to leave school, but he was fine. I knew then that people would always revolve around him. He would have a big life and I wanted to be part of it," she said, breaking into a smile. "Like everyone else, I glommed onto him."

In an instant her happy expression faded. "Somewhere along the line, I started to resent your dad for the very thing that attracted me in the first place." She turned to me and said, "Don't be like me, Finn," the way she had when I'd blamed her for Jeff's—and Dad's—leaving.

When we got home after church, John was awake. He certainly was devoted, jumping up to get Mom a glass of water and rearranging the pillows, the stool, the blanket to make her comfortable on the sofa. He even rubbed her stockinged feet. She thanked him with an appreciative gaze. They couldn't have been more intimate if I'd surprised them in bed. I'll bet he would have hated hearing that Dad had hurt her, though. Out of allegiance to Dad, I hoped Mom hadn't told John about Dad and Billie.

When John proposed an afternoon drive, I told Mom to go. I didn't have much choice. It was clear she wanted to make up for lost time with him. I went for a drive myself and wasn't surprised at where I ended up. Neither was the crone who pointed to the bench, said, "Sit down," and, with a wink, "Don't run off this time."

"I won't," I said, and when I slumped and dumped my troubles on her, she absorbed them.

"Well, that's a damn shame," she said of Mom's cancer diagnosis, but when I said I was worried Mom would die like Dad, she raised a finger to shush me and said, "Don't borrow trouble."

"I know," I said. "Don't worry before it's time. The thing is, what if it is her time?" I was afraid the crone would think I was challenging her, but she was understanding.

"I wish I could tell you it isn't her time," she said.

CHAPTER THIRTY-SIX

During the week, I resumed daily visits to Cassie's apartment, crawled into her bed, and clung to her. Distracted as I was about Mom, I was surprised and grateful Cassie let me stay. I didn't want to be alone. Unlike Francine, who was empathetic when I talked about Dad, Cassie was unemotional about Mom's situation. "You know there's nothing you can do," she said, and she was right. The surgery's outcome was out of my hands. I'd be in limbo until we learned the results.

On Sunday, Cassie drove me home for the operation on Monday. We found Mom and John side by side on the couch cuddling like couples in the dorm lounges at school. Cassie waggled her eyebrows at me, but I couldn't laugh. Now that Mom could be with John again, how cruel would it be if she didn't get the chance.

Cassie and I walked around the block and stopped at Grandpa's, where he led us out to the backyard to check on seedlings he'd planted in a cold frame. Pete cleaned and ran the mower over the yard, although the grass had hardly grown since winter.

Their restlessness mirrored mine. Only Mom and John were still.

"There's plenty of food," Mom called when we got back from Grandpa's. "Fix something for yourself and Cassie."

"I think we'll go out," I said, looking into the living room.

"Suit yourself," she said, waving a hand in the air without turning to look at me.

As Cassie drove downtown, I told her about the theater, the coffee shop, and the other new businesses that were revitalizing Danton. I tossed in tidbits of history too, the way Dad had on our tour of the town with Billie.

"You like it here," Cassie said as though the fact had just become apparent.

"I do," I replied. And with that, I realized I'd made my decision. "I can't go to New York with you," I said, confident it was the right choice but concerned how the news would land.

"I figured as much," Cassie said as though it was no big deal, but it was and I hurriedly tried to explain.

"It's not for me. I wouldn't feel right. I'd only spoil it for you. Don't be mad." I wished she would say something in response and I wished I could feel as settled about Mom.

Had I been able to see through the steamed windows of the new pizza place, I might have steered Cassie to the sub shop instead. When we stepped inside and the bell over the door jangled, a couple in line turned to look at us—Francine and some guy I didn't know. She gave me the warm smile she'd always saved for me and introduced Brad, a fellow student from the community college. I introduced Cassie.

"Oh, the famous Finn," Brad said. He extended his hand to shake mine as Francine blushed and Cassie eyed me sideways. "These two really had the hots for each other in high school," he said to Cassie. He draped an arm around Francine like she was his personal property, but with his gaze, staked a claim to my girlfriend too.

"Four of us now," he told the hostess, and when she showed us to a table, he positioned himself across from Cassie and gawked at her while he pulled out the chair next to his for Francine.

"So, what do you guys like?" he asked as he studied the menu. I like Francine. I wasn't surprised at the thought. Looking as good as ever, she held her own with Cassie. I willed her boyfriend to pick up on what I was thinking and be jealous. You asked what I liked, Braaad. Then I wondered whether Francine really liked him. He seemed like a jerk, but it could have been the situation. Guys fell all over themselves around Cassie. His attention wouldn't faze Cassie, but he shouldn't have been ignoring his date to concentrate on mine. To compensate, I asked Francine about her classes, her family, our friends from high school, anything I could think of.

When Cassie asked, "What are you talking about?" I said, "Nothing," and redirected my attention to her. "How's your pizza?" I asked. She didn't reply.

When we'd finished eating, Brad grabbed the check and I didn't fight him for it. He probably thought he'd impress Cassie if he paid. Outside, as we approached her car, Brad lost it. "Wow. You don't see one of these every day." He was probably imagining himself behind the wheel of the MG with one arm around Cassie and the elbow of his steering arm out the window. What an asshole. I wondered what Francine saw in him, why she bothered with him.

Cassie didn't speak again until we were close to home. "You never told me about Francine," she said.

Uh-oh. "I didn't?"

"You know you didn't," she said.

I thought for a moment before I replied. "I guess I wanted to forget her."

"So, she broke up with you?" Shoot. Too late I realized how

that might make a difference. Don't worry. I'm not hung up on her anymore. That's what I should have said, regardless of whether it was true.

Inside the house, Cassie went upstairs while I turned off the lights in the living room and kitchen. Mom and John were already in Mom's room. I found Cassie in the guest room, looking through a book she'd brought from school.

"I've got some reading to do. I'll stay here tonight," she said.

"You don't have to," I said as I put my arms around her.

She extracted herself from my embrace. "I think I should."

"Mom won't care. She won't even know." I tried to kiss her, but Cassie turned her head.

"It's not that," she said.

"What then?"

"You've got to be up so early. You'll need to get some sleep. Go," she said, as she pushed me out the door.

Giving up too easily, I slept alone in my room with no midnight visit from Cassie.

Being in the hospital is harder on the family than the patient. Mom was knocked out, oblivious. Grandpa and Pete, John, my aunts, and I—we were the anxious ones. Before a nurse whisked her away, Mom smiled and told us not to worry. She said she'd be all right, but no one looked convinced.

The monolithic city hospital dwarfed Danton's in size, and there were so many people, we shrank into insignificance, held at bay by the procedures in place to manage a crowd. Watch the electronic board for patient updates, we were told. We yawned and shook ourselves to stay awake. We startled when a door opened or the intercom screeched. At first, we were solicitous of each other, taking turns to go for coffee, but an hour and a half after Mom's scheduled procedure, worry wore us down. We fidgeted and muttered the same phrases repeatedly.

"Where is the doctor?"

"It wasn't supposed to take this long."

"Why doesn't somebody tell us something?"

"Where is that doctor?"

My mind wandered to how my parents had worried when I was a newborn in the NICU and when I'd had that appendicitis attack. I pictured Billie holding the towel for me when I threw up and running along with us when Dad carried me out of the apartment. She'd been worried too. I fought to keep my focus on Mom, but leaning forward in my seat, elbows on my knees, I was distracted by the pattern of gold dots in the blue rug.

"Grandpa," I said, pointing down, "remember that game you taught me? Taking turns to draw lines to connect the dots. Making boxes for our initials." He patted my back.

My aunts jumped in. "Try not to worry," Rina said.

"I'm sure your mom will be all right," Rachele added.

But at that moment, I wasn't worried about Mom or even thinking about her. I was putting Bs in boxes I imagined drawing on the rug. Not Fs for Finn. Bs for Billie.

When I began to think Mom's doctor had forgotten us, maybe even finished his shift and gone home, he pushed open the swinging door with one hand and rubbed his eyes with the other. Just before he reached us, he drew that hand down over his weary face to reveal a smile like he was a magician as well as a physician.

"She did really well," he said. How odd for him to imply that Mom had played any role in the operation when she'd been unconscious, but coupled with his casual stroll away from us, his words were consoling. Surely, if there was anything to be concerned about, he wouldn't be so nonchalant. I released the breath I'd been holding and relaxed. She's going to be all right.

Everyone agreed that Grandpa and I should go first to see Mom. A nurse led the way and warned us she'd be groggy. We joined a procession of other family members trooping past the row of beds, each one bearing a patient monitored by a bank of beeping, blinking machines. Mom's expression was serene. I took her hand.

"John?" she asked. Again, I thought about Billie. If I'd asked for her after my appendectomy, it would have devastated Mom.

"It's Finn and me," Grandpa said on her other side.

She sighed and squeezed my hand. When she mumbled something, we asked her to repeat it.

"Make yourselves a sandwich," she said.

The nurse at her bedside tittered. "She won't make much sense for another hour or so. Why don't you go get something to eat like she suggested?"

When we went back to the waiting room, I told an anxious-looking John, "She asked for you. You should go see her next."

An hour later, Mom was opening and closing her eyes and starting to focus because she said my name. Then she smiled wider and reached for John. In another hour, she was sitting up, sipping ice water through a straw, waiting to be admitted to a room for the night. John said he'd stay with her until she was settled or maybe all night depending on how she was feeling. The rest of us went home to the dinner Cassie was making. Driving solo, I was the last to arrive because I'd taken a detour past Billie's apartment.

"Your aunts said the operation went well," Cassie said after I entered the back door and met her in the kitchen.

"Yes," I said, finally letting go of some of the day's tension as Cassie handed me a shot of whiskey. "The doctor says she's going to be all right."

I knocked back the shot then poured a tumbler half full of whiskey that I nursed through dinner along with my preoccupation. Everyone thanked Cassie for her efforts, but I was lost in the past, sixteen again, sitting outside Billie's apartment in Mom's car. Forget Pete, forget Dad, forget Cassie even.

"We'll see you tomorrow at the hospital," Rachele said as everyone left.

"You come, too, Cassie," said Rina.

When they were gone, the house creaked and groaned as though telling me to get a move on if I was going to go.

"I think I'll take a ride. Get some air," I told Cassie.

"Let me get my jacket," she said. "I'll go with you."

"No, stay. I won't be gone long," I insisted.

She followed me to the door and put her hand over mine on the knob. "Is it Francine? Are you going to see her?"

"What? No. Where'd you get that idea?" I said, trying to dismiss her question. "I just need to clear my head." She wouldn't move her hand.

"Billie, then," she said evenly. "What is it? Are you in love with her?"

"Jeez. No." It was too sharp, too sudden a protest, a knee-jerk reaction to an accusation that had hit the mark. Cassie went in for the kill.

"Oh, I get it. You think Billie's in love with you."

Her sarcastic tone triggered my unfeeling response: "And you think you know everything." I should have left it at that, but I didn't stop. "You know what? You can leave now if you want. I've got my own car. I can drive myself back to campus." Stunned, Cassie withdrew her hand and I wrenched open the door.

In the car, I revved the engine and backed up, then slammed on the brakes when a car blew its horn and roared down the street a few feet from my bumper. Framed in the doorway, Cassie brought her hand to her mouth, but then put her hands on her hips, challenging me to relent and stay or change my mind and take her with me. I almost went back. Once I cooled down,

I'd be embarrassed and I'd have to apologize for my overreaction, but then I fumed again at what she'd said: "You think Billie's in love with you." Cassie made it sound preposterous, but why not? Hadn't stranger things happened somewhere, sometime to someone? Why not me?

I backed into the street, gassed the car, and took off.

CHAPTER THIRTY-SEVEN

Tires crunched the gravel as I pulled into the apartment driveway and parked behind a 1986 Camaro. It was tomato red, not candy apple, with a curvy front end that contrasted with the boxy shape of Billie's first vehicle. How she'd laughed with Dad at her fixation: "I could live on Tobacco Road, but I'll always have a shiny new sports car in front of my shack."

That was as good an explanation as any for why Billie remained in the house that was already old when she'd moved into it. The second story especially was smaller than I remembered and sad looking. Peeling paint on the siding exposed patches of bare wood turned a silvery-gray like the stairs—stairs, I realized, that led not to a simpler time, but to the time when life got complicated for me.

Still, I went forward, counting the steps the way I had as a kid: thirteen, fourteen, fifteen. On the landing, I paused. Billie had always greeted me like a child herself, innocent in her excitement. What if she wasn't waiting for me? What if I was projecting a desire she didn't share? Just then she parted the curtains and yanked open the door. Her smile sparked a familiar surge. Her voice still tantalized. "Finn! How you've grown."

That's right, Billie, at least six inches and seven years. But I hadn't closed the gap. Billie had aged, too. Why hadn't I expected it? Her face was fuller as was her body. Her hair had darkened from that bright coppery color to an auburn, but she still lit up the kitchen. The low, sloped ceiling cropped the room, cutting it down in size. Had it seemed like that to Dad? Like a playhouse? Billie gestured toward the table, the chair that had been his, and I sat down. Her eyes roamed my face and she said, "You look more like your dad than ever." I didn't want to hear about him. I wanted her to focus on me, but then she turned my attention to Mom. "I was sorry to hear about your mother. How is she?" Right. Pete would have told her, but Billie's genuine concern surprised me. Hadn't she and Mom been rivals? For a second, I thought sharing details might be some sort of betrayal of Mom, but I couldn't hold back.

"The surgery was today. The doctor said she'll be all right."

"You must have been so worried," Billie said. Whether it was her sincerity or the day's toll, my tears welled without warning. I tried to blink them back, but had to wipe them away.

"Mom didn't tell me she was sick," I said. "When my grandmother got cancer, she died." I shuddered, and when Billie patted my arm, I wanted to reach for her hand the way I'd taken Francine's or Cassie's.

"Would you like a Coke or something stronger?" Billie asked, tapping the pint of locally distilled whiskey on the table. There it was. The evidence. What would she say if I let her know I'd noticed?

"That's the brand my uncle Pete drinks," I said.

She didn't flinch. "A lot of people do around here," she said. She went to a cupboard for two rocks glasses and poured a couple fingers of the whiskey in each. When she handed me a glass,

I examined the amber liquid as though it could confirm when she and Pete had become an item, that St. Patrick's Day in the pub or, even earlier.

"Oh. I should have asked," Billie said, pointing to my glass. "Water? Ice? Soda?" I shook my head. I'd drink it neat like Pete. When Billie raised and tilted her glass toward me, I lifted mine and we tapped the rims. She surprised me with a toast. "To Monica and Aidan. And their very fine son." She swirled the whiskey in her glass, smiled and sipped it, her eyes on mine. There was an expression for what she was doing. Drinking me in. I gulped and gripped my glass. Maybe I should have stayed at home with—

It was my last thought of Cassie.

Bringing the glass to my lips, I inhaled the fumes, took a sip, and held the fiery liquid in my mouth. As I swallowed, warmth and well-being spread through my torso, my limbs. I relaxed. Time slowed.

Billie reminisced about my previous visits, drawing me further into the past. She didn't mention our dancing, but she recalled the games we played, my favorite TV shows, and how much I'd loved Ginger. That's what had been missing, the whimpering, the scratching at the bedroom door, the tapping of paws on the kitchen floor.

"Where is Ginger?" I asked.

Billie's face fell. "It's been a couple of years now," she said, "but I haven't had the heart to replace her."

Right. And Pete's allergic to dander. I drained my glass and Billie refilled it.

When she mentioned the incident on Halloween, I apologized for scaring her, but she waved me off, went to the cabinets again, and removed a large shallow box from a drawer. Her languid movements evoked the memory of our dancing. If I took her in my arms now, I'd be a more adept partner. Where might our dancing lead? When she set the box in front of me, I straightened in my seat and opened it. Inside, atop a pile of Monitor clippings, was the letter Mom had made me write.

"I'd like to keep it since you sent it to me," Billie said.

"Oh, yeah, sure," I replied. That second drink set me on a path I was too curious not to take. "Technically I kept my promise," I told her. "I didn't bother you, but I didn't exactly stay away. After I got my license, I sometimes drove here and parked across the street."

"You did?" she asked, her interest piqued.

I rushed to add, "I wasn't stalking you or anything."

"Of course not," she said with a slight smile, and after a pause, "It's nice to know you thought about me."

"I thought about you all the time, Billie," I said, then groaned inwardly. It was the whiskey talking, making me sound like a lovesick puppy. "Don't think I'm weird," I said. She shook her head, but smiled more broadly. I gulped the whiskey left in my glass.

Billie had saved so many clippings that, if I took time to read them all, I could stay with her all night. There were photos and stories about my grade school basketball and Little League baseball teams and programs from my honor society induction, confirmation, and commencement. In every article, photo caption, or program, she'd highlighted or underlined my name. So, Billie had her own box of treasures, but while I wanted to regard them like mine, Billie acted more like a proud parent than a long-suffering lover. She was like Mom.

"I'm sorry my mom was mean to you," I said, and when Billie looked puzzled, "I was just thinking. After Dad died, you didn't get to see him."

"Oh, but I did," Billie said, and it was my turn to be confused. "The funeral director called and told me your mom said I could go to the funeral home between visiting hours and sit in the choir loft during the funeral."

I was stunned to think Mom had considered Billie's pain when Billie's involvement with Dad had been the cause of her own.

"It was a beautiful service," Billie said. "So many people loved your dad."

But what about me, Billie?

"And you," she said, as though she'd read my mind, "you looked so grown up in your suit, but I felt so sorry for you. I knew you'd be lost without your dad."

I refilled my glass and took more than a sip. I didn't want Billie to get hung up on Dad, but I had to acknowledge the memorial ads for him.

"I really appreciated these," I said, fingering a couple of them.

"They're beautiful, aren't they?" Billie said, growing contemplative. "When your mother came to the paper to place the first one, I was surprised that she spoke to me. She said, 'I want Finn to read something inspiring.' I took a chance and told her your dad had a whole book of Irish sayings that might work. I tore out the inscription I'd written to him and dropped the book off at school for her, but she must have known I'd bought it for him."

Turning her attention back to me, Billie said, "Your mom did a good job picking just the right phrases, didn't she? Those ads sounded just like your dad."

"For a while, I thought you submitted them," I said.

"Me? Oh, no," Billie said firmly. "It wouldn't have been my place."

Fingering the clippings again, I dared to bring up the incident that had preoccupied me for years. "Why were you naked that last time I was here?"

Billie didn't miss a beat. "It didn't scar you for life, did it?"

Her tone was teasing, but rankled too, making me feel like a kid again and I struck back.

"Dad was going to leave you," I said.

She caught her breath. I'd caught her off guard, hurt or upset her, but she got the last word. "Yes, thanks for reminding me," she said. She'd known.

Immediately I was sorry and said so, but Billie got up from the table and left the room. I followed too late to catch her. She was behind the closed bedroom door, cutting me off the way I'd been shut out by Dad years before. I waited as I had back then. If she was startled when she opened the door, she didn't show it. Pressed to her breast, she held the blanket and pillow she'd used to make up a bed for me all those years ago.

"You've had too much to drink to drive home," she said. "You can sleep it off on the couch."

She sent a mixed message, though, when she took a step back into her room. It reminded me of how she'd drawn me into the field before the storm that day we'd met and how she'd taught me to dance. Did she want me to follow her now the way I'd followed her then? Or did she want me to take the lead? I could. I knew what to do.

With a forgiving smile, Billie touched my cheek and with pursed lips moved toward me to kiss the other one, the way Mom might. That split second clarified that I might have mistaken her interest, her caring for love. Of me. Maybe Billie wasn't my destiny after all. But it was the chance I'd yearned for and I took it. I turned my head at just the right moment to capture her lips, taste, and part them with my tongue, but then pulled back, puzzled.

Billie looked intrigued, as though the thought of being with me hadn't occurred to her before but now that it had—

She kissed me back.

After years of waiting and wanting Billie's affection, I should have been aroused, right? Then where was the passion I'd felt with Cassie, the delight I'd shared with Francine? And what was all this flashing before my eyes? I was drunk, not dying.

Mom, Dad, Jeff, Tim, Cassie, Pete: "Finn will be the hero of his life…beautiful women unleash terrible trouble…go for it… once you choose, you're responsible for your choices…you think Billie's in love with you…what's it to you anyway?"

Pete. I couldn't do this to Pete.

"I've got to go," I said, turning away from Billie. "I'll sleep in the car." I steadied myself with a hand on the walls, the table, the fridge to keep from stumbling as I left her apartment. Outside, as the cold cleared my head, I recognized the close call I'd escaped and the reality of the situation. Some hero I was. My whole life, I'd chased a fantasy, her name a prayer, an incantation, but Billie hadn't cast the spell. I'd let myself become obsessed.

In the morning, I woke to a knocking on the car door window and a muffled voice calling my name. When I opened my eyes in a squint, Cassie's worry-creased forehead was inches from mine on the other side of the glass. Her MG idled behind her. She stepped back as I opened the door, sucked in a mouthful of chilly air, and expelled it. "Hey," I said.

"Hey, yourself," she said, her eyes searching mine. "Are you all right?"

"Yeah, sure," I lied, my head a massive ache. "I'm just stiff." I unfolded myself from the driver's seat, stretched and flexed my muscles.

"Is this where you slept?" she asked.

"Yeah. I couldn't drive home. Too much to drink last night."

"With her?" Cassie glanced toward the house that looked too weary to stand.

"Yes," I said, my memory clearing. "With Billie."

I wrapped my arms around Cassie, squeezed her puffy pink

coat to get hold of her body, and said I was sorry for storming out on her.

When Pete drove up, he didn't ask what we were doing there. I said Cassie would take me to the hospital before we drove back to school. He said he would take my car back home. I wondered how Billie would explain my presence to him. Lost in that thought, it took me a minute to size up the situation with Cassie. When I did, I shivered, but not from the cold. Standing in my embrace, her arms stiff at her sides, Cassie wasn't hugging me back.

I fell asleep on the drive back to campus and woke up, surprised, when Cassie pulled up to my dorm. I'd expected to go to her apartment.

"Shall I come over later?" I asked.

"Tomorrow," she said. Fair enough. I'd put her through a lot, and I was too drained to protest. As she drove away, though, I resolved to walk to her apartment later that day, but after I took a shower and lay down on my bed, I fell asleep again.

In the morning, I woke in a panic that pursued me all the way to Cassie's nine o'clock class. When I didn't see her in the room, I bolted from the building and ran to her apartment. Her car wasn't there, but I took the steps two at a time anyway and pounded on her door even as I sensed it wasn't any use. What's that ironic phrase to describe the thing you'd always expected yet hadn't seen coming? Right. I was shocked but not surprised.

"Hey," Cassie's landlady yelled from the bottom of the stairs. "If you break that door, you'll pay for it." Her frosty tone and icy stare blamed me for the sudden loss of her tenant. With crossed arms, she waited for me to descend the stairs then delivered the news that Cassie was gone. And, no, she hadn't left a forwarding address or phone number, at least not for me. Instead, she'd lopped off a piece of me and taken it with her.

When I called Mom later that day to check on her, she

said, "I've been thinking, Finn. Maybe you should go to New York for the summer with Cassie. It could be a fantastic experience." I couldn't tell Mom that wouldn't be happening. Even if I knew where Cassie was working, where she was living, I couldn't imagine she'd be pleased if I showed up. She'd moved on to launch a photography career in the most exciting city in the world. When she found another man, he'd be equally talented, driven, and comfortable in that mecca of commerce and culture. It didn't matter that I wasn't done with Cassie. She was done with me.

And I was a fool for believing I ever had three women available to me when now there were none. Or, maybe one.

CHAPTER THIRTY-EIGHT

It was an eventful summer at home. John asked Mom to marry him and she said yes. Grandpa said he was fine with Mom giving herself away. He was just glad to be around as a witness. Pete told Mom about Billie, and she surprised everyone when she said he should bring Billie to the wedding, and while he was at it, marry her. He said all right; he would.

I wasn't ready to face Billie, so when Mom asked Pete to invite her to dinner, I lied and said I couldn't be there because I had to meet some friends from college in the city.

When I showed up at Tim's place where he and David were preparing a meal they invited me to share, Tim teased, "I heard your mom was giving a dinner party. Weren't you invited?"

"Too awkward," I said. "First Dad, now Pete."

"When you thought Billie was yours," Tim said.

"Don't remind me," I groaned, and Tim clapped my back.

"So it happened," he said. "The question is, what do you do about it now?"

When I drove by the side of our house almost three hours

later, Billie and Pete were still there, standing on the porch saying one of those long goodbyes to Mom and John. They all looked like old friends. I should have pulled into the driveway, gone up the steps, and gotten the awkward encounter over with. Instead, I drove to Billie's apartment, parked across from it in my old spot on the side street, and waited for Pete to bring her home.

It turned out to be a good decision. As Pete followed Billie up the steps and into the apartment, it was like they were starring in a movie that had no role for me. I wasn't angry. I wasn't envious. It wasn't my story. Billie was a loose end I'd had to tie up, even if I'd done it clumsily. My consolation? I wasn't the only one who'd fallen for her.

Considering how Mom felt about cemetery visits, she surprised me when she asked me to go with her to Dad's grave. As we walked among the headstones, she said, "I don't think your dad would mind that I'm marrying John. He always felt bad we'd lost touch with a good friend."

"Did you think about John when you and Dad were married?" I asked her.

"Sometimes," she said. "I don't think you ever forget anyone you've cared about. I was sorry I'd hurt John, but I was never sorry I married your dad."

"Not even when Dad left?" I asked her.

"You mean when I threw him out, don't you?" she said with a rueful smile. "Well, maybe a little." She stooped down to brush the dried shreds of mown grass from Dad's headstone, and perhaps to look away from me. "Does it bother you that I'm getting remarried?" she asked.

No, it didn't. Seeing how compatible she was with John made me think he'd been her destiny, and with Dad, she'd gotten off track. "This is what bothers me," I said, stooping beside her, tapping the engraved letters of her name. "Someday you'll be here too, and I'll be alone."

"Oh," she said, sounding wounded. "Not for a long time, I hope." I helped her stand and she searched my face. "When I'm gone, you'll be able to bear it. You're my hero, the hero of your life, remember?" Her gaze swept the cemetery. "Not everyone is called to save a life, but anyone can try to live a heroic life. You know how to do that, don't you? You keep going when things are hard, even when you think you can't. You try to do what's right, but when you do wrong, you own up to it, especially to yourself. Anyway, that's what I believe," she said.

Back at home, Mom called me into the living room where she sat at Dad's desk. She took Billie's gift book for Dad from a drawer and handed it to me. "You should have this now," she said. "It's full of wisdom. Find your own inspiration."

As I headed upstairs, I rubbed my thumb over Dad's embossed name on the cover, and in my room, I flipped those gilt-edged pages until I came to a slip of paper. I'd have to ask Mom whether she or Dad had marked the passage. Either way, the highlighted words gave me hope: "A hero is no braver than an ordinary man, but he is brave five minutes longer."

Mom said I should stop moping around and call Francine, but I didn't do it, not right away. I didn't want to ricochet like a pinball. I wanted to be Pac-Man, charting my course, outrunning my ghosts. I retrieved Francine's letters from the drawer where I'd buried them and taped together the ones I'd torn apart. Then I reread them, reviving the memories, reliving everything we'd experienced. Only then did I propose resuming the journey I'd once thought we were meant to share. I took her out for pizza and drove to the hillside covered in new growth. I parked and we necked.

"I'm sorry I blamed you for Jeff's leaving town," Francine said. "Sorry I wouldn't listen to you. I'll never do that again."

"You don't have to apologize," I told her. "I love you. I never stopped loving you." And I wasn't just saying it. It was true.

Mom also urged me to get to know John. "He won't replace your dad," she said, "but he's a good man."

Grandpa, Pete, and I took John to Jake's for sandwiches and beer. They picked the still-wobbly table where Dad and Billie and I had sat years earlier, but relocated to another one. I pulled the darts from the old dartboard on the wall, stepped back, and threw them. All of them hit the board and several hit the bull's-eye. As I pulled out the darts, John complimented me for my prowess.

"A few of those holes are mine," I said, pointing to the pin-holes in the wall as I handed him half the darts for a match.

"Well then, you've gotten better," John said. Maybe I had.

My aunts spread the word that anyone was welcome to come to the ceremony, and that Saturday at the end of August, it looked like everyone had. The church was packed with happy people, the Eye of God gazed benevolently, and I believed Mom was right that even Dad would be happy for her and John.

As John took his place in the sanctuary with Father Damian, and the organist played the first few notes of the processional, someone poked my arm, hard. I wasn't about to move over and make room for just anyone in the reserved front row, but when I stood for a confrontation, Jeff grabbed me in a bear hug, slapped me on my back, and leaned around me to give a thumbs-up to Francine and Tim and David who grinned like the coconspirators they were. Jeff was back and not just for the wedding. He whispered that he planned to stay in Danton for a while, give the town another chance. Settled in the pew with the four of them, I grinned too. The organ that had moaned and sighed through Dad's funeral trumpeted joy.

When Mom and John left on their honeymoon, Pete and Billie took off for Florida in her Camaro, and I invited Francine over and up to my room. This time we weren't nervous and we weren't interrupted. I was with the right girl. There was nothing wrong with the picture until—Billie? No, Cassie.

So, Mom was right when she said you never forget anyone you cared about. But how long would she hover? Would she think about me? When Francine put her hand on my chest and reclaimed my attention, I pulled her close, pointed out the images on the ceiling, and let Cassie drift away like a cloud.

QUESTIONS FOR DISCUSSION

1. The best characters are neither all good nor all bad. What are the flaws and redeeming qualities of the characters in For Love of Billie? Who was your favorite character? Which character changed the most?

2. If you are a woman reader, did you identify as Finn's mother, one of his girlfriends, or as Billie, the "older" woman who infatuates him? Why were you drawn to that particular character?

3. Psychologists say the greatest threat to one's ability to function is loss. How is this demonstrated through the reactions of Monica, Finn, other family members, and friends to Aidan's death?

4. What examples of magical thinking can you cite in the book? What life situations prompt people to illogically believe that their thoughts, feelings, or actions can directly influence events?

5. With which characters, and how, does Finn experience infatuation? Love?

6. Monica tells her son, "You never forget anyone you cared about." If Billie—or Cassie—continues to occasionally cross Finn's mind after he chooses to be with Francine, is that normal or does it mean he's still obsessed and his relationship with Francine is doomed?

7. Monica wants her son, Finn, to be the "the hero of his life," and at the end of the novel, she gives him her definition. How do you define the concept of hero?

8. Finn is considered an "unreliable narrator" in that his first-person point of view cannot be counted on to accurately reveal what other characters are thinking or feeling. But what can you discern about other characters and their relationships from what Finn does express or think?

9. How, if at all, did this book relate to your own life? Did it evoke any memories or create any connections for you?

A NOTE TO READERS

Thank you for spending time with *For Love of Billie*. I hope this story stays with you long after the final page.

If you feel inclined, leaving a brief rating or review on your preferred book retailer or reading platform can help other readers discover the book. Even a short note or star rating makes a difference.

Thank you again for reading — and for supporting authors and the stories they share.

— Patricia Vido

WHAT I LEFT OUT

Writers are advised to "murder their darlings"—the words, sentences, paragraphs, perhaps whole chapters they love—but that fail to advance the story.

I murdered many darlings while revising *For Love of Billie*. Some are resurrected here:

Meeting Billie that end-of-summer Saturday in 1979 was like encountering a tremor in the Force. She fissured my world. I'd leave it at that, as though it was all her doing, as though my parents weren't already on shaky ground, and I'm not responsible for what I thought and felt and did when I was with her—or wished I were. But Tim, Mr. Weiss, would say be honest. Nobody's perfect, not even a hero. Write about your mistakes.

Dad backed the car into the street, drove toward my grandpa Dom's house at the other end of our block, and tapped the horn sounding two quick beeps. Grandpa waved without looking up from his newspaper, and I wondered whether he'd agree with the day's editorials. If he didn't, he'd grunt and grumble, fling the paper off the porch, but then get up to retrieve and finish reading it. He forgave the occasional lapse in judgment on the opinion page because the monitor kept tabs on our town like its masthead proclaimed, and he defined unfamiliar words instead of telling me to look them up like Mom did. "Grandpa, what's d-e-c-a-p-i-t-a-t-e-d?" I'd asked him once while reading the report of a grisly car wreck. I almost puked when he told me.

For a long time, Mom blamed herself for the early onset of labor. Maybe it was the meatballs she ate straight from the refrigerator after midnight or moving the couch back into place by herself after Dad finished painting the living room.

"Don't torture yourself, Monica," Dad said. "Finn turned out all right." She'd relax until she recalled a particularly frightening episode in the NICU or read an article like the one about a high rate of suicide among children who'd been premature. It had something to do with the idea that an infant who once teetered on the border of life and death could more easily go over the edge as a depressed teen.

"Monica, please!" Dad protested. "That's enough."

Inside the barbershop, two old men sitting in the chrome and cracked vinyl chairs motioned for me to go ahead, and I hop-stepped to Sam on the black tiles of the checkerboard floor. His barber chair wheezed as he pumped the bar with his foot bumping me up until my head was level with his. I steeped in the manly scents of citrus and sandalwood, menthol and mint.

"Just get it out of his eyes," Dad said to Sam. If those other customers had looked up again, Dad would have talked to them, but they were engrossed in their magazines, the ones Sam said were for men not boys. They cleared their throats and shifted in their seats as they studied the pages.

At the end of the school year, my friend Greg swiped one of those magazines and smuggled it out of the shop in his backpack. Days later in the woods behind Grandpa's house where he and Matt and I ware building a cabin with scavenged scraps of wood, Greg smirked, well acquainted with the women inside. I was dying to meet them but wary because of Dad's warning: "What's been seen cannot be unseen." To deny Greg the satisfaction of making me beg, I crossed my arms to feign indifference and challenged him with an offhand, "What's the big deal?"

"Jugs. That's what," he said, whipping open the magazine and pointing to a grainy black and white photo of a naked woman with breasts as big and round and mottled as cantaloupes. Whoa. Dad was right. The picture seared my brain and sapped my resolve to play it cool.

"Wait. Go back," I said, when Greg turned the page past another nude figure on all fours, her long hair a tangled mane. He sneered at my excited shout and tossed the magazine over my head to Matt who flipped it back to Greg when I lunged for it. "Forget it," I said, as I turned away, seething at how I'd been tantalized by the image and teased by my friends.

"Billie's new here," Dad said. No Miss or Ms. No last name, the way he usually instructed me to address adults. Billie was just Billie from the start. Maybe that's why she seemed so young or young enough.

Clad in fake wood paneling, the ad department was crammed with clunky gray metal desks and stubborn-drawered filing cabinets. Pushed together facing each other, Dad's and Billie's desks formed an island in the sea of scratched and dented office furniture. Dad got to look at her and listen to her and breathe in her scent every day. No wonder he fell in love with her.

"Happy little clouds," Mom called them, mimicking the soft-spoken artist with the poof of hair that made him look like a dandelion gone to seed. He painted every afternoon on our PBS station with a brush the size a house painter would use to cut in the trim. I knew his deft scritch-scratching created the picture by applying dabs of paint to a blank canvas, but sometimes it seemed like he was wiping away a coating of white to reveal an already completed scene. It was always so perfect.

Billie's apartment had a Dutch door. It was different and kind of neat, I guess, except that there really wasn't anything exceptional to look out at when the top half of the door was open. A door with a name like that should look out onto a garden. With tulips.

I liked the richness of the vestments, the odor of incense, the statues that represented holy people who'd lived long ago. The mysticism of the mass and the majesty of our church's architecture bridged the gap between earth and heaven. The worship spaces of other churches were plain and ordinary, too much like a house or other secular building for me to believe God would be there. They never seemed worthy of him.

Mom's first task was to acknowledge the neighbors who'd sent us food. She wrote out her thanks on the little black-bordered notecards from the funeral home, put the notes in the empty casserole dishes and sent me out after school to return them. When men answered my knock, they coughed or cleared their throats, took the pans, and lifted a hand in silent acknowledgement before they shut the door. Women, though, invited me in to sit at their tables, eat some cookies, and drink a glass of milk. They tried to smile, but sniffed and wiped the corners of their eyes with a finger or an apron edge. Every single one of them asked, "How's your mother?" and when I got up to leave, they ruffled my hair or touched my shoulder. In the few minutes I was with them, their houses grew somber. I should have apologized for bringing the gloom.

A wave of sadness gave way to curiosity. I knew the dream meant more than the fact that Dad was gone, and in his book about dreams, I found the interpretation. Shoes signify being grounded and in touch with everyday life, I read, and recognizing a specific pair of shoes means the dreamer needs to make a change in attitude. I wrestled with that for a while. Did it have to do with Billie? If it did, forget it. I wasn't about to stop thinking about her. I wasn't about to let her go.

ACKNOWLEDGEMENTS

My dear friend and fellow author, Dawne Allette, was the first person to be intrigued by Finn's infatuation with Billie and encourage me to tell his story.

Family members, especially Nancy Vido Senatore and Shirley Fisher-Ciancetta, kept me on track by inquiring regularly about my progress.

Friends and fellow authors R.A. Boyd, Leslie Kain, and Laura Jane Willoughby of the Charm City Writers group read multiple drafts and gave insightful critiques.

Friends and avid readers Debra Duncan, Sue Ann Klaus, Jim and Debbie Pollino, and Sharon Thomas Chandler responded enthusiastically to an early draft, and Cindy Lisiak to the final version.

Poet and memoirist B. Morrison gave my manuscript a professional quick-look assessment, and Lynn Auld Schwartz of the Writer's Wordhouse provided a thorough developmental edit. My meticulous copyeditor was Katherine Pickett of POP Editorial Services, LLC.

An avid book reviewer and aspiring author, Meredith S. K. Boas of Grunge Muffin Designs and Grunge Muffin Press, partnered with me to both publish my book and design my website, newsletter, business card, sales sheet, and social media posts.

Many family members, friends, and acquaintances subscribed to my monthly e-newsletter, and fellow members of the Maryland Writers Association shared their writing and publishing experiences.

I derived information and inspiration from instructors and fellow participants in programs at Baltimore County Community College, the Johns Hopkins University Odyssey program, Maryland Writers Association, and Towson University's Baltimore Writers Conference.

Story Engineering/Mastering the Six Core Competencies of Successful Writing by Larry Brooks helped me plot my novel. *The Author's Checklist* by Elizabeth K. Kracht modeled how to develop and edit my manuscript.

I kept in mind author Susan Perabo's admonition to regularly visit my "hoarder's head" of characters (even when I didn't write every day) and author Jeffrey Deaver's advice: "Write in the genre you enjoy reading, organize your story ahead of time, and have fun."

Thank you. I'm grateful to all.

ABOUT THE AUTHOR

Patricia Vido honed her writing and editing skills as a reporter, features writer, and features editor at newspapers in western Pennsylvania always most interested in stories that explored—and tried to explain—why people do what they do.

A married mother of adult twin daughters, she loves quirky independent films, playing mahjongg, and rooting for the Baltimore Orioles and Ravens from her home in Owings Mills, Maryland.

She is a member of the Maryland Writers Association. *For Love of Billie* is her first novel.

Website: patriciavido.com